EAST ATLANTA

How to Get Away with Myrtle

THE MYRTLE HARDCASTLE MYSTERIES

Premeditated Myrtle

How to Get Away with Myrtle

ALSO BY ELIZABETH C. BUNCE

A Curse Dark as Gold

StarCrossed

Liar's Moon

How to Get Away with Myrtle

A MYRTLE HARDCASTLE MYSTERY

Elizabeth C. Bunce

ALGONQUIN YOUNG READERS 2020

Published by Algonquin Young Readers
an imprint of Algonquin Books of Chapel Hill
Post Office Box 2225
Chapel Hill, North Carolina 27515-2225

a division of Workman Publishing
225 Varick Street
New York, New York 10014

LIBRARY OF CONGRESS CATALOGING-IN-PUBLICATION DATA

Names: Bunce, Elizabeth C., author.
Title: How to get away with Myrtle / Elizabeth C. Bunce.
Description: First edition. | Chapel Hill, North Carolina :
Algonquin Young Readers, 2020. | "A Myrtle Hardcastle mystery." |
Audience: Ages 9–12. | Audience: Grades 4–6. |
Summary: When someone commits robbery and murder
aboard the luxurious train on which Myrtle Hardcastle,
her Aunt Helena, her governess Miss Judson, and cat Peony
are traveling, Myrtle is determined to find the culprit.
Identifiers: LCCN 2020018053 | ISBN 9781616209193 (hardcover) |
ISBN 9781643751184 (ebook)
Subjects: CYAC: Mystery and detective stories. |
Railroad travel–Fiction. | Murder–Fiction. | Stealing–Fiction. |
Great Britain–History–Victoria, 1837–1901–Fiction.
Classification: LCC PZ7.B91505 How 2020 | DDC [Fic]–dc23
LC record available at https://lccn.loc.gov/2020018053

10 9 8 7 6 5 4 3 2 1
First Edition

How to Get Away with Myrtle

1

EXTRADITION

Just as no scientific or military expedition would set off without adequate supplies, equipment, and reconnaissance, the same is no less important for leisure travel.

—Hardcastle's Practical Travel Companion:
A Compendium of Useful Advice for the Modern Tourist,
Including Select Destinations of Note, Vol. I, 1893

"Think of it as an academic exercise."

Miss Judson, my governess, dropped another armload of chemisettes onto the bed. Peony let out a mew of protest and sought refuge in the trunk.

"In what discipline?" I surreptitiously withdrew two petticoats from my luggage, replacing them with the latest edition of *English Law Reports* and three volumes of my encyclopædia. Taking the whole set seemed excessive, but I could not be sure Fairhaven would have a bookshop or a lending library. The Brochure had not specified.

"Put that middy* back," Miss Judson said. "Aunt Helena will expect to see you in it. And *discipline* is exactly right. You and I shall be practicing our Exceptional Forbearance."

"I thought we were going to frolic on sunny beaches and partake of Family Amusements." The Brochure had likewise not specified what, precisely, a "Family Amusement" entailed, but I suspected nothing good. "Besides, that dress is ridiculous! I'm not a naval recruit."

I felt like one, though, press-ganged into a Seaside Holiday by ruthless schemers who were entirely unsympathetic to my objections.

Miss Judson retrieved the garment and folded it anew. "We have been over this. Your aunt wants to take you on holiday—"

"No, she doesn't."

"*Myrtle.* You have exhausted your appeals. Accept your sentence gracefully." As soon as she said that, I could tell she wanted to take the words back.

"My sentence?" I cried. "I *am* being punished." I threw down the heap of petticoats.

"Of course you're not," said Miss Judson. "Stop getting carried away."

"What happened this summer wasn't my fault!

* a garment inexplicably fashioned after a midshipman's uniform; *id est*, a sailor suit

2}

Father told me that himself." Arms crossed, I willed Miss Judson to prove me wrong.

"He meant it. This holiday is to get away from all of that—"

"Father went all the way to Paris to get away from *me*."

She stepped back a pace, hand to her chest. "Is that what you think?"

I turned away and shoved the chemisettes into the trunk. If this were a proper holiday, Father would be coming with us, not separating us with a whole ocean.* On a Proper Holiday, Father and Miss Judson might even frolic on the beach together. They'd Promenade on the Pier *together*. We could be a Proper Family, just the three of us. Instead, Miss Judson and I were being Exiled to the seaside, while Father got as far away from us as possible.

Miss Judson turned me to face her. "You may not believe this, but your father just wants you to have a good time—"

"I'd have a good time in Paris. With him."

"—doing something that does not involve *murder*."

I glowered at her. "An ordinary holiday. Like an ordinary girl."

"Exactly. I'm sure you can manage that. Rumor has it you're clever and resourceful."

* 262 miles. I'd measured.

She plucked the Ballingall Excursions brochure from my hands and slipped it into my valise. "Finish packing. We're going to miss the train. Be downstairs in fifteen minutes, and if that hat is not on your head when you appear, I shall make you sit next to Aunt Helena for the entire trip."

She would, too. Peony offered a little warble of sympathy.

Defeated, I beheld the sea of garments before me. My great aunt Helena had been sending shipments of new clothes for weeks. My Holiday Wardrobe was now three times the size of my regular wardrobe, and included the aforementioned sailor suit (for yachting), a Promenade Ensemble (for walking), a Walking Dress (for . . . ?), and a perfectly horrifying bathing costume, of which no further mention shall be made, for the protection of the Reader's delicate sensibilities.

Objections aside, the *notion* of a holiday was not necessarily unwelcome. The past several weeks had been rather trying. The Redgraves Murder was national news, but even I'd stopped collecting newspaper clippings about it. I hadn't been called upon to testify *at all*, despite having (almost) single-handedly solved the crime myself! It had been my first professional triumph as an Investigator, but Swinburne's Prosecuting Solicitor—that is, Father—had engineered matters to keep my name out of the official version of events, and refused to see the logic in permitting me to give evidence. Instead, while the case proceeded miles away in London (an entirely reasonable destination for a holiday, I might point out, boasting the Natural History Museum, Madame Tussaud's waxworks, and the Central Criminal Court), I had already been judged, and this was Father's verdict.

And where was Father to be, during all the Family Amusements? In Paris! At the *Symposium International sur la Médecine Légale*, a conference on forensic science. The most brilliant criminologists from all over the world were going to be there, sharing the latest developments in crime-scene analysis and post-mortem pathology. Famous French experts like Dr. Lacassagne, founder of Europe's most prestigious forensics school, and Mssr. Bertillon, the policeman who invented mug shots and anthropometry,* would be speaking, and there was going to be a debate on the merits of fingerprinting.

While *I* languished in sunny Fairhaven, collecting seashells.

"Exceptional Forbearance, indeed," I said to Peony. "Assuming I don't die of boredom." I hadn't yet seen a case that could *reliably* cite Tedium as a cause of death—but if I had to be the first case study, at least the holiday wouldn't be a complete waste of time.

"Mrrow," Peony agreed.

---

* also called bertillonage, his clever system of measuring prisoners to identify them later. I wondered if it was as tedious for the criminals as being fitted for Aunt Helena's wardrobe had been.

"It's all very well for *you*," I said. "You'll be here with your sunbeams and your fish heads and Cook." With a final wretched sigh, I picked up The Hat–the crowning humiliation, quite literally, of this ordeal. With its enormous puce* bow, tiny velvet pumpkins, and sprig of dried wheat, it looked like a rotting autumnal meadow. All it lacked was a couple of flesh-eating beetles.

Peony hissed and swatted at the ribbon.

I beheld Peony. I beheld the hat. I beheld my trunk crammed full of holiday clothes and not nearly enough books. Peony beheld them as well.

"*No*," she said, firmly.

"If I have to do this, so do you." I scooped her up and dropped her unceremoniously into the hatbox,† along with a nice flannel petticoat and a leftover biscuit. Before closing the trunk, I defiantly tossed in my magnifying lens, slingshot, and a sturdy pair of Wellies that may or may not still have been wet from earlier. The hat, like a martyr, I wore.

❧

We took the tram to the railway station in Upton, where a painted banner proclaimed, WELCOME, FAIRHAVEN

---

* named for the French word for *flea*, the flattering hue of digested blood

† Lest you fear for her safety, she had been sleeping in that hatbox for the better part of the week, and it was quite the latest in hatbox engineering, sturdy pasteboard and mesh, so there was perfectly adequate oxygen.

EXCURSIONISTS! Aunt Helena marched along the platform, brandishing a walking stick like the drum major in a military parade.

"*She* seems to be enjoying herself." I shifted my grip on the hatbox, willing its contents to remain still and silent.

Miss Judson murmured, "Perhaps if she's very good, they'll let her drive the train."

I bit my lip to keep from emitting a highly unladylike snort, which Aunt Helena would *certainly* have noticed. It was a blustery October afternoon (and if that strikes you as a curious time for a seaside holiday, Dear Reader, you are not alone), and the station was crowded with expectant passengers juggling umbrellas, hatcases, and timetables. Everyone seemed to be admiring the waiting train, a modern affair of shiny purplish-black cars and a locomotive emblazoned BALLINGALL EMPRESS EXPRESS. A long red ribbon stretched the length of the platform, blocking off the train.

A stout gentleman dressed like a circus ringmaster strutted about, smiling broadly through his copious sandy whiskers. I recognized him from his Brochure as Sir Quentin Ballingall, Excursion Impresario, the fellow behind this scheme of Aunt Helena's. She'd spoken of him frequently over the last few years, always in glowing terms, and often signed on for his holiday packages. She'd been on some sort of seaside tour with him most of the summer. But this was the first time she'd roped Miss Judson and me into going with her.

"Ah, Judson. Here you are at last." Aunt Helena turned her severe gaze to me. "Helena Myrtle. What on earth is that thing on your head? That can't possibly be the hat I ordered for you."

I gave them both a look of outrage, but my protest was forestalled by the arrival of a harried young woman in a severe black frock, toting a knitted bag and a rolled-up travel rug. "Miss Hardcastle," she panted, "they said if you want to change your dinner order you'll have to take it up with the staff on board."

"Has Aunt Helena fired another round of housemaids?" I said sympathetically, but the girl just looked at me blankly.

"Miss Highsmith is my Paid Companion." Aunt Helena spoke as if this were a great honor. "The Ballingalls have engaged her on my behalf. Ladies of Quality do not travel *alone.*" She turned to Miss Highsmith. "Never mind about that, Cicely. Go and see what the delay is. Sir Quentin can't mean to keep us standing about in a draft." She withdrew a coin from a beaded reticule. "Helena Myrtle, fetch yourself something to read on the train. I won't have you disrupting the journey with your mindless chatter."

I swallowed my retort when I saw the money: a whole shilling, more than enough for a week's worth of papers, which just goes to show you how many newspapers Aunt Helena had bought. Before Miss Judson could make me return it, I scurried across the platform toward the station. A woman waiting at the ticket window gave me a friendly nod as I slipped inside.

The newsagent's was well stocked, and I spent a few moments fortifying myself for the next fourteen hours. I selected *The Times*, *The Strand*, and *Illustrated London News*, which was not exactly reputable, but had the most entertaining headlines. Mindful of Miss Judson's eyes on me (even through the station's brick walls), I dutifully added a copy of the *Girl's Own Paper*, in which to conceal the others.

I took my newspapers, the hatbox, and my generous handful of change and returned to the platform, to Observe that Aunt Helena had gone off to complain about the Intolerable Delay, and that Miss Judson was now absorbed in sketching the *Empress Express*.

She made a striking image herself, in her dark green traveling suit, far more elegant than her habitual attire. It set off her deep complexion, but looked exceptionally prone to being stained by salt water and sand. She'd brought along *three* trunks, in addition to her valise, and though I knew one was stocked with easels, pastels, her watercolor set, and fresh sketchbooks, I was powerless to imagine how she could need as many clothes as she seemed to have packed. I didn't even know she *had* that many clothes.

An alarming thought struck me. Miss Judson originally hailed from French Guiana, a part of the world known for its shining tropical beaches.* I bit the fingers of my gloves and considered this. Was she expecting to enjoy herself on this holiday? I felt a curious sting at this thought—something akin to betrayal, although I could not quite work out who was betraying whom.

Well, I might have been crimped into a fortnight's holiday, but that was no reason to let my skills get rusty. A busy railway station made an excellent venue for honing my Observational Techniques. I set up post by a brick pillar with a pasted notice warning passengers to be alert for Suspicious Characters, giving me an unobstructed view of the whole platform and the length of the snaky purple train. I tucked the hatbox neatly against my ankles and disguised myself behind my newspapers to survey the scene.

Black-clad railway guards and porters swarmed the platform and the train, preparing for the journey. An identical pair of elderly ladies, clutching matching baskets, twittered and pointed, their fluffy white heads bobbing like pigeons, as a fellow with an oversized valise skulked by, hat pulled low, concealing his features in a manner that could definitely be considered suspicious. I made a mental note to track his movements aboard the train. A nurse pushed through

* and a considerably less shining French penal colony, where her parents ministered to the prisoners

the crowd, wheeling a frail-looking young woman in a wicker bath chair. She waved down a porter, who helped her wrangle the contraption and its passenger past the red ribbon and into one of the passenger carriages.

As I Observed, the lady in red left the ticket window without buying anything and continued on to the platform—directly toward the *Empress Express*. She eyed the train with a critical manner that was entirely unlike the other passengers. She seemed oblivious to the fanfare, instead intent on her study of the train itself.

Dear Reader, I need hardly note the danger posed by saboteurs on railways. The sensational newspapers were full of warnings about anarchists planting explosives aboard locomotives, knocking out bridges, or disabling signals so trains would derail. Though I would not mind should something happen to derail this holiday *before* it got started, I rather hoped to avoid disaster once it had begun. Juggling Peony's hatbox and my newspapers, I decided to get a closer look.

I followed the lady. Carefully, of course—I had been practicing Mr. Holmes's shadowing techniques. Although my efforts to pursue Peony with stealth had met with some challenge, I was getting better at Observing Cook unawares.* I hung back a bit and

* So she told me, at any rate.

pretended to focus on my newspaper—not, I'll grant you, the most convincing of diversions (a twelve-year-old girl reading *Illustrated London News* does raise an eyebrow or two). Peony uttered a discontented warble from within the hatbox, barely audible above all the bustle and noise.

My subject was somewhat older than Father, with curly fair hair beneath a red hat and carrying a well-worn carpetbag with her brolly stuck in the handles. She didn't stand out especially from the other middle-aged ladies in their smart traveling costumes, but she was unduly attentive, striding up to the loco and peering into the cab and beneath the wheels. A commotion from inside the cab caught both our notice: the driver was arguing with a stocky, red-faced guard. I could not hear what they were saying without creeping too close and being discovered, but the woman paused to listen.

A moment later, the guard stormed off the cab and disappeared down along the train. My subject moved on, evidently having decided to plant her sabotaging device elsewhere, and took a quick glance about the platform. I froze and focused on the sketch of a steamship explosion in Prussia, bodies flung everywhere. "Be glad we're not *sailing* to Fairhaven," I told Peony—and looked up in time to see the woman in red duck beneath the ribbon to climb aboard an unguarded passenger car.

I darted after her, arriving at the vestibule mounting block just as a red flounce disappeared inside the carriage. I slipped under the ribbon, shoved Peony's box before me up the stairs, and sneaked aboard the *Ballingall Empress Express.*

Whereupon I was momentarily distracted from my quarry. I let out my breath and stared, quite overcome. I'd been aboard trains before, of course, but this was less like a railway carriage than somebody's overstuffed parlor. Every inch of it was purple—everything that wasn't polished brass or glittering crystal or burnished wood or gilded fretwork, that is. A glass ceiling arched overhead, hung with electric lights that shone on the plush purple carpeting and plump velvet furniture. Even a piano had not escaped the decorator's attentions.

Now that I'd followed the saboteur onto the train, the jig was up: she could see me as plainly as I could see her. But she ignored me. She'd dropped her carpetbag and brolly by the piano and was inspecting a cloth-covered case set on a plinth, like in a museum, and she looked downright unhappy about it. Forehead deeply creased, she was jotting in a notebook, shaking her head.

"No, no, and no." She punctuated this with jabs of her pencil. "Not satisfactory, not at all."

"Are you supposed to be in here?" I said loudly. The woman in red didn't even turn around.

"One might ask the same, Myrtle Hardcastle. This is the Ladies' Lounge, and I am—last I checked—a lady."

A quiver of surprise went through me. "How do you know my name?"

"It's my business to know."

What did she mean by that? "Sir Quentin wouldn't like you in here," I hazarded.

She looked up at last, with a laugh. "No, he would not. Come here. Tell me what you think."

I hesitated. But curiosity got the better of me—about her, and about what was in the case she was so upset about. I crept forward, bracing myself for something ghastly (rattlesnakes? shrunken heads?), and she pulled off the cloth.

Inside was a crown, huge and delicate, glittering with diamonds and vast greeny-purple stones. A placard read:

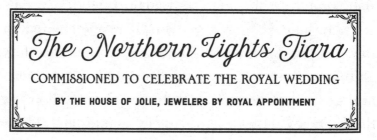

The Northern Lights Tiara

COMMISSIONED TO CELEBRATE THE ROYAL WEDDING

BY THE HOUSE OF JOLIE, JEWELERS BY ROYAL APPOINTMENT

"Is that real?" The stones' color shifted as I looked at them, like an enchantment in a fairy story. "What's it doing here?"

The woman clapped her notebook shut. "That, Miss Hardcastle, is my question. This is not what I agreed to at all."

"Is it yours?" I took a better look at her. She seemed to be an ordinary sort of woman, and her worn bag and practical suit hardly suggested wildly expansive wealth, let alone a penchant for tiaras.

She gave another laugh. "You might say so! And yet, no. But I *am* responsible for it, and this arrangement"—she waved a hand at the case—"is entirely unacceptable."

"You won't get away with stealing it," I declared. "I'll go and tell Sir Quentin that you're in here, messing about with his—tiara." That sentence limped to an improbable end, and I heard a judgmental meow from my sidekick in the hatbox.

The woman turned away from the case. "And what will you tell him, exactly, Miss Hardcastle?"

"That you've boarded his train without a ticket. I saw you being turned away from the ticket counter. This is a subscription excursion. You can't just buy a fare at the last moment. And you've sneaked aboard the Ladies' Lounge for obviously nefarious purposes. I can tell you're trying to figure out how to breach that jewel case's defenses."

She broke into a wide smile. "Oh, brava!"

She had no chance to elaborate, for at that moment,

the heavy vestibule door squealed open and Sir Quentin himself burst in.

She pounced before he had a chance to speak. "*Mr.* Ballingall, this is a clear violation of your insurance policy. The tiara is to be kept in the train's safe at all times—not on display like fruit at a greengrocer's!"

"Now, Mrs. Bloom." Sir Quentin wove through the furniture, holding his arms open. His ringmaster's jacket matched the purple velvet upholstery. "Don't get your dander up. That case was made for me by the same chaps who supplied them for the Crown Jewels. Or don't you trust the Tower Guard?" He had a booming voice that echoed above the roar of the steam engine and the expectant shudder of the carriage.

"Not especially," Mrs. Bloom said. "Even young Miss Hardcastle spotted the faults in your security straightaway."

"Why *do* you know my name?" I asked again. It was seeming less likely that she was a thief or saboteur.

"Because she's an interfering busybody, that's why."

Evidently I'd blundered my way into a quarrel and should have extricated myself, but I was brimming with curiosity.

Mrs. Bloom handed me a calling card. "I am a representative of Albion Casualty Insurance, engaged by the owners of this tiara to ensure its protection en route to Fairhaven. Miss Hardcastle, where do you stand on breach of contract?"

This was like standing for an exam I hadn't studied for, bewildering and a little exhilarating. "Er–against it?"

"Quite right. Mr. Ballingall, I'll be revoking your policy." She moved to pick up her carpetbag, but Sir Quentin stepped in front of her, a hand gripping her elbow.

"You wouldn't dare," he said in a low voice.

He was twice her size, like a mountain standing in her way, but Mrs. Bloom tipped her head up and regarded him coolly. "I think you'll find it isn't advisable to threaten me."

This time his laugh felt forced. "I'm not threatening you, woman! I'm sure we can come to some agreement. Let me show you what I've done before you make up your mind."

Seizing my shoulders, he steered me round the case, thundering in my ear: "Laminated glass!" He rapped heartily on the panes. "Practically unbreakable. And a solid steel frame, so it can't be smashed." He gave the whole display a shove, and it didn't budge. "Bolted down!"

"What about the lock?" I pointed, and Sir Quentin beamed as proudly as if I'd admired his baby.

"World's most advanced combination-dial lock. Six wheels, and nobody knows the code but me. Absolutely unpickable. You see, ladies? *Perfectly* safe. You'd have to be mad to try anything aboard the *Empress Express*!

I've thought of everything on this train, I have. Mrs. Bloom, if you'll stick around, we might manage to impress you yet."

She didn't *look* impressible. Just then she was eyeing Sir Quentin with undisguised disapproval. "I doubt that, Mr. Ballingall. And don't worry. I have no intention of going anywhere. I'm not letting that tiara out of my sight."

2

Caveat Viator

Railway travel is by far the most efficient means of seeing our fair island. The comforts of the modern rail carriage permit the traveler to enjoy the sights of England, without having to endure its climate or people.

—*Hardcastle's Practical Travel Companion*

Aunt Helena and Miss Judson were not well pleased to find me alone in the company of Sir Quentin and Mrs. Bloom. They stormed aboard, trailed by the harried Miss Highsmith, now toting the knitted bag, the travel rug, a picnic hamper, and a tennis racquet and looking like she was about to faint.

"Helena Myrtle!" my aunt barked. "Where have you been? You gave Judson a terror, disappearing like that!"

I had never seen Miss Judson in a terror, but she certainly looked piqued. Eyebrow quirked, she beckoned me with a crook of her finger. I hung tight to Peony's hatbox and composed my defense, but Sir Quentin made it unnecessary. And impossible.

He grabbed me in another bone-crushing squeeze. "Helena, give the girl some credit! She's a plucky lass, just like you."

Now Aunt Helena spotted Mrs. Bloom. "I might have known," she said, charging down the carriage like a bull. "You haven't made a pest of yourself with decent people enough, Mrs. Bloom, that you must go about accosting their children!"

She yanked me toward her. I was going to get a concussion at this rate.

"Nobody accosted me! I *followed* her."

"Myrtle suspected I might be planning to sabotage the train." Mrs. Bloom said this with complete gravity, and not to make the other adults laugh. "She was naturally concerned."

"Naturally," Miss Judson murmured.

"Sabotage?" Aunt Helena sniffed. "On an *English* train? I hardly think so."

Miss Judson coughed politely. I freed myself and Peony at last and hastened over to her.

Aunt Helena was not finished with Mrs. Bloom. "You are a disgrace to respectable company, and I'll see Sir Quentin throw you out on your ear." She banged her stick against the carpeted floor for emphasis. Aunt Helena was irascible and disapproving as a rule (you could classify her scientifically by the trait: *Amita helena irritabilis*)—but this seemed out of proportion, even for her.

"Well, you could try," Mrs. Bloom offered conversationally. "But Mr. Ballingall and I have come to an agreement. Isn't that right? Miss Hardcastle, do sit down before you topple the train, and Miss Highsmith, you're not a pack mule. Don't let her treat you like one."

Sir Quentin tried to be appeasing. "Mrs. Bloom is merely here to, shall we say, oversee the arrangements. Isn't that right, Myrtle?"

I didn't like being drawn into their disagreement, and I wasn't sure how to answer that. But I was saved from replying when the vestibule doors once more made their shrieking announcement of the arrival of yet another party.

"Father! Where have you got to? Everyone's waiting for your speech!" This was delivered by a younger, female version of Sir Quentin. Several years older than Miss Judson, she was squat and plump, with colorless hair scraped back into a knot, and birdlike eyes in her round face.

"Temperance!" Sir Quentin boomed. "Come and meet our guests. We've assembled early. Jumped the gun, so to speak."

Miss Ballingall clomped aboard, clad in a drab plaid cape over a faded walking skirt. Her right arm was bent at her waist, the fist balled up as if hiding something, and in her left she bore a startlingly large pair of gleaming gold scissors.

"Oh, good," said Aunt Helena. "I assumed Cicely had lost them."

"It was ever so kind of you to lend them, dear Helena," said Miss Ballingall. "You know how Father loves his ceremony!" She held the scissors out to Sir Quentin, who replied with a disappointed scowl.

"You've all invaded my train before we could *have* the ceremony," he huffed. "Not much point to it anymore."

"Father, don't be silly. You've prepared your speech. That's all that matters. We'd love to hear it."

"Nope, nope. Won't hear of it now. I'll go and tell them to take down the ribbon. Where's that porter? Must get the ladies settled." He took the scissors and bustled out the opposite door, behind the piano.

Miss Ballingall came smiling through the carriage. "Well. What a muddle! Father won't soon forget this," she said, with a wink. "He'll be telling that story for years. Everyone, come and sit down, or should I fetch the porters so you can all see to your compartments? Yes, that's best, isn't it?"

She reached up with her left arm and tugged on the signal wire, which swagged along the length of the ceiling. "Don't do this while we're running, though—it will stop the train."

She turned to me, solemn and merry at the same time. "Miss Myrtle, we are Very Glad Indeed to have you aboard. I hope you enjoy our little Excursion. Dear Helena speaks of you constantly, and I feel I've known you—and you, Miss Judson, of course!—for years."

She moved on to Mrs. Bloom. "I'm sorry we didn't have a chance to meet earlier. I hope Father wasn't too dreadful."

"Not at all, Miss Ballingall. I hope you've been well."

Miss Ballingall's face clouded, and she rubbed absently at her arm. "Life with Father on one of his schemes is always such a whirlwind!"

"I'm sure he'll make a great success of it, my dear," said Mrs. Bloom.

Miss Ballingall tried to laugh. "Well, we'll try at any rate! Sunny Fairhaven awaits. Good thing you've brought your umbrella." Still rubbing her arm, she set off toward the vestibule door. "Let me arrange a compartment for you. We're not so full up as all that."

☙

Under the cheerful direction of Miss Ballingall, we got settled in our compartments, such as they were.

"How can you be disappointed?" demanded Miss Judson, surveying her bed in all its gilded and flounced and befringed glory, the glittering crystal chandelier, the Turkish carpet. "This is positively luxurious!"

"The Brochure said Pullman sleeping cars." I'd expected clever convertible furniture—settees that turned into bunks, or berths that folded down from the ceiling. "These are just bedrooms. Isn't anything on here a *proper* train?"

Miss Judson shook her head and stashed her valise in a cubby sized for exactly that purpose. Peony, liberated from the hatbox, immediately settled atop my pillow in the adjoining compartment. I followed her in but could still hear Miss Judson through the communicating door.

"Did you see the *Tiare Aurore*?" She pronounced this with a decidedly French accent, making it sound even more alluring. "I wonder if I can capture those colors. I ought to have brought my oils."

"Sir Quentin was supposed to store it in the safe." I summarized his quarrel with Mrs. Bloom.

Miss Judson swung into my compartment. "Perhaps we'll be beset by highwaymen."

"We're on a *train*." Although that did happen all the time in America.

"Or maybe even"—she scooped Peony up and dandled her white forepaws—"*cat* burglars."

"*No*," Peony said, wriggling free.

I could not decide whether or not to be disappointed in Miss Judson's utter lack of reaction to my smuggling of Peony aboard the train—but I decided not to remark on it, if she wasn't going to. Instead, I just stuffed the Decaying Hat into a cubby and gathered up my newspapers.

"Ahem." Miss Judson held out an expectant hand, and I handed them over. She gave a little sigh.

"What?"

"You know perfectly well what." She sorted through them, frown intensifying. "This goes against our express purpose of being here. You are on *holiday*." She waved her hand at the Positively Luxurious compartment for emphasis.

I watched the newspapers with a visceral longing I could scarcely explain. Especially with Father in Paris, someone had to monitor things. "I need to know what's going on. In London. At—at the sessions." I couldn't bring myself to say *trial*.

Her frown softened. "Your father is keeping abreast of the case and has promised to inform you of any important developments."

"They're all important!"

"Really." She flipped through the *Upton Register*. "What revelations do you expect from an interview with Mr. Ambrose's first-form teacher?" She tossed the papers over to Peony on the bed, shuffled me into the corridor, and shut my compartment door with a decisive click.

☙

Back aboard the Ladies' Lounge carriage, everyone was admiring the tiara. The cover had been removed from the case, and the jewels glowed blue-green in the afternoon sun. Our party had been joined by the matched pair of elderly ladies, as well as the invalid woman with her nurse, and even her weary eyes were drawn to the gemstones.

"Aren't they stunning?" twittered one of the old ladies. The tiara was twice the size of her head, and she had to stand on tiptoe to blink myopically into the case.

"Stunning," her companion chirped back.

Aunt Helena peered through the glass with her lorgnette. "I was *at* the Royal Wedding* myself, of course." She made it sound as though she'd been a guest, and hadn't merely crabbed for a view through the crush on Marlborough Street like thousands of other people in London. "What a *coup* for Sir Quentin to have them here on his train for us to see up close."

"They're such an extraordinary color—colors." Cicely gazed at the jewels, dark eyes huge and luminous.

"Aren't they?" said Miss Ballingall. "Alexandrite stones appear green in sunlight, but take on their enchanting violet cast by artificial light. Father had the electricity installed especially to show off the Northern Lights to their best advantage. The effect is so much more brilliant than by gas or candlelight."

---

* Princess Mary of Teck to His Royal Highness Prince George, Duke of York, 6 July 1893. It was a national sensation. If you like that sort of thing.

"They really do evoke the aurora borealis," said Miss Judson. "What do you plan to do with them in Fairhaven, Sir Quentin? Forgive me, but I don't think they'll go with your suit."

Sir Quentin's laugh rumbled like cannon fire. "They'll be the centerpiece at my new hotel. Crowds will come from miles around to see them—maybe even convince the House of Jolie to open up a branch in town."

"It seems a shame to keep them locked up." I Observed that Miss Judson was working on a sketch of some unknown woman, face not yet filled in, coronet of dark braids crowned by the tiara.

"They'd look smashing on *you*, Miss Judson! Ought to have you model them for me. Catch all the rich young men's eyes."

Miss Judson regarded him mysteriously. "Hmm."

I glanced over to Observe Mrs. Bloom Observing all of *us*, watching us with cold calculation, as if working out who was most likely to "make a move" on the stones. It made me uncomfortable, and I tugged at the collar of my coat. She'd taken out some knitting, and her flicking needles reminded me of Peony's sensitive whiskers, seeking out danger.

While Aunt Helena's attention was elsewhere, I approached Mrs. Bloom and took the chair opposite. "Do you really think there's any risk something might happen to the tiara?"

Clickety-click went the needles, as the wheels rumbled away underfoot, a stimulating rhythm that thrummed into my bones. "Miss Hardcastle, I make my living assuming there's always a risk."

I still had her calling card, and now I finally gave it a proper inspection. An engraving of a cloud-ringed mountain sat above text which read:

MRS. ISID. BLOOM, INVESTIGATOR
ALBION CASUALTY INSURANCE CO.
MANCHESTER • LEEDS • LONDON

"Investigator!" I breathed, scarcely believing it. "Like the Pinkertons or something?"

"Hardly anything so melodramatic. I'm an insurance investigator."

"What's that?" I hadn't realized there was anywhere in England a woman could be a professional Investigator. I'd been expecting to make my way to America and the Pinkerton National Detective Agency, if Scotland Yard didn't work out.

"Loss prevention. I make sure all the claims made against stolen or damaged goods are authentic." She rummaged in her carpetbag and held out a paper package of sweets. "Humbug? Assuredly *not* poisoned. We hardly want a repeat of Bradford, do we?"

My eyes widened in appreciation. The infamous case of arsenic-laced candy from 1858 had killed twenty-one people and led to important laws to protect food from contamination. I took one and sucked on it companionably as Mrs. Bloom knitted. Checking up on insurance fraud didn't *sound* terribly interesting–not like investigating murders–but even so! "What makes you think the tiara is at risk?"

With a shrewd look, Mrs. Bloom produced a newspaper of her own, the *Portsmouth Evening News*, dated a few days ago. The front page was dedicated to John Monson's upcoming murder trial in Scotland (yet another place we might have gone instead of Fairhaven). "Have a look at page three."

I glanced at Miss Judson, reluctant to commit this particular transgression without waiting a few minutes, at least, but she was absorbed in her sketchbook. Flipping through, I spotted a small item wedged into the corner:

BRIGHTON BANDIT
STRIKES AGAIN!

Police in Brighton, Southsea, and Eastbourne report that the thefts of jewelry plaguing holiday resort towns this summer——previously thought to have slackened——have recommenced. The thief or thieves have thus far absconded with properties surpassing £100. No suspects are yet identified, and none of the stolen items has been recovered.

I let out all my breath and my eyes flew over the edge of the paper to Mrs. Bloom. Jewel thieves! In seaside holiday towns! "That's why you wanted the tiara stored in the safe."

Mrs. Bloom sat back into her purple armchair. "Still, Sir Quentin's probably right. You'd have to be mad to try something on a moving train."

"Or daring," I said, thinking of Billy Garrett, my favorite penny dreadful hero. I glanced around the carriage, trying to see the other passengers as Mrs. Bloom did—as potential thieves. "How *did* you know my name? Do you know everyone aboard?"

Now she gave me the shrewd look, indicating her bag. "Passenger manifest," she said. "And employee rolls. Provided by Eastern Coastal Railways." She had an air of satisfaction that reminded me even more of Peony. "I know more about this train than Sir Quentin, and he built the thing."

Such a vast amount of information to possess—about us, about everyone. I couldn't decide whether to be envious or uncomfortable. Yet preventing crimes *before* the fact—there was a novel idea. I wanted to know more. "What other cases have you worked on? Is it all famous jewels?"

"Wouldn't that be fun! No, accidents, mostly. Sometimes suspicious deaths." Her eyes slid toward me. "But nothing like what *you've* been up to, Miss

Myrtle Hardcastle of Swinburne. The Redgraves Murder? Impressive."

I could feel my cheeks color. "That was in the passenger manifest?" I said meekly.

Her grey eyes glittered. "I have my sources. But I would love to hear the *real* story."

Twisting my fingers together, I glanced across at Miss Judson—she'd played a major role, as well. "I'm supposed to be on holiday." My voice was faint and soggy.

Mrs. Bloom nodded. "I understand." I couldn't help the flood of disappointment that washed through me. "Perhaps another time."

"Will you be staying in Fairhaven, too?"

"Indeed I shall."

"On business?" My voice was eager.

"Visiting old friends. How long will Hardcastle and Associates be there?"

"A fortnight," I said, with a tortured sigh.

She dipped into her carpetbag and handed me a thick book with a faded black cloth cover. "Here. If you run out of things to do, the shoreline hereabouts is an excellent source."

"Source?" The book, *Figures of Characteristic British Fossils* by William Hellier Baily, was full of detailed sketches of snails and ferns and otherworldly creatures like insects gone nightmarishly awry. *Trilobite*, declared the caption: *Actual Size.* I shut the book again with a shudder.

"I find it a very satisfying sort of detective work," she said. "The idea that the past is never buried for good, but always ready to reveal itself to someone determined to find it."

I liked that. It did describe Investigation quite nicely.

"Keep that," she added. "See what you can dig up on that beach."

"But don't you need it?"

Mrs. Bloom shook her head. "I've done my digging in Fairhaven," she said—and the *way* she said it, the way adults often say such things, made me think she meant something entirely different.

"What do you mean? Are you here to 'dig up' some other old mystery?"

She just smiled that cryptic smile again. "It seems you're being Summoned."

With dismay, I turned and followed her gaze across the car, to where my impertinent chatter had drawn Aunt Helena's attention. She was staring daggers at the both of us. "I'd better go," I said. "She'll say I'm bothering you."

"You *aren't.*" Mrs. Bloom's voice was firm.

"When can I see you again?" I asked. "I have so many questions."

"Perhaps breakfast tomorrow, if your party can spare you? Dining carriage, seven o'clock?"

"They can spare me." I wouldn't miss that appointment for all the alexandrites in Russia.

⁓

At night, the *Empress Express* seemed even more elegant. After dinner in the dining car (during which I was subjected to Aunt Helena's Strong Opinions on everything from the Disgraceful Mrs. Bloom and Respectable Jobs for Ladies to the deplorable state of the drains in Most Seaside Towns), we assembled once more in the lounge carriage. The elderly ladies, who were called Miss Causton and Miss Cabot, sat together like eager children, bouncing in their seats and whispering, while Nurse Temby fussed over the sickly Miss Penrose. Sir Quentin had changed his ringmaster's costume for a deep aubergine dinner jacket, but Miss Ballingall was nowhere to be seen. The glass case with the tiara had been covered once more, and I was itching to peek under the cloth. I wanted to see the exotic coloration of the stones come alive under Sir Quentin's electric lights.

Miss Judson had drawn no fewer than four studies of the tiara, from all angles, trying to capture its shifting colors. But she had put away her sketchbook and we all sat in rapt expectation, waiting for the evening's Entertainment to begin.

We did not have to wait long. A few minutes after ten o'clock, as we rumbled contently along the coastline, a porter heaved open the vestibule door, admitting a draft and Miss Ballingall. I let out a gasp, for she was transformed. Gone was the dowdy plaid, and in its place an elegant swish of loose blue velvet, long silvery gloves, and a hairstyle that must have taken all evening to achieve—upon which was perched, in a crest of dazzling violet, the Northern Lights.

Mrs. Bloom was on her feet in an instant, quivering with outrage, but as Miss Ballingall glided through the carriage like a frosty peacock, she made herself take her seat. She sat at the very edge of the plush armchair and fixed Sir Quentin with an accusing look, which he flagrantly ignored.

He had bounded to his own feet to take his daughter's hand. "Now, my good ladies, I present to you the true treasure of the *Empress Express*, my precious songbird herself—in an exclusive debut performance, my daughter, Temperance!" He held her left hand aloft as she dipped a surprisingly graceful curtsy.

"Oh, thank you all," she said, round cheeks glowing. "If you'll forgive me, I may be out of practice . . ." She gave a nervous cough.

Another movement in the carriage caught my eye. Nurse Temby rose to her feet and seized the handles of the bath chair. "Please excuse us." She was a small, sturdy woman of middling years, with iron-grey hair held up by a white peaked cap. She wheeled the bath chair into the aisle. "Miss Penrose isn't feeling up to this much company, I'm afraid."

"Yes, do forgive me." Miss Penrose's voice was thready and ethereal, like she was speaking across a great distance. Her pallid skin looked translucent in the lamplight, and the hand she offered Miss Ballingall trembled. Miss Judson had said she was only twenty-two years old, but it was hard to believe.

"Dear Maud, there's nothing at all to forgive!" Miss Ballingall gave them a kind smile. "Don't trouble yourself about my little business here." She watched them depart, concern creasing her brow—unless that was the weight of the tiara. "Poor girl," she murmured.

Miss Penrose's departure cast a pall over the carriage, but Sir Quentin set us back on track. "We need a little musical entertainment more than ever now, my dear." With a snap of his fingers, the electric lights dimmed, and Cicely slipped to the piano. A hush fell over the carriage, Miss Ballingall coughed again, and a moment later, a tremulous song, wan and wispy as Miss Penrose, made its hesitant way past her lips.

We had to strain to hear her. In the low lights, the carriage felt cavernous and echoey. Every sound seemed amplified: each slight rustle and intake of breath, sour note of the piano, uncomfortable shift of backside against velvet. Miss Ballingall's song—an Italian melody that might once have been on its way to an opera, but got lost and found Miss Ballingall instead–tried to work through the crushing silence, but her voice wavered and broke and caught back on itself.

I bit my lip to push back a dreadful–I think it was Sympathy, Dear Reader. Like watching a fledgling take its first awkward foray out of the nest, before plummeting to the earth with a splat.

The song finally splintered to its brittle end, and Miss Ballingall took a tiny, shy bow.

"Brava!" Miss Judson clapped with far too much enthusiasm. A painfully long moment later, Mrs. Bloom and the Bird Ladies joined her.

"I keep telling you, Quentin, she ought to have pursued a career on the stage," Aunt Helena said rapturously, shocking me. For one thing, I had never heard Aunt Helena give the faintest suggestion that a woman should pursue anything other than the delicate art of decorating a drawing room. For another, it was not like Aunt Helena to be–well, nice.

Sir Quentin didn't seem to notice. "That song was written specially for her." His voice rang with pride. "Wait till you see the stage I've built for her in Fairhaven!"

Miss Ballingall beamed, the tiara sparkling. "You're too kind. Are there any requests for my next piece?"

The Bird Ladies chirped in unison: "'Spanish Ladies,'" suggested one, while the other said, "'Onward, Christian Soldiers'!"

Faced with these polar opposites, Miss Ballingall balked—but at a nod from Sir Quentin, Cicely struck up a lively march, and Miss Ballingall relaxed and caught up. She was a little more confident this time, her voice warming to a popular current song with a chorus everyone could join. And all the while, there was the tiara. As Miss Ballingall's head bobbed in time to the music, the electricity and mirrors sent the alexandrites and diamonds into a shimmering shower of dazzling purple light—exactly like the celestial display from which the Northern Lights took their name.

Cicely's piano hit a devastating crescendo, and Miss Ballingall's voice rose to a pitch and volume that shuddered the crystals on the chandeliers. And our eardrums. She had just taken a great breath when, abruptly, the electricity failed, plunging the carriage into darkness.

Miss Ballingall's voice cut off immediately, but it took Cicely a couple more keystrokes to catch up. I stared around me, fruitlessly, as everyone murmured protests and alarm. Miss Judson's arm reached for me, and on instinct, I caught her hand and squeezed back.

"No one move." I think that was Mrs. Bloom. "Temperance, kindly be on your guard."

"What's happened?" said one of the Bird Ladies. "Is this part of the entertainment? How exciting!"

"Exciting!" Her companion clapped her hands.

"No, no, just a power surge, I'm sure. Nothing to fear, ladies! I'll be along to check on it." I heard Sir Quentin lever himself from his chair. An electrical dynamo might take some time to repair, and the modern carriage, outfitted with its modern fixtures, was ill equipped for primitive catastrophes like this.

A moment later, I heard the squeal of the heavy door, followed by a rush of icy air.

Followed by a little cry.

And then a shriek. "My jewels! The tiara! It's gone!"

3

HIGHWAY ROBBERY

Thanks to the advances of the modern railway, travelers need no longer fear the hazards that faced our forebears on their arduous journeys across the lawless countryside.

—*Hardcastle's Practical Travel Companion*

After that, it was pandæmonium.* Miss Ballingall kept screaming, drowning out the wail of the train whistle and a confusion of gasps, cries, and panicked rustles. Aunt Helena fought to be heard above it all.

"For heaven's sakes, someone fetch a light!" she bellowed. "The poor girl's being murdered!"

Miss Judson's crisp voice came from beside me: "Myrtle, the signal cord."

"Of course!" I was closest, but lacked reach. I felt something pressed into my hand—Mrs. Bloom's

---

* A splendid word coined for us by John Milton: the capital city of Hell in *Paradise Lost*, it means "Place of All Demons" in Greek.

umbrella! Flailing overhead in the pitch dark, I finally caught the handle around the electrical cord that would signal the locomotive and open the brake pipes, bringing the carriage to a shrieking halt. I gave it an almighty yank, expecting the alarm to sound, and braced myself for the crash.

Nothing happened. Frantically, I tugged again and again.

"It's not working!"

Was it the faulty electricity? I tried to scramble free of the seat, with the thought to make it to the next carriage down and pull *that* cord—but I thunked into somebody's skirts. A shower of red light flared up, casting a devilish halo around Mrs. Bloom's pale face.

"Fusee," she said. "Signal flare. Standard equipment on every English train. Never travel anywhere without them." She held the torch aloft—it wasn't terrifically bright to see with, being intended to be *seen* by, but it was better than nothing. "No one move!" she called out again. "Myrtle, take this."

It was not at all like holding a well-behaved household candle. The fusee wasn't much larger than an ordinary taper and felt nicely substantial—but it threw off a spray of wild red sparks, a sort of roaring hiss, and a huge, erratic, leaping flame. It's a miracle I didn't set the whole carriage ablaze. But I managed to keep hold of it, and crept behind Mrs. Bloom. Miss Judson produced a box of candles (she no doubt had them stashed on her person, for just such an eventuality), and we used the flare to light all four, jamming them into the lamps and sconces. It was only a mild improvement over the complete darkness, a few bright dots here and there.

Miss Ballingall's cries finally subsided, as she succumbed instead to a swoon. She lay cradled in Cicely's arms, strands of colorless hair scattered across her face—clear evidence that, indeed, the Northern Lights had been wrenched from her head. Cicely froze, like a terrified rabbit caught in the light of my flare.

Mrs. Bloom bent over them. "Get her up. Has anyone smelling salts? Miss Hardcastle?" She held out an expectant hand to Aunt Helena, who recoiled.

"Get away from the poor girl! She's suffered a terrible fright. We all have." Aunt Helena tried to shove Mrs. Bloom aside (in a ladylike way, of course), but Mrs. Bloom would not budge.

"She will be fine. The smelling salts, if you please. There's been a robbery. The tiara is missing. We need to find and apprehend the culprit as soon as possible."

I held the flare as high as I could, trying to get a better view of the whole scene. "Is anyone else missing anything?" I said.

"Good thinking. Everyone, please check your belongings."

"Ooh, how thrilling!" The Bird Ladies' voices rippled through the gloom. "So realistic!"

"How are we expected to do anything in this dark?" grumbled Aunt Helena.

"Like so." Mrs. Bloom crouched beside Miss Ballingall—not, it appeared, to coax her back to wakefulness, but to examine her for clues. I held the light over them, but there was no sign of the tiara, no wink of violet-green leaping out from the shadows in the flash of the flare.

"Get off her! What do you think you're doing? Guards! Guards!" Aunt Helena shrilled, somewhat belatedly.

"She's looking for evidence," I said. "We should do as she says."

"Perhaps we ought to fetch help," suggested Miss Judson.

"Wait." Mrs. Bloom's voice was firm. "Everyone stay exactly where you are. We need to contain the scene. *I'll* go. Why didn't the signal cord work?"

At this moment, Sir Quentin returned, crashing back through the vestibule door.

"Some problem with the dynamos. Should be back up any minute." He halted, taking in the scene. "What the blazes happened in here?" Then he spotted the crumpled heap of Miss Ballingall. "Dolly!" He wrenched his daughter away from Mrs. Bloom and heaved her upright. Her eyelids fluttered. "Someone please, get us some water. Dolly, speak to me!"

On the whole, I'm afraid that the Ladies' Lounge passengers did not acquit ourselves admirably in a crisis. Cicely failed to calm Miss Ballingall; the Bird Ladies chattered on like excited audience members at a melodrama; my flare sputtered out, singeing my fingers, and I dropped it on the purple carpeting (also singed); Aunt Helena quarreled with Mrs. Bloom; and Sir Quentin roared at everyone. Thankfully, Miss Judson's level head prevailed, and she managed to get Miss Ballingall onto a settee, with her feet propped up on a cushion.

"Now, Dolly, tell me what's happened." Sir Quentin reminded me more than ever of a lion, bluff and golden in the candlelight.

"I'm not sure." Her voice wavered. Miss Causton had produced a flask of brandy ("for medicinal purposes, of course"), and Temperance was giving it unladylike—not to mention *intemperate*—gulps. "I was singing, then the lights went out—"

"I know, pet, I was here for that." He rubbed her hand as though she were suffering frostbite instead of a shock.

"Something—some*one*—yanked at my head." She touched her disheveled hair and heaved a sobbing breath. "The tiara's gone, Father. I'm so sorry."

"Hush, it's not your fault." He was red-faced with fury, staring around the compartment like he couldn't believe how we'd been violated. "Where the blazes are those guards? Er, excuse me, ladies."

I could no longer hold my tongue. "Shouldn't we—somebody—go after the thief? Before he gets away?"

"Train's moving too fast," said Sir Quentin. "He can't have got off. We'll catch him while he's still aboard." He bounded to the vestibule door and hailed two of the train guards. They appeared from the darkness like will-o'-the-wisps, bodiless pale heads in black-and-purple Ballingall livery.

"What the devil took you so long? There's been a robbery! Search the cars. You two go that way, and send two more guards toward the loco. The man can't have gone far." At his word, the guards disappeared once more.

"Or *woman*." I eyed my fellow passengers. Heavy skirts were a better hiding place than the comparatively few layers of men's clothing—and ladies, with their Delicate Sensibilities,* were less likely to be subjected to a thorough search. According to the Billy Garrett stories, that is. I sucked in an excited breath. This was just like being in a penny dreadful adventure. A jewel thief—right here aboard our very own train. Family Amusements, indeed!

---

* Science has yet to identify what, precisely, constitutes a Delicate Sensibility, but remains convinced that the female *Homo sapiens* comes burdened with an excess thereof, which interferes with her efforts to pursue any number of interesting endeavors.

"We must stop the train immediately," said Aunt Helena. "This is outrageous!"

"That's exactly what we must *not* do, Miss Hardcastle," Mrs. Bloom said. "If we slow or stop the train, he'll make good his escape."

"Perhaps he has already." Miss Judson stood at a window, contemplating the passing countryside. "How fast are we going? About thirty miles an hour? Someone might well survive such a jump."

Everyone turned to stare at her, but she regarded us serenely. I had a sudden apprehension of Miss Judson trying this for herself—or to an unsuspecting volunteer—and inched away from her.

"Unlikely," Mrs. Bloom said. "It's a hundred miles to the nearest town."

"This was well orchestrated," Miss Judson countered. "He—or she—must have planned this down to the minute." Tapping her chin, she elaborated. "He knew exactly when Miss Ballingall would be singing, so he'd likewise have known exactly where along the route we'd be at that point. He may well have a hideout nearby."

It was hard to see Mrs. Bloom's expression, but she paused to weigh my governess's theory. "Or he may still be aboard the train."

"Or even the *carriage*," Miss Judson returned. "We should all be searched, in case he slipped the jewels into our skirts or bags." She was doing her best to hide it, but Miss Judson was plainly enjoying herself, too.

"Oh, yes!" One of the Bird Ladies applauded this suggestion. "Do me first. I don't *think* anyone's hidden a tiara in my petticoats, but I should like to know for certain!"

I gazed round the dark carriage, trying to piece together exactly what had happened. "Did anybody notice someone enter or leave this car? For all we know, the thief might be one of us!" (Although we'd barely managed to scrape together candles. Clearly no one in present company was capable of engineering such a heist.*)

"Helena Myrtle!" Aunt Helena snapped. "What an absurd suggestion. I don't intend to be 'searched' by anyone—and nor will you."

Mrs. Bloom tossed up her hands in exasperation. "Then we'll call in the guards to do it."

"We shall do no such thing, Bloom." All pretense of friendliness had left Sir Quentin. "Can't you see you're upsetting everyone? Accusing my passengers of thievery!" (Actually, Miss Judson and I had done that, but nobody corrected him.) "We're the *victims* here!" He bundled Temperance to her feet. "I'm taking my daughter to her rooms now. Don't even think of disturbing her."

Mrs. Bloom tugged on her gloves, watching them leave. "This is far from over, Mr. Ballingall."

---

* with the exception of Miss Judson, apparently

46}

He paused in the doorway, arms around his daughter, who sagged against his shoulder. "Your meddling isn't going to help anything this time. What do you suppose your superiors will do when they find out you've let the tiara disappear, right under your nose? Don't think *you'll* get away from this scot-free, either." His face was nearly as purple as his jacket, and he might have meant to keep on berating her, but Miss Ballingall emitted a warbling sigh, as though about to swoon again.

Aunt Helena shoved past all of us. "Let me help, Sir Quentin. Come, Cicely." She snapped her fingers at the girl, like she was a trained spaniel. Cicely gave us all an apologetic look.

"I could—" she said tentatively, glancing helplessly around the carriage. "If you need . . ."

Lips pursed, Mrs. Bloom just sighed. "No, Miss Highsmith. It's all right. Go on ahead."

I watched this unfold with dismay. This wasn't proceeding sensibly at all! We had no more idea what had happened to the tiara than when Miss Ballingall started screaming her head off, and now the crime scene was dissolving before our very eyes. I turned to Mrs. Bloom. "Can't we do anything?" I pleaded. "You'll never see that tiara again!"

Mrs. Bloom's jaw was set as she watched everyone leave. "Don't worry. Unlike our thief, they're not going anywhere. And we still have work to do." She hoisted up her carpetbag and gave me a businesslike nod. "Coming, Myrtle?"

For a moment I couldn't speak. "Do—do you mean me?"

Her eyes sparkled. "Is there *another* Myrtle Hardcastle aboard?"

Faintly dazzled, I looked between her and Miss Judson. "May I?" My voice was a sorry little squeak, tripping over my disbelief.

Miss Judson's expression was inscrutable. "Don't make a nuisance of yourself, and I expect you to return to our compartments immediately if there's any danger." She paused, met Mrs. Bloom's eyes, and repeated: "*Immediately.*"

"Yes, Miss!" I retrieved my notebook from my seat and hastened to make myself look as Professional as possible for a twelve-year-old girl on a train who has been dressed by her great-aunt. But as I scurried at Mrs. Bloom's heels, Miss Judson watching us depart with satisfaction, a mad little laugh threatened to bubble out of me.

Aunt Helena couldn't have picked out a better holiday if she'd tried.

4

DERELICTION OF DUTY

The success of every enterprise depends on the quality, training, and dedication of its staff. The Excursion Industry is no different.

—*Hardcastle's Practical Travel Companion*

I hastened after Mrs. Bloom through the dining carriage, notebook and pencil clutched tight. Assisting a real Investigator in the search for a jewel thief! I could scarcely believe my good fortune.

The broken dynamo had only affected the Ladies' Lounge, and the lights were still functional here. The staff had cleared up from dinner, and the car was dim and empty. The train rumbled along, my heart keeping pace in my chest as we swooped through the dark night. Not breaking her stride, Mrs. Bloom sniffed the air.

"Smells like someone burnt their supper," she said.

Belatedly, I noticed that, too, chagrined I hadn't picked up on it right away. I could learn so much from Mrs. Bloom, about what to look for, what to . . . smell for. Did Insurance Investigators take on apprentices?

"Now, Miss Hardcastle, what's our next move?"

My breath caught—was she asking for my opinion? Or was she quizzing me? Either way, I knew the answer. "We interview the witnesses."

"Exactly. We've covered the Ladies' Lounge. Now let's go check up on the gentlemen. Next stop, the Smoking Carriage."

Here I balked. Behind the next door, beyond that vestibule, was a Foreign and Mysterious Land, full of cigar smoke and leather and men with their boots off. It was one thing seeing Father at home in his shirtsleeves, or even visiting his club (which I had done *once*, in an emergency), but a railway car full of strange gentlemen at midnight? I bit my lip, wishing for Miss Judson, who would be entirely unfazed by the threat to propriety.

But my present companion was unfazed, as well. Mrs. Bloom was, I decided, most definitely Irrepressible—and I was beginning to see what a virtue that could be, for a grown-up. I ventured a personal question. "What does your husband think of you being an Investigator?" She wasn't dressed like a widow, so I'd already surmised there was still a Mr. Bloom. Perhaps they were even in the Insurance Investigation business together!

Hand on the door handle, she quirked her mouth. "Well, to tell you the truth, I haven't asked him lately." That curious tone again. She turned to me, answering the question I hadn't figured out how to ask. "One day, I decided I was done letting Bertram make up my mind for me. And here we are."

I had no idea what she meant by any of that, but had no chance to ask more. She'd yanked open the vestibule door, letting in a swirl of October night, brisk and smoky, and we stepped out. The Smoking Carriage was blocked by a tall, stocky guard I recognized as the man who'd been arguing with the driver in Upton. He reminded me of a Staffordshire terrier: arms broad as sleeper beams crossed over his chest, jaw jutting out defiantly. Something small and rectangular bulged his uniform jacket pocket.

"No ladies beyond this point," he growled.

"That's all right, then," Mrs. Bloom said smoothly. "We're on duty. No ladies here."

"Did you see anyone come through here?" I asked eagerly. "Anyone out of the ordinary? Besides us, I mean," I added. The guard's eyes had narrowed perceptibly.

"Been at my post," he grunted. "Just got off. Minding my own business, I am."

I held my tongue. A railway guard's business *was* looking for anything out of the ordinary on his train— for instance, a fellow sprinting down the corridors with a massive great purple crown—but apparently this one saw his job as making sure that Mrs. Bloom and I didn't step out of line as Ladies of Quality.

Mrs. Bloom flipped through her notebook, never taking her eyes off the guard's broad chest, or his brass nameplate, I realized. "Now, let's see here . . . You are Bartholomew Coogan, is that correct?"

"Bart, aye."

Mrs. Bloom made a *tsk*. "Mr. Coogan, I see that you've been written up three times this quarter for disorderly conduct. Twice for drinking on duty, and once for—oh, dear—brawling with another guard?"

"He weren't no guard." Mr. Coogan was scornful. "Some desk man in Portsmouth. And it weren't a *brawl*." He drew out the word. "Just a friendly disagreement between men."

"Glad to hear it." Mrs. Bloom looked up at him. "What was the disagreement about, if you please?"

"Don't remember."

She jotted notes in her book—far too long to be any of Mr. Coogan's curt answers—until he and I were both fidgeting. "Is there anything else you 'don't remember,' Mr. Coogan? Anything that *didn't* happen tonight, for instance? Perhaps something you didn't happen to see while you weren't taking a nip from that flask I don't see in your jacket pocket? This is a temperance train— no alcohol permitted. This would be your third such offense. A man might lose his post for so many demerits. I'd hate for Mr. Ballingall or Driver Urquhart to hear about it."

Mr. Coogan stretched up taller to loom over her, but I could see Mrs. Bloom was making him nervous. She was making *me* nervous, and I hadn't done anything wrong.

I hoped.

I appealed to Mr. Coogan. "You must have seen something," I urged. "Someone coming from the Ladies' Lounge carriage about an hour ago? Or maybe tampering with the dynamos?"

Mr. Coogan was still glaring at Mrs. Bloom like a thwarted watchdog, but he unfolded his arms and eased back a breath. "What time you say this was? About half ten? Now you mention it, somefin' did 'appen. There were a fire in the kitchen on the dining car—cook spilt some oil on th' hob. Weren't serious, but it did fill up wiv smoke, and the boys 'n' me, we got pulled off our stations to help put it out."

"A fire?" I exclaimed. "We didn't hear anything about a fire!"

"It's our job to make sure you *don't* hear about it," Mr. Coogan said with pride.

"Hmmm," Mrs. Bloom said, scribbling in her red journal. Her eyes lifted over the edge, peering back toward the carriage we'd just come through.

"Could it have been a diversion, do you think?" I asked. "To distract the guards at the crucial moment? Our thief wasn't acting alone."

Mrs. Bloom snapped her notebook shut. "No, Miss Hardcastle, I don't believe he was. I'll need the name of that cook, if you please."

Mr. Coogan shook his head. "Coulda been anyone. Two chefs an' three undercooks on the dinner shift. You'd 'ave to ask them."

She eyed him, long and steadily, in a gaze that recalled Peony stalking squirrels. Finally, she said, "Thank you, Mr. Coogan, you've been very helpful. If you remember anything else, please let me know."

He nodded warily. "We're square, then? You won't say nuffin' to Ballingall about—" He waved his hand vaguely in the direction of his coat.

"I make no promises, Mr. Coogan. If I find the guards might have prevented the theft, you'll have much bigger things to worry about. Good night." She heaved open the vestibule door without Mr. Coogan's help. I could still feel his bulldoggy eyes on us as we stepped into the overheated, choking air of the Smoking Carriage.

In truth, it was really no different from the Ladies' Lounge, with the exception that the piano had been replaced by a billiard table, and they didn't have their own tiara. But there were the same plush purple furniture and electric chandeliers, and half the occupants wielded pipes or cigars. A middle-aged gentleman in evening dress rose to his feet.

"Ladies," he said, as if speaking on behalf of the whole car, "are you in the right place?"

I was speechless with uncertainty about that—but had enough presence of mind to Observe the occupants. A black-coated footman with a coffee trolley stared at us, white-faced and wide-eyed, barely turning back in time to catch his coffeepot before it poured all over the young moustachioed gentleman he was serving. Two men circled the pool table, careful not to impale innocent by-sitters with their cue sticks, as the billiard balls haplessly fell prey to the motion of the train.* A sheepdog roughly as large as the locomotive was squeezed into an armchair, snoring away, white fringe puffing with every breath. I saw no sign of the tiara (although it could have been beneath the dog), and everyone here seemed perfectly calm—not at all as if their peaceful journey had been interrupted by a jewel thief. Either the culprit hadn't come this way, or these fellows were all being maddeningly Victorian about it, and pretending not to have noticed.

"Ah," said Mrs. Bloom. "You're Mr. Penrose, am I correct?"

"Yes," said the man who'd stood to greet us. "But I'm afraid you have the advantage of me." He was tall

* not, perhaps, Sir Quentin's most successful contribution to the field of Luxury Rail Travel

and straight-backed, with neat silver hair and a warm, velvety voice.

"Bloom and Hardcastle, on official business."

I felt a flutter of responsibility and pride as she said my name, and stood a bit taller myself. Penrose— he must be the invalid girl's father. As soon as Mrs. Bloom spoke, his face drew tight with concern.

"What's going on? Is my daughter all right?"

"Miss Penrose? Oh, yes, she and Nurse Temby retired before everything happened."

Mr. Penrose's fingers tightened on his coffee cup. "*What* happened? I insist you tell me at once." His calm voice vibrated with command. Mr. Penrose was a man accustomed to getting his way about things, without raising his voice or lifting a finger.

Mrs. Bloom didn't tell him at once. Lips pressed together, she took a few more steps into the Smoking Carriage, gaze skirting the occupants, who had all turned to gape at the Wild Females in their midst, uninvited and unwelcome.

"Who's this, Penrose?" That voice, thickly but indeterminately accented (German? Swedish?), belonged to the man with the blond moustache. Moustaches, really: they seemed to sprout from every possible location and swirl in all directions, like a tamarin monkey's. "Madam, what are you looking for?"

I scurried to Mrs. Bloom's side. "What do you see?" I whispered.

"What do *you* see?" she countered.

Throat tight, I looked round the carriage, straining to spot hidden clues, as though she might have concealed them here in advance to test me, and would know exactly what I missed. But—"Nothing," I said, voice droopy with failure. "It doesn't look like he came this way at all."

She turned to me. "Agreed. Well done. Why?"

I stood up straighter still. A moment later, and you'd have to tether me down so I didn't drift away like Billy Garrett in a hot-air balloon.

"Well," I said slowly, "everyone is too calm. In our carriage, we were all shrieking and carrying on, and Miss Ballingall fainted." I didn't expect any of the gentlemen to faint, naturally, but even so. There ought to be some commotion.

"Excellent. What else?"

I took a deep, stalling breath—and had it immediately, as I was overcome with coughing. "Nobody's been in or out of this carriage in hours. There's no fresh air."

Mrs. Bloom broke into her "brava" smile again, but this time she merely nodded. Giving the space a last look, she spoke up, voice clear and commanding. "Gentlemen, I must advise you to be on guard. There was a robbery aboard the Ladies' Lounge carriage tonight. No one was harmed, but some quite valuable jewelry was taken. Please alert me or the staff if you hear or see anything unusual. My name is Bloom, and I'm in Compartment Two-F."

"Robbery! By the gods!" The Swedish fellow was on his feet, looking thunderstruck. "Pickpockets?"

"I'm afraid not," Mrs. Bloom said. "But do mind your own property, as the thief is still at large. That is all."

"No, that is not all." Mr. Penrose stepped between Mrs. Bloom and the door. "You can't just drop news like this and then flounce away again. Tell us everything."

"Mr. Penrose, I'm afraid I'm not at liberty to share any more details. If you wish a full report, you'll need to take it up with Sir Quentin. Or perhaps you'd care to check on your daughter, instead? She left the carriage complaining she felt unwell." This speech was delivered in a kindly, maternal tone that instantly calmed Mr. Penrose down. He slumped into his armchair, undrunk coffee sloshing.

"No, she's always unwell." He sighed. "Melancholia. That's what Nurse Temby tells us, anyway. The doctors don't know. She seems to do better at the seaside."

With a lurch of painful recognition, I realized how drawn and strained Mr. Penrose looked. That was exactly how Father had seemed, years ago in the months before Mum died. I bit my lip and considered what Mr. Penrose had said. "She gets better with sea air?" I said. "Does she have green wallpaper?"

"Green—? Young lady, I hardly—"

"*Does* she?" Mrs. Bloom's tone made it impossible not to answer.

Mr. Penrose answered faintly. "I'm not sure."

Keenly, I explained. "You know that wallpaper often contains arsenic—from the dyes—and the fumes can be toxic. Green is the most common culprit." That could cause muscle weakness in the legs.

Mr. Penrose's warm eyes widened. "Is—is that true?" he asked Mrs. Bloom.

She gave an ineffable shrug. "I have it on good authority." I very much suspected that the "good authority" was actually me. But it *was* true, Dear Reader: an American physician had done up a study on it, publishing quite a sensational book some years ago.*

"Oh," said Mr. Penrose. "Well, thank you, young lady. I had no idea. I'll investigate that immediately. Anything to help poor Maudie."

As Mrs. Bloom and I made our way back from the Smoking Carriage, I considered Poor Maudie, and the Swedish Gentleman (when I inquired, Mrs. Bloom informed me that his name was Victor Strand, and he was a traveling salesman, which accounted for the huge valise I'd seen him lugging about the station), and Mr. Coogan. The gruff guard had decamped

---

* *Shadows from the Walls of Death*, R. C. Kedzie, 1874. Father had refused to obtain a copy, as Dr. Kedzie had used actual samples of the toxic wallpaper in the book, and it was a poisoning hazard. (Honestly, did he think I planned to *lick* the pages or something?)

from his post outside the Smoking Carriage and was nowhere to be seen.

"If the thief didn't head that direction, what happened to him?"

Mrs. Bloom's pale hair ruffled in the night air. "Exactly, Miss Hardcastle. What, indeed?"

I recognized that as a Socratic Method sort of question, the kind Miss Judson preferred in her own lessons, meant to inspire me to think critically. "Either he got off, like Miss Judson said . . ." I began.

"Or?"

The thrill rippled through me again. *"He's still aboard?"*

"Perhaps." She didn't sound convinced. "We must explore every possibility, including that this might have been an inside job. Where to next?"

"The lights might be back on in the Ladies' Lounge by now," I said carefully. "Maybe we should get a better look at the crime scene?"

"Very good. After you, Miss Hardcastle."

I happily led the way, but we never made it. We had to pass through the sleeping carriage, and there, charging down the corridor like an oncoming locomotive—steaming and unavoidable—was Aunt Helena. She had her giant gold scissors, and pointed them at us like a skewer.

"You!" she thundered. "How dare you lead my niece astray like this!"

I didn't *feel* astray. I felt quite well in hand, focused and responsible, and I was enjoying myself enormously (the express purpose of this holiday, so I'd been told—not that I was daft enough to say so).

Mrs. Bloom stepped between us. "Miss Hardcastle, please—"

"I told you, I don't wish to hear your ridiculous accusations, and I won't have you poisoning my niece's mind, either. Helena Myrtle, go to your compartment at once."

"I'm helping her." That came out small and miserable, and I'm afraid I couldn't help it—I cringed away from Mrs. Bloom. She might not have experienced my aunt's wrath before, but I had.

Aunt Helena took a dangerous sniff, like they say angry rhinoceroses do before trampling you. "Helena Myrtle. Compartment. *At once.*"

"I—" I dithered, biting my lip. I didn't want the evening to end so ignominiously, nor did I wish to leave Mrs. Bloom alone at the mercy of Aunt Helena. I was certain Mrs. Bloom could handle herself, but it still seemed cowardly to desert her just when she was facing down such a formidable opponent. And I still couldn't see why Aunt Helena was so angry with her.

"What did Mrs. Bloom ever do to you?" I burst out—causing all the color to vanish in an instant from Aunt Helena's creased face.

Mrs. Bloom stepped in before Aunt Helena could

reload. "It's all right, Myrtle. You've been a great help tonight. I'll see you at breakfast."

"Not if you know what's good for you!"

"But—"

The argument had drawn attention. All along the carriage, compartment doors cracked, releasing slits of golden light. I saw the white hair of one of the Bird Ladies and Nurse Temby's dour face. The vestibule door eased open, and the bulky form of Guard Coogan took shape, a dark shadow behind Aunt Helena. My own compartment door opened, and Miss Judson poked her head out, holding Peony. I took that as my cue to retreat, although I felt more cowardly than ever, deserting Mrs. Bloom in the corridor with my aunt.

5

VENI, VIDI

The first murder aboard an English railway occurred in 1864, when Franz Muller beat banker Thomas Briggs to death on a London commuter train, then accidentally took the victim's hat by mistake. This also marked an early example of another common travel hazard: mixed-up luggage.

—*Hardcastle's Practical Travel Companion*

Eager to meet Mrs. Bloom the next morning, I scarcely slept and woke before dawn, well ahead of both Miss Judson (an early riser) and Peony (who believed in all-day breakfast). I hastened into yesterday's dress and thence to the dining carriage to scope out a spot far from where Aunt Helena would want to be.

I claimed a noisy, drafty table for two near the vestibule, and settled in to study my notes from the Investigation. The *Empress Express*'s exceptional staff had done their job, and there was no trace of the smoke smell from last night's fire.

As the sun rose, the rest of the Excursion passengers filed in. The Penroses were present—that is, grim-faced Mr. Penrose and Nurse Temby, seated unspeaking across a table, but not Poor Maudie. The sea air had not yet had a chance to do its revivifying work. The Bird Ladies flitted in together, swallowed up by their frilly and lacy morning dresses. Miss Causton (or perhaps Miss Cabot) led the way, clutching her reticule for dear life. Her companion's wide-eyed gaze flicked to each passenger they passed, as if hoping we might leap out at them, seize their valuables, and provide another thrilling entertainment this morning.

They alit beside the unsuspecting Mr. Strand, the salesman, who moved aside his catalogues (and his moustaches) to make room. Miss Judson appeared with Aunt Helena, trailed by Cicely, wobbling somewhat beneath her armload of fur stole, Aunt Helena's walking stick, the knitted bag, and a small needlepoint footstool. I Observed Aunt Helena's face darken as she spotted me in the corner, and I suspect mine did something not dissimilar. But Miss Judson deftly steered them to the far end of the carriage and chose a seat that put Aunt Helena's back to me. I gave her a salute with my teacup.

The footmen brought me a pot of tea and a dish of marmalade. Then a neat little stack of toast. Then a covered plate of kedgeree. But as the car filled up, there was no sign of Mrs. Bloom.

"Have you seen Mrs. Bloom?" I asked the next footman to appear, with a second pot of tea. The footman's expression did not change. "The Insurance Investigator?" I persisted. "You must have seen her last night, after the robbery." She'd probably questioned the rest of the staff after I'd deserted her.

"No, Miss," he said, in a gloomy, sepulchral voice, then vanished with no further word.

Where was she? I sloshed my tea around, trying to tell myself that Mrs. Bloom had important business to attend to and I mustn't be disappointed. I knew I was only a twelve-year-old girl she was being nice to, but *she'd* arranged this breakfast meeting. She wasn't the sort to be flighty and forget—or dismiss it. If she hadn't meant to meet me after all, she'd have sent word.

While I waited, I reviewed my notes and Observed the other passengers. Mr. Penrose, absorbed in his newspaper, never looked up from his coffee, and Nurse Temby crumbled her toast to bits and glowered out the window. The Bird Ladies appeared to be recreating the events of the robbery for Mr. Strand. Miss Causton pantomimed singing, then succumbing to a swoon, as Miss Cabot swooped in to swipe an imaginary tiara from her snowy-white head.

I closed my notebook and sighed, looking out the window. We were still hours from Fairhaven, our

winding coastal route having been chosen not for efficiency, but to give the Excursionists a Luxury Rail
Travel Experience, including dinner, breakfast, the
finest sleeping accommodations, and a jewel theft.
Gloomy clouds hung over the vast, desolate empti-
ness. The coastline bumped past in rocky clusters,
scrubby hillsides breaking into occasional flashes of
dark water. What had become of the thief and the
tiara? Had they disappeared into the night, after all?
Perhaps there'd been a boat waiting nearby. They could
be halfway across the Channel by now. Discouraged
and confused, I finally packed up my notes and wandered back to my own party.

"Helena Myrtle. How kind of you to join us at last."
Beady eyes studied me through the lorgnette.

"I had a breakfast meeting with Mrs. Bloom," I
said pointedly, then turned to Miss Judson. "She didn't
show up."

Miss Judson's brow furrowed, but with sympathy,
not concern. "I expect she had important work."

"*No one* has seen her this morning. I asked."

Miss Judson started to rise from the table, but Aunt
Helena uttered an exasperated sigh. "Don't encourage
the girl to meddle, Judson. Sit down, Helena Myrtle,
like a civilized person. Don't stand about loitering in
the passage."

Sulking, I squeezed in beside her, since Cicely and
Miss Judson hadn't left any other place free. "The

porters and footmen haven't seen her, and she didn't send word that she wasn't going to meet me. What does that say to you?"

"That she's careless and inconsiderate," put in Aunt Helena. "Not the sort of person you ought to be associating with. Cicely, what are you doing to that tea? I want it sweet, girl, not jellied."

"We'll be in Fairhaven shortly," Miss Judson said. "You can find her then." She tapped her spoon against her teacup with finality. I glared at my tablemates. None of them understood.

"Perhaps we should speak to Sir Quentin." I glanced about the dining car, but there was no sign of the Ballingalls.

Cicely took a hasty gulp of tea. "They have their own carriage. They always take breakfast together. I expect they're still shaken up, after last night." This was the longest utterance I'd heard from her, and she seemed worn out from the effort.

"Poor Temperance," Aunt Helena cooed. "Such a shock to her, after everything she's been through."

"I barely slept at all last night," Cicely said, with a shiver. "It was all so awful. Those beautiful stones." Her fingers nervously brushed a brooch at her throat, as if the thief were still lurking aboard, ready to strike again.

"Mrs. Bloom will find them," I said.

"I wouldn't put too much stock in *that*," said Aunt Helena. "She's no doubt off somewhere trying to salvage whatever's left of her post. I can't imagine it looks good to your superiors, having the item you're supposedly insuring disappear right under your nose."

I Observed that Aunt Helena used the same words Sir Quentin had last night. Like a mynah bird.

"That was Sir Quentin's fault," I said. "He's the one that put the tiara at risk. Miss Ballingall wasn't supposed to be wearing it!"

Miss Judson intervened. "Let's put the blame where it belongs, on the thief–"

"Thank you," murmured Cicely. She was probably worried that if this argument continued, Aunt Helena would figure out some way to make it all *her* fault.

"–and hope the police do the same." Miss Judson drained her teacup and rose from the table, hat feathers brushing the signal cord. "Myrtle. Come. You need to pack."

"I haven't *unpacked*," I grumbled, but was only too happy to make our escape. I tried to explain my concerns again as we crossed between carriages. A frigid wind, thick with coal smoke, buffeted our hats.

"I'm sure Mrs. Bloom is just busy." Miss Judson's words were sympathetic, but I heard doubt in her voice. "Aunt Helena wasn't far wrong. She will have an awfully big report to write after what happened."

"Then where is she? Why hide from everyone?"

"Yes, I'm sure she's *hiding*. Let's think about this sensibly. You're not proposing that Something Has

Happened to Her?" I could hear the capital letters in her voice.

"No," I said. "Her absence is *strange*, not suspicious—"

"Excellent! Strange we can tolerate, and suspicious is not our purview."

I grudgingly followed Miss Judson back to our compartments. We passed Mrs. Bloom's, and at my pleading look, Miss Judson stopped to rap on her door.

"Mrs. Bloom?" she called in her firmest governess voice. "It's Miss Judson and Myrtle Hardcastle. Are you in?"

There was no answer, and Miss Judson's furrowed brow did not relax. I reached for the door, which opened easily at my touch.

"It's not locked," I said, nudging it wider. "Mrs. Bloom?"

The compartment was empty. Miss Judson put a hand to the doorframe, blocking my path.

"We ought to check," I insisted. "There might be some clue to her disappearance."

"Don't get carried away. You can hardly 'disappear' on a moving train."

Thankfully, I hadn't left my gloves in my room. With mounting respect for finger-marks as evidence, an Investigator had to be careful not to contaminate a scene with her own greasy mitts. (Mine were clean. Miss Judson insisted on it. But still.)

There wasn't much to see, really. Mrs. Bloom's carpetbag sat at the foot of the settee, closed but unlatched, and a half-empty teacup waited on the side table. I put a hand to the cup. "Cold."

"About an hour, then. At least. Assuming she didn't simply forget about her tea before leaving."

"Or it's from yesterday. Maybe she never came back to her compartment. Her bed hasn't been slept in."

"Unless she made it herself." But she sounded doubtful; that was the maids' job.

Mrs. Bloom's red ledger book lay open across the arm of the settee. I reached for it, but Miss Judson forestalled me.

"That crosses the bounds of privacy," she said. "Whatever's in that book won't tell us where she is right now."

I sighed, but she was right. It really did look as though Mrs. Bloom had simply stepped out for a moment, intending to return straightaway.

"Why didn't she lock her door when she left?"

"We'll ask her when we see her at the station." Miss Judson's tone was final, signaling that this Investigative foray was, to her mind, concluded.

ళ

The *Empress Express* pulled into Fairhaven Station at 8:38 on the morning of 8 October, 1893, precisely on schedule. Sir Quentin wouldn't have it any other way. The shrill whistle and squealing brakes announced our arrival, and as we eased along the platform, a black pelican perched upon a shiny green railing regarded us with sleepy eyes, then lifted its improbably large body aloft and flapped lazily away.

Like the train, the station sparkled with newness. It sat against the black hillside, a bright spot of cheery red brick and green roof and yellow signs. As we all queued up for a glimpse out the train windows, I Observed the stationmaster hanging a freshly painted sign on the side of the building: FAIRHAVEN-BY-SEA. Another version of weathered wood lay propped against the brick façade. I could barely make out the peeling letters, but it looked like it said EELSCOMBE.

We decamped en masse, a more subdued and jittery party than Sir Quentin might have wished, but he was doing his best to drum up the holiday atmosphere (although the *actual* atmosphere had more than a hint of fishiness about it). A boy my age with a camera suspended from his neck awaited us, and Miss Ballingall, looking much recovered after last night's drama, swept us all together for a group photograph. The boy had warm brown skin, sharp black eyes, and a shock of dark curls, and carried an impressive knapsack and a tripod nearly as tall as he was.

Mrs. Bloom was still nowhere to be seen. Perhaps she'd disembarked first and rushed into the station to wire Albion Casualty and the Railway Police. Or perhaps she'd captured the thief already and had him detained with the guards! I was even more disappointed to miss *that* than breakfast.

I tried to shake off the gloom, which was easier than expected, given Peony's contribution to the effort. She had been . . . reluctant to be returned to the hatbox, so I was now carrying her, the hatbox, and my valise, which left me at least two arms short of what was required by the enterprise. I wondered how Cicely managed it, and eyed the photographer's bulging knapsack with envy.

"Here now, Clive, lad, do our ladies credit!" Sir Quentin said. He'd donned his purple ringmaster's coat again, though it was getting spotted by a salt-tinged mist. Sir Quentin shuffled me and Peony into position front and center, between him and Miss Ballingall.

"Right-o, sir," the young photographer said, readying his equipment. "Hold still, then, everyone." He squeezed the bulb for the shutter, then took a few moments to slide a new photographic plate into the slot on the back of the camera before taking a second picture. "That should do it, sir."

"Better take another," called Sir Quentin. "For posterity!"

After the photographer was done, Miss Judson released me to scurry over and inspect Clive's equipment. I introduced myself and Peony.

"Is this your camera?" It was a beautiful contraption—a small box of polished wood, fitted out with shiny brass knobs and hinges and a black leather bellows that expanded like a concertina, then collapsed so the whole affair could be folded up and carried by its handle, like a tiny suitcase. It looked gloriously modern (and expensive).

Clive looked pleased. "Thornton-Pickard Ruby, finest field camera there is!" While I watched, he opened a window at the back of the unit and withdrew a rectangular plate of glass—the exposed image he'd just captured—and swapped it out for a fresh one. "I'm shootin' holiday views for Sir Quentin right now, families on the beach and the like. But I mean to do pictures for the press. I reckon the *Times*'ll want a look at Sir Quentin's new train."

I was impressed. "Miss Judson has sold some drawings to the newspapers." I indicated my governess, who was even now sketching the passengers as they awaited the opening of the baggage car. I was itching to say what *sorts* of drawings, but even I knew you did not strike up an association with someone by mentioning murder in the first breath, and Clive seemed a more interesting sort of fellow than the Brochure had promised.

"Here," Clive said, setting up the camera once more. "Stand over there."

I gamely went where he indicated and struck a jaunty pose, chin up and facing Peony toward the camera. She was more or less cooperative.

Clive peered through the camera's rear window and slid the bellows back and forth to adjust the focus. "There. I'll bring this round once it's printed. You're at the hotel, then?" He said this as if Fairhaven possessed only one hotel.

"The Ballingall Arms," I clarified, and Clive nodded.

"She's the one. Me dad's the manager." He swiftly added, "We came out from Brighton. We've a boarding'ouse of our own, back home. Impressed Sir Quentin so much, he hired Dad right on to run his new hotel." He proudly stuck his thumbs in his purple bracers. "Mum and the girls"—he pronounced this *gells*, in an accent I'd not heard before—"stayed on at our place, but I came wiv Dad, to make my own fortune."

"I've heard Brighton's nice," I said politely. What I meant was I'd heard it was a larger, even more Amusing version of Fairhaven, positively infested with holidaymakers.

"Well, she's not Fairhaven," Clive said with a laugh, although I wasn't sure what was funny. "Here, then. Let's have another." He started to reach for a new photographic plate, but Peony had had enough of being an artist's model. She squirmed free of my grip and darted off toward the train.

I uttered an Inappropriate Word, searching the crowd.

"There she is!" Clive pointed toward the train, where a dot of white was weaving in and out of legs and skirts. "We'll have her back in a snap." Hoisting up his tripod and kit, he made off across the platform. Quick on his heels, I followed his knapsack, right into the porters preparing to unload our luggage. They'd pulled a trolley to the edge of the platform and were sliding open a set of arched doors. Peony, unable to resist an open door, saw her opportunity and leaped into the baggage car.

"Hey, now!" cried a porter. "Wot's that cat doin' 'ere?"

"I'm sorry, sir," I said. "She's with me. May I–" I gestured apologetically to the carriage as Clive clambered up to search for her. The porter tossed up his hands in surrender and helped me aboard.

Inside, the open doors and large windows made the carriage bright enough to see easily. Our trunks were stacked neatly on racks, and the car also held cargo, barrels and cartons and crates and great heavy sacks of coffee and flour.

"For the hotel," Clive explained. "He's been sending shipments like this for months. This'll be linens."

He clapped a hand against a crate with a fancy label from an Irish draper.

"Peony!" I called. "Here, kitty, kitty . . ." Not that she was especially responsive to this.

"I see her." Clive pointed over a stack of trunks. A familiar arch of furry black perched atop a suitcase, hair on end and a low, ugly growl issuing from deep in her throat.

"What'd you find, gell?" Clive asked her. "Looks like somebody's trunk spilled . . ." He pointed to a heap of red cloth on the floor among the crates. A lady's skirt.

And her shoes, scuffed black lace-up boots, worn soles peeking out amid a fluff of petticoats.

"Clive, wait—" I reached for him, but he beat me there. I heard his tripod hit the floorboards with a sickening thunk.

"Is that—" He clapped a hand to his mouth, eyes huge. My heart had jolted to a stop, jammed in my throat, and I couldn't answer.

We'd found Mrs. Bloom.

6
UNCLAIMED BAGGAGE

Pickpockets, luggage thieves, and confidence artists abound at railway stations, preying on the unsuspecting. Travelers are well advised to keep a vigilant eye on their belongings.

—Hardcastle's Practical Travel Companion

For a breathless moment, I couldn't think or move. I just stood there staring blindly, not even taking it in. Behind us, the bustle on the platform continued, trunks scraping and passengers chattering, while underfoot the carriage shuddered with the uneasy rhythm of the idling steam engine. I shook myself out of my stupor.

"Don't touch anything," I managed.

"Blimey—why would I *want* to?"

I forced myself to look closer. Mrs. Bloom had fallen between the luggage rack and the trunks stacked in the aisle and was wedged in—not at all a natural position. I squeezed past Clive and knelt down beside her.

"Hey, now! You said *not* to touch her!"

"I'm checking for a pulse," I said, knowing it was useless. Her hand was cold, arm stiff. She'd been dead for hours.

"Who is she? Wot's happened to her?"

"I'm not sure what happened," I admitted. "There's no obvious sign of trauma . . ."

"You mean like bloomin' great scissors stickin' outta her back?"

I jerked up. "What?"

"Look—" He pointed, and sure enough: Just visible between the shadowy trunks was a glint of gold. A massive pair of German repoussé sewing scissors, jammed with some considerable force into poor Mrs. Bloom's back.

Aunt Helena's scissors.

After that, everything happened at once. A porter climbed aboard and spotted us, letting out a great sharp yelp when he saw Mrs. Bloom's body. That drew *everyone's* attention, and before I could secure the crime scene, the baggage carriage was overrun. I found myself bustled off into the ready arms of Miss Judson.

As soon as Miss Judson looked at me, she realized what was wrong. She squeezed through the press of jabbering porters on the carriage and stomped her foot twice, like a music hall girl onstage. The sound smashed over the chaos, and everyone froze.

"There's been an accident. You, there—Clive, yes? Get the police."

"Yes, Miss." Clive hopped down to the platform and dashed off.

"Myrtle, find the stationmaster."

My job was easier. The man I'd seen earlier, hanging the sign, had forced his way to the open carriage doors. I crouched down and in hushed tones rattled off the situation. He stared at me in disbelief, so I repeated myself. "A woman's been murdered. We need to secure the crime scene and telegraph Scotland Yard."

"Crime scene?" he echoed in a faint voice.

"Hold it together, man!" I offered the bolstering encouragement often employed by Billy Garrett in such crises. The stationmaster was a solid-looking fellow of middle age, quite smart in his dark red railway uniform with its polished name tag. "Mr. Clark, can you secure the scene?" If I had to, I'd Deputize the entire Eastern Coastal Railway staff. He kept staring blankly, so I waved a hand at the crowd. "Keep everyone away from the body—the whole car, actually. Get some men to help you. Sir."

The stationmaster was probably unaccustomed to taking direction from a twelve-year-old girl, but he looked relieved to have something productive to do. I knew how he felt. He moved on, barking at the crowd. "Move back, back up now, please, folks. We don't want to disturb anything. Come along, ladies, let's move along, into the station . . ."

As he stepped off, a vise clamped itself around my arm, making me squeak. "Ow!"

Aunt Helena had reached into the carriage and had me in a grip like iron, her face a deadly mask. "Get down from there," she hissed.

I stared back for a moment, heart pounding, as she tried to pull me from the carriage. I didn't care. I didn't have time. I wrenched my arm free.

The Ballingalls arrived, Miss Ballingall's tweedy cape flapping like an injured sparrow. A porter hastened to prop a mounting block in place so Sir Quentin could barge aboard. He took in the scene, his bluff, lionlike face turning red.

"Good God," he swore. With a grip like Aunt Helena's, he tried to steer his daughter back to the platform, but it was too late. She spotted Mrs. Bloom's body and let out a scream that shook the carriage windows.

Miss Ballingall pulled away from her father. A shift came over her, and her soft face hardened. "Quickly. We must cover her up." She hastened toward the crates. "Fetch some blankets."

"No!" I flung myself between Miss Ballingall and the body. "Don't touch anything. Don't *disturb* anything, until the police come."

"The police!" she shrieked. I gave Miss Judson my most pointed and imploring Look.

Miss Judson took over. "Sir Quentin, Miss Ballingall could use some air." Her tone was impossible to disobey, and Sir Quentin nodded dumbly, leading his daughter away in an ominous echo of last night's drama. Aunt Helena bundled her in an embrace, as if *she* were the one who'd been stabbed. I was glad Aunt Helena had turned her attention to someone besides me.

Finally! It was just me, Miss Judson, and a couple of workers from the train. Distantly I recognized the familiar sound of Miss Judson's swift sketching, and that grounded me. I studied the scene with clenched fingers, wishing for my satchel with its specimen collection kit—the satchel packed neatly in my trunk, somewhere nearby, yet agonizingly out of reach.

I would have to do without it. Or my notebook. Sherlock Holmes would memorize the scene in just a passing glance. I might have very little more time than that. I cast a swift look about the carriage, but other than Mrs. Bloom's body jammed between the trunks, head crunched to the side, there didn't seem to be signs of a struggle.

"How did she get here?" I said. "Did her killer catch her unawares? Or was she moved here afterward?"

Miss Judson, having no more answer than I, did not reply.

I knelt beside the body, heart lodged in my throat, and tried to be brisk and businesslike. There was surprisingly little blood, beyond a darkening of her dress around the scissors. *Think, Myrtle!* The answer was right here, in this carriage, on her body, and I hadn't a second to waste. But I could only stare, stupidly, my mind clunking like a broken dynamo. Last night Mrs. Bloom had been formidable and vigorous, the way she'd taken charge after the robbery. And now, lying here, she looked—diminished, somehow. Smaller. Not much taller than I, I realized.

Maudlin thoughts about Mrs. Bloom would not help her now. She needed a skilled Investigator to solve her murder. Not *me*, necessarily—but at least until the proper police showed up.

A moment later, a breathless, panting Clive came careening up the hill, trailed by a tall, wispy reed of a man in a blue police uniform. Relieved, I rose and wiped my sweaty hands on my skirts.

The stationmaster let them through, and the constable scrambled awkwardly into the carriage, took one look at Mrs. Bloom's fallen body, and fainted.

⁊

After Constable Hoskiss's histrionics disrupted my orderly crime scene, the stationmaster dispersed the crowd. Which included, to my ignominy, adolescent Aspiring Investigators. I'd been shuttled away and dumped in Aunt Helena's supervision, and now we sat on the hard bench outside the station, waiting for someone with authority to tell us we could leave. I wasn't holding out much hope.

Miss Judson sat on the bench opposite, pressing a cool damp cloth to Constable Hoskiss's forehead. I clutched Peony to my chest. She seemed happy to be clutched, and hung on tight, claws hooked into my collar. Aunt Helena beheld the scene with a cold, indifferent impatience that made me shiver.

"It must have been a vagrant," she said, staring straight ahead, hands clenched on her stick.

I bit my tongue before I could blurt out all the questions bubbling up inside me. How would a vagrant have got on the train? And where had he gone?

And how did he get Aunt Helena's scissors?

Rubbing my arm where she'd grabbed me, I tried not to think too hard about the obvious explanation, about the argument last night in the sleeping carriage, about Aunt Helena pointing those scissors threateningly in Mrs. Bloom's face. I stole a glance at her—she couldn't have killed someone.

Could she?

Don't be silly, Myrtle. My gaze slid to Sir Quentin, now arguing with the stationmaster. He'd been quarreling with Mrs. Bloom, too, since she first got on the train. Or maybe the thief had still been on the train after all, and he'd killed her when she caught up to him. I searched the crowd, but I wasn't sure what I was looking for. *Whom* I was looking for. Peony butted me in the chin, trying to distract me. I scratched absently behind her whiskers.

The railway platform was crowding up with spectators, not just *Empress Express* folk milling about in distress, but local villagers who had wafted out of their cottages and shops like the sea mist. It was mostly ladies in drab woolly shawls, a handful of small children, and an assortment of domestic ducks. I glared at the ducks, who were getting white feathers and duck mess all over the crime scene. The villagers would be tromping off with souvenirs, soon, too, if somebody didn't put a stop to it. Why couldn't Aunt Helena be of any use when you needed her?

I watched everything fall apart with growing desperation. Mrs. Bloom was a professional Investigator, and deserved the courtesy and respect of a proper, professional murder investigation—not have her death trampled over by a befuddled and incompetent village constabulary. The very *idea* that her murder would be in the hands of someone like that Hoskiss fellow was unthinkable.

I kicked my heels into the ground. I had to do something. But what? Except for the buzz of people around the baggage carriage, the rest of the train seemed abandoned. No one was paying any attention to the other cars, to the Ladies' Lounge where the robbery had occurred, to the dining car, to the passenger carriage. The passenger car! I hopped to my feet, struck with sudden Investigatory Inspiration.

"And just where do you think you're going, young lady?" Aunt Helena sounded weary.

"I left my—I left something in my compartment," I lied.

"Oh, very well. Just don't get in anyone's way. And send Cicely over with my powders. I have a beastly headache. Where can that girl have got to?"

Before she could change her mind, I hoisted Peony more firmly against my shoulder, grabbed my valise, and slipped off toward the *Empress Express*, just as I had yesterday afternoon. Nobody saw. Nobody was paying me any notice at all. Not even Miss Judson, too absorbed in the plight that was Constable Hoskiss.

We squeezed through the vestibule door, right into a sturdy black uniform. *"Ooph."* Peony squirmed from my grip.

I looked up, into the face (well, chest, rather) of Mr. Coogan, the guard from last night. His eyes narrowed, but before I could extend my apology—or accept his— he pushed past me and hastened out of the carriage, down to the platform. I straightened my hat and fol- lowed Peony. Mr. Coogan's gruff manner was even more understandable this morning.

"Don't get lost," I warned Peony.

"No," she said scornfully, and set off straight for Mrs. Bloom's door. The maids hadn't been in yet,

thank goodness; the compartment was just as it had been when Miss Judson and I had searched it earlier this morning. Mrs. Bloom's notebook lay where she'd left it, waiting for her to come back to work. The work of tracking down the jewel thief and recovering the tiara, which she'd never have a chance to finish, now. All the notes from her own Investigation were bound to be in that book. I picked it up and closed it carefully. I started to slip it into my own bag, but Peony was rubbing her head against the carpetbag. "Mrrrr," she said.

"The bag, too?" I asked her.

"Mrrrm."

I couldn't carry it all—not my bag, and Peony, and Peony's hatbox, *and* Mrs. Bloom's bag—but Peony had a point. There wasn't time to go through everything now, and someone was bound to realize I was missing. Eventually. I contemplated my own valise. All it had was spare clothes, extra stockings and chemisettes that hadn't fit in my trunk after I'd filled it with essentials. (Which I would definitely be needing now, thank you very much!) It looked similar enough to Mrs. Bloom's that nobody would notice—probably—if someone were to switch them.

"*Now*," said Peony.

"I'm sorry, Mrs. Bloom," I said aloud, with real regret. "I wish I could do more." With that, I shoved my own valise into the storage cubby. Then I slipped Mrs. Bloom's ledger into her bag, snapped the latches shut, grabbed the worn handles, and hastened back to the platform.

With Mrs. Bloom's bag in hand, I immediately felt better. More composed. More Official. The bag had a comforting weight to it, and I felt the handles molding to my grip, like they belonged there. I strolled back into the throng of adults like *I* belonged there, and thrust myself into the conversation.

They had covered Mrs. Bloom's body with a sheet—over Miss Judson's objections—and Stationmaster Clark was trying to question Sir Quentin and the driver, Mr. Urquhart.

"What about this robbery, then?" Mr. Clark asked. "Did you not stop to give chase?"

"We wanted to, of course, but Sir Quentin, he wouldn't hear of it."

Here everyone turned to Sir Quentin, who puffed up his chest. "We'd a schedule to keep," he said, with great importance. "Wasn't much point trying to chase the fellow down on foot. He'd made good his escape by the time we could even sort ourselves out."

"But it seems he *didn't* escape," Mr. Clark pointed out. "Or else this woman would still be alive." He scratched his head, frowning toward the carriage. "She must have been killed when she confronted the thief in the baggage car. Fairly straightforward, I suppose."

"It's not straightforward at all," I objected. "There are a lot of unanswered questions. What was Mrs.

Bloom doing in the baggage car? Was she killed there, or *moved* there? Was it one of us—someone aboard the train, I mean—or has the suspect already fled?"

Stationmaster Clark's mouth actually dropped open, but he closed it slowly, pondering this. He glanced over to the constable.

"There's been a robbery, and now a murder," I pressed. "Do you think Constable Hoskiss there knows how to investigate a homicide?"

Constable Hoskiss looked like he wasn't certain how to button his uniform, and put his head between his knees again.

"Now wait just a minute," Sir Quentin began, but the driver forestalled him.

"The lass is right." He was a distinguished older man with neat white whiskers and an air of authority. "Railway crimes are the purview of railway police. A crime on my train will be handled through proper channels."

"Scotland Yard," I suggested.

"It's *my* train," Sir Quentin said. "And I say what happens. It's obvious how she got herself killed. Don't take Scotland Yard to work that out."

"She didn't 'get herself killed'!" I cried, incensed on her behalf. "Someone did that *to* her—someone *on the train*. Ask the guards—someone must have seen something. There's that Mr. Coogan, now."

Mr. Urquhart's countenance hardened. "Coogan!" he bawled, startling the stocky guard, who hunched his way over.

"Aye?" His voice was wary.

"Report! This lass seems to think you might know sommat about all this."

Mr. Coogan looked at me sharply. "Didn't see aught. I were at my post, like allus." Despite the cold morning, his face was sweaty, and he rubbed his hands together.

"Did you see Mrs. Bloom again after we left you?" I asked.

"Nay, nay. Never saw the woman," he insisted.

"But—" I started to protest, but was cut off by Mr. Urquhart.

"See here, Coogan, I'll have none of your attitude now. Did you see anything suspicious or not?"

Mr. Coogan shifted from foot to foot, not looking at any of us, a sharp change from his belligerent behavior last night. "No, sir," he mumbled. "Didn't see aught."

Mr. Urquhart shook his head. "It's obvious he can't help. Get off w'ye."

He couldn't have spoken fast enough. Mr. Coogan bolted, faster than I'd have imagined someone so large could move through such a crowd.

Sir Quentin coughed, a mighty, throat-clearing sound that rivaled the steam engine. "There's no reason to hold this up any longer. Send for your coroner, or whoever, so we can get that woman off my train!"

The stationmaster glared at the crowd of people (and livestock) disrupting his lovely new platform. "The Coroner will have to come in from St. Mary's up the shore," he said. "Take a few hours. But I don't see why we can't have the lads move her somewhere more–suitable."

I turned to the stationmaster. "No, you *can't*," I pleaded. "You have to preserve the crime scene until the Detective Bureau have a chance to see it." Didn't he know how many murders went unsolved because people went about blindly disturbing evidence?

"Oh, for the love of–" Sir Quentin's face went dark enough to match his purple jacket. "Who do you work for, man? Are you going to listen to reason, or to this–child?"

The stationmaster flung up his hands. "Enough! My station, my decision. Sir Quentin, Mr. Urquhart, you can have the rest of your train back, but I'm hereby impounding the baggage carriage, pending the arrival of someone with more experience and authority with crimes like this. Now, can we all go on about our business? I think you have folks who'd like to start their holidays."

I could have hugged him. The driver looked satisfied, as well, and set off back for the train, already barking orders for uncoupling the baggage carriage from the rest of the cars. I felt a surge of triumph and relief. Now Mrs. Bloom would get the investigation she deserved.

Abruptly, Miss Judson picked up her valise. "I think," she announced, "that Myrtle and I shall be off to the hotel. That is, if you're quite through with us, Constable?" He nodded weakly, still clutching her handkerchief. "Very well. You know where to find us if you need anything else. Come along, Myrtle!" Whereupon she clasped me by the arm like a toddler, and set off—in the opposite direction from the train platform.

"Where are we going? There's been a murder!"

"Exactly." She dragged me—and by extension, Peony—down what was evidently Fairhaven's main thoroughfare, a twisting cobbled track flanked by parked wagons and hillsides shored up with stone, the clamor of voices fading as we descended the precipitous slope.

I was trying to concentrate on the important matter of Mrs. Bloom's death, and the slightly more pressing matter of not tripping over my own feet, but I could not help an impression of the scenery. The winding streets and jumbled houses stacked atop one another looked like they were about to fall into the sea. It gave the place a disorienting air, like an off-kilter storybook.

I don't think Miss Judson really knew, or particularly cared, where she was taking me just then, so long as it was away from the crime scene. Mrs. Bloom's bag was weighty in my grip, like a magnet pulling me back to the murder scene. "We have to go back," I said again. "They need our help."

Here she stopped and released me, straightening her hat, which had not in the least shifted out of place. "That is exactly what we shall *not* be doing."

"But—"

"Myrtle, you know perfectly well your father sent you on this holiday to get you *away* from murder. Imagine, for a moment, his reaction should news reach him that you managed to involve yourself in one, on your very first day."

"Make up your mind! One minute you're sketching the body, and the next you're dragging me off before we have a chance to help!" I held Mrs. Bloom's bag all the harder, shocked Miss Judson hadn't mentioned it yet.

A squat woman pushing a handcart laden with barrels of fish shoved her way up the hill, and we moved aside to make room. When she was past, I appealed to Miss Judson's sense of justice.

"Father would *want* us to help. He'd never turn his back on a victim, and he'd expect us to do the same."

"Overruled," Miss Judson said.

Behind us, the fish lady rattled her squeaky cart into the village, and before us lay the barest scrap of a Vista, our first glimpse of the sea. It peeked out between a curve of road and a strip of dull October sky, a smudge of wavery black in the distance. Out in the water, white flecks might have been fishing boats, waves, or the flash of gulls' wings—none of which were aware of or even cared about poor Mrs. Bloom, lying dead in the train car, waiting for Scotland Yard. I reaffirmed my grip on the carpetbag.

"She was one of us," I said. Miss Judson's eyebrow lifted a fraction of an inch more, inviting elaboration. "An *Investigator*. She came along on the Excursion to prevent a crime—and now she's the victim of one." I looked fiercely at Miss Judson.

"You must realize that's even *more* of a reason for us to stay out of the affair, if we can."

"That doesn't make any sense!"

Her lips were pressed tight. "Yes, it does. How do you suppose your father will react to the news of a female investigator murdered on the job?"

It didn't take me long to catch up. "Oh."

"Oh, indeed. Your father already thinks you're too involved in dangerous affairs. You must *promise* me, Myrtle Hardcastle, that you will stay out of this."

I looked down at the sea, then back up the hill, where the train platform had already disappeared into the warren of old streets. I hid Mrs. Bloom's bag behind my skirts and tried to tell myself I was not about to lie to Miss Judson.

"I'll *try*," I said. "But that's the best I can do."

7
GRAND HOTEL

The modern hotel comes equipped with every luxury today's travelers could wish for. Expect nothing less than the most up-to-date amenities: electricity, indoor plumbing, private baths, and other marvels await the discerning guest.

—Hardcastle's Practical Travel Companion

I trotted down the hill, hard pressed to keep up with Miss Judson's determined stride. Honestly, I'd agreed to her terms. There was no need to add a forced march to my sentence. Peony bounded from boulder to brick stair to empty fish barrel. As we left the village behind, Miss Judson's pace slowed. She gripped her valise in one gloved hand, the Brochure in the other, and now stopped, surveying the terrain.

"It doesn't look much like the Brochure," I volunteered.

Miss Judson's knuckles tightened on the valise handles. "It has its own . . . austere beauty," she declared, as a blast of sea spray threw a fishy mist across us. Below lay not a soft white beach dotted with colorful bathing machines for wheeling swimmers out to sea in perfect modesty, but a harsh inlet of churning water ringed by black rocks. "It will be a *Lovely Holiday.*"

She headed straight down the hill—or as straight as possible, at any rate. The road canted left and right and finally gave up altogether, stranding us in a tangle of brush and oily scree. Miss Judson marched onward, only turning her booted ankle once as she forged a path toward the Ballingall Arms Hotel.

Reader, the Ballingall Arms is now so famous that I scarcely need describe it. Indeed, when one can buy stereographs and decorative spoons in shops as far away as London and Liverpool, or simply turn to the front page of their dailies for yet another view of Sir Quentin's Folly (as the press have dubbed it), it hardly calls for yet more ink squandered on it. But until you have stood in its shadow yourself, it is impossible to conceive of just how grand it really was. All five stories, gleaming white against the dim grey sea and sky; the colonnaded archways; the green tile roof and balconies; the purple flags billowing at every cupola, garret, tower, and belfry—all this it had, and more besides. The edifice dominated the seascape, perched precariously at the tip of a sheer promontory, like one wrong move would send the whole thing crashing to the sea below.

"Goodness," Miss Judson said. Even Peony stared, one eye critically dilated more than the other.

"What's it doing *here*?" I wondered aloud–aware I was echoing my sentiments upon seeing the Northern Lights tiara yesterday. Like the stolen jewels, Sir Quentin's gem of a hotel looked out of place. "And what's happened to the Family Amusements?"

A gust of surf crashed against the black rocks, spraying us anew. Miss Judson consulted the Brochure again, although it was fruitless. There was no beach, the Yacht Regatta was a fleet of dilapidated fishing boats, and the Frolicking Families just one lone gaffer in a weatherproof securing (or perhaps robbing) one of the sorry vessels. A Pier jutted out over the water, but half of it was missing– unfinished or destroyed, it was impossible to tell– skeletal metal girders stretching into nothing. The remains of a carousel had been swallowed by the scree, faded circus-tent roof cracked through, weather-beaten steeds abandoned.

"Perhaps Sir Quentin means to restore it all." Miss Judson sounded doubtful. "We'd best get inside."

Trying not to quail under the grandeur, I pressed close to Miss Judson. The lobby was large enough to hold my entire neighborhood, with room to spare for the Swinburne Ladies Auxiliary Social Hall, and a couple of small farms. There was a pond, *inside*, with a school of huge, deeply unhappy-looking goldfish.

"*No*," I told Peony, and scooped her up. "You cannot eat the decorations."

At the front desk, a man who must have been Clive's father greeted us warmly. Behind him hung a painting of a steamboat plowing up choppy black water.

"Here from the Excursion? You've beat the rush." He opened a leather ledger to the very first page.

Miss Judson took the pen he offered. "New register?"

"New *hotel*," replied the manager, whose name badge said Mr. Roberts. "You've the honor of being the first to sign, Miss . . . Judson. Welcome to the Ballingall Arms."

On the lower level of the counter sat a striking photograph of Mr. Roberts with his wife and daughters, four Young Ladies of Quality in lacy dresses surrounding their parents—"Mum and the gells," back in Brighton. Mrs. Roberts held a plump toddler with a huge white bow in her dark, downy hair, and looked like she was holding back a laugh.

"Clive's work?" Miss Judson inquired (an excellent deduction, as Clive himself was absent from the group). "He has a good eye."

"That he does." Mr. Roberts spoke with obvious pride. "But be careful asking him about it—the lad'll talk your ear off."

"Miss Judson's an artist, too," I said, indicating her sketchbook. It was, rather unfortunately, still open upon the page showing Mrs. Bloom's body in the baggage car. "Erm," I concluded.

Miss Judson set it atop the counter and carefully closed the cover. "I'm afraid there was an unfortunate incident on the train," she explained. "Your son might have seen something upsetting."

Mr. Roberts nodded grimly. "We heard something about it. Don't be surprised—word travels fast in a place like Eelscombe. Do they know what happened?"

"They're sending for the authorities now," Miss Judson assured him. I let her handle this exchange, since I rather hoped I might see Clive (and his marvelous camera!) again. Confessing to his father that I'd involved him in a murder within approximately thirty seconds of meeting him was *not* the ideal way to ensure that.

"Sad business." Mr. Roberts shook his head as he handed over the key. "Mrs. Bloom was popular hereabouts."

I was ready to leap in to ask what other information Mr. Roberts might be able to provide about the victim, but Miss Judson swiftly seized the key. *"Thank you."* Her voice was so final even Mr. Roberts got the message and changed the subject.

"Are they sending the rest of your luggage down?"

Whereupon Miss Judson and I shared a Belated Revelation. She closed her eyes briefly. "Sadly, no," she said. "The baggage car has been impounded by the stationmaster. We seem to be left with just the clothes on our backs."

"We can send to the shops for any necessaries," he offered, "but I'm afraid Eelscombe's a bit thin in that regard."

"Why do you call it Eelscombe?" I asked.

"Well, we're not supposed to, really," Mr. Roberts said. "Hard habit to break, that. Sir Quentin reckoned the village would attract more tourists with a more appealing name than the one it's had these three hundred years."

"Like Greenland,"* I said.

"Exactly. The lads can take you up to your suite. We have you in the Nile Rooms, on the fourth floor. The lift's round the corner, past the ballroom and the Orpheum. If you reach the tiger, you've gone too far. Shall I send someone up to unpack?"

Miss Judson declined. "Seeing how that's hardly necessary," she noted on the way to the lift, "since you had the stationmaster impound our luggage."

"There was evidence at stake!" Surely she knew I would not have sacrificed my specimen collection

* largely an icy wasteland, but given a better name by Erik the Red in the hopes of luring gullible Norse settlers

kit–not to mention my encyclopædia!–for anything less than a genuine criminal crisis.

"Remember that when you have no clean stockings or petticoats," she said.

"Petticoats don't get dirty."

"Not under typical circumstances. But *your* petticoats are somehow subjected to a great deal more mud, blood, and explosions than average."

From the looks of our rooms, Sir Quentin had felt an English Seaside Holiday was not ambitious enough, and that Ballingall Arms guests would appreciate having every holiday at once. Our suite– two bedrooms, a sitting room, and private bath–was fitted out like an Egyptian palace, complete with papyrus-themed wallpaper, a lapis-blue ceiling, and a golden bed carved like the Sphinx, which Peony approved.

"Very nice," Miss Judson agreed. She peeked into the other room, past a doorway guarded by a statue of Anubis. "I'll take the Sphinx. This one is more to your taste." The other bed looked unmistakably like a giant sarcophagus.

"Hey!" But she'd already disappeared into her room. Since I had no unpacking of my own to do, I set Mrs. Bloom's bag upon the sarcophagus bed's scarab-beetle coverlet. If there were any clues to her murder within, I should make haste to find them.

I did not get the chance. A moment later, Miss

Judson returned, carrying her jacket—but halted midway, keen eyes trained on the carpetbag.

"I trust," she said, "that there is an excellent explanation for *that*."

Excellent? Hardly. "It's Mrs. Bloom's."

"I see," she said, in tones suggesting quite the opposite. "And where is *your* valise?"

"In her compartment on the train."

"Well, that explains everything." With an air of resignation, she draped her jacket across one of the hippopotamus armchairs. "I seem to recall having this very conversation not a quarter of an hour ago."

"I couldn't very well hand it over to the police," I said. "You saw that constable! He's completely unprepared to investigate a murder."

"In his favor, I feel I should note the fact that he's not a twelve-year-old girl."

"He might as well be," I scoffed. "He *fainted* when he saw the body."

"That is not a character flaw," she pointed out. "So your intent is to hand that off to the proper authorities at the first opportunity." That was not a question.

"Of course."

"And that is *all* you will do with it."

I bit my lip. Peony sat very still and innocent beside me. "It wouldn't do any harm to take a peek," I said.

"You removed evidence from a crime scene, and now you're considering tampering with it, and I cannot believe the words that are coming from my mouth at this moment." She put a hand to her head, looking pained. "Myrtle."

It's never good when she says my name that way. "I followed proper custodial procedure. The bag has been in my care the entire time."

"We're not police officers."

"You don't need to say it like that," I said. "I merely think that the responsible thing would be to take a thorough inventory of Mrs. Bloom's possessions. There could be important"—I stopped myself short of saying *evidence*—"information in there."

She eyed me narrowly, face drawn so tight her neat eyebrows nearly met. I could tell she was warring between being a governess and her own burning curiosity. "If your father were here, he wouldn't allow any of this."

I didn't bother saying that she and I had long since mastered the knack of getting around what Father did or did not technically "allow." (For that matter, very few middle-class English families include "Thou Shalt Not Get Involved in Murder Investigations" in their household rules, and ours was no different. Although, to be fair, someone really ought to rethink that.)

"If Father were here, there would be a proper Investigator present!" I said instead. "But there's not. There's *us*. And we have a moral responsibility to do what we can. Mrs. Bloom's murderer must be brought to justice, and we are the only ones here who can do it."

Miss Judson took a moment to compose her counterargument. "That we have a duty to justice I do not dispute. However, it does *not* therefore follow that you and I have a duty to investigate the crime! Don't forget that I also have a duty to your safety, and that you have a duty to your father. And, I would hope, to me."

"Of course!" How could she question that?

"Good. Then I propose a compromise. We will retain possession of the bag, in its current unopened and untampered-with condition, until the arrival of a person we agree is competent to take charge of it, at which point we shall surrender it to his custody, without further discussion."

"How is that a compromise?"

"Because your other option is taking it straight to Constable Hoskiss, where the poor man will drop dead of fright. I'm sure you don't want that on your conscience."

To punctuate the finality of her decision, Miss Judson set Peony on the floor. Peony hopped straight back onto the bed and rubbed her chin against the carpetbag.

"*Mine*," she said smugly, lay down atop it, and went to sleep.

"Well," Miss Judson sighed. "I suppose that settles that."

Miss Judson inspected my appearance with a critical eye, straightening my collar. "Not much to be done about it now, I suppose."

"Why?" I said, suspicious. "Where are we going?"

"If you had bothered to read the Brochure, you would know that this Excursion includes tea this afternoon with the rest of our party. Perhaps it escaped your notice that we missed luncheon."

"*No*," said Peony, whose notice it had *not* escaped.

Much as I chafed at the notion of sitting through tea with Aunt Helena and the others, I revised my opinion as we descended on the lift. Aside from the thief—who was still at large—the members of our Excursion were the most likely suspects in Mrs. Bloom's murder. I knew Miss Judson wouldn't let me question anyone—but it would be an excellent opportunity to Observe them, at least. And I hadn't promised not to *think* about the murder, after all.

Apparently everyone else had, however. The Bird Ladies flitted about the lobby, cooing and pointing. Sir Quentin escorted Aunt Helena on his arm, stopping to show off a massive crystal chandelier. Cicely trailed behind with Aunt Helena's shawl, fan, lorgnette case, and a purple cushion. I felt sorry for her, forced to spend an entire fortnight at Aunt Helena's beck and call, pretending to be her friend. Couldn't she have found a better job? Like being a grave digger?

"Sir Quentin," Aunt Helena gushed, "this is an *outstanding* achievement." Her predatory eyes shone, and she grasped Sir Quentin's velvet sleeve in her talons. "What a lovely spot this would be for a wedding." Was I hallucinating, or did she actually bat her eyelashes at him?

Sir Quentin's laugh echoed off all the marble. "My, my, Helena, always scheming."

Even Miss Judson looked mystified. What was going on here?

Miss Ballingall came rushing in from the labyrinth of branching corridors. Her face was blotchy, like she'd been crying. "It's too late to cancel tea," she said. "But the kitchens can send everyone's dinner up to their rooms. Mr. Roberts has phoned the railway, but they're not sure about rescheduling the return train. We might have to wait until the regular rail service comes through, and goodness knows what will happen with our trunks now." She shuddered.

Sir Quentin scowled. "Tea? Rescheduling? What's this, now?"

"Canceling the Excursion, of course."

"Cancel? Ridiculous! Won't hear of it."

"But, Father! Think of our poor guests."

"Exactly," said Sir Quentin. "They've paid good money for a holiday, and a holiday they shall have."

"But what sort of holiday could it be now, with a black cloud hanging over it?" Miss Ballingall rubbed her bad arm. "We can't have the Hardcastles caught up in this awfulness. We *must* send them home."

"No!" I burst out. "If we leave now, we'll never find out what happened to Mrs. Bloom—or the tiara!"

Aunt Helena shot me a withering look. "That is hardly our concern."

"Well, it *ought* to be," I returned, forgetting my vow to Miss Judson. "How can anyone think about a holiday right now?"

"Myrtle's right," said Miss Ballingall. "We can't possibly go on as if nothing's happened. Everything's spoiled."

"Nonsense," said Sir Quentin. "Give in at the first inconvenience? We're going to buck up and soldier on. Isn't that what we Ballingalls do, Dolly?"

But instead of Soldiering On, Miss Ballingall burst into tears.

"Oh, dear." Miss Judson took charge, putting an arm around her. "Here, now. None of that. Why don't we all go in for tea. It would be a pity for all that lovely food to go to waste. Did you plan the menu, Miss Ballingall?"

Miss Ballingall wailed, "Father did! Father plans everything."

Between Miss Judson's coaxing and Aunt Helena's bossiness, we all made it inside the grand dining room and settled round a table set for a royal banquet, with a white cloth and silver-edged plates and a battalion of teacups and water glasses and inexplicable forks. At a nearby table, the moustachioed salesman sat alone, sipping coffee from one of the delicate cups as he read a newspaper.

"Judson!" Aunt Helena tapped Miss Judson's sleeve. "There's that nice young Swedish gentleman from the train. Go and invite him to join us."

Miss Judson was a master of the art of Exceptional Forbearance, but this command gave her pause. "Aunt?"

"Well, he shouldn't have to dine alone."

"Perhaps he *wants* to—" Miss Judson's protest was fruitless.

"Nonsense. He'd be in his room if he wished to be alone. Go and bring him over."

"Yes," chirped Miss Causton. "He's ever so friendly!"

"*So* friendly!" echoed Miss Cabot.

Miss Judson looked helplessly at our companions, and I saw my chance.

"I could do it," I volunteered, in the sweetest voice I could muster. I rather doubted my ability to coax a Swedish salesman to tea, but it was worth the attempt, both to get away from my current party and to question him about anything he might have seen on the train this morning.

"*No.*" Miss Judson and Aunt Helena quashed that suggestion in unison, and Miss Judson rose to her feet. "I shall go."

As uniformed servers melted out of the wood-work and heaped our table with sandwiches, cakes, and dainties, I watched Miss Judson with Mr. Strand. Was it too much to hope she was taking his witness statement? He glanced at our table, sandy moustache twitching, as Miss Judson held out her graceful, light brown hand. He rose to give her a small, polite bow—then pulled out the opposite chair and helped Miss Judson seat herself. For a dumbfounded moment, I could only stare at them, but she did not meet our eyes, chatting instead with Mr. Strand, helping herself to *his* tiered stand of petit fours, a smug little smile at her lips.

Furious, I turned away. That was so unfair! She'd managed to make her escape, and I was still stuck with Aunt Helena and the Bird Ladies.

Aunt Helena scrutinized them through her lorgnette. "Hmph," she said. "I've always said that travel is a great way to broaden one's mind, but that's taking things a bit too far, if you ask me."

Broaden the mind? It clearly wasn't working for Aunt Helena.

No one was interested in talking to (much less hearing from) me, so as the meal dragged on, I studied my companions. At Aunt Helena's end of the table, Cicely stirred listlessly at her consommé and flinched every time Sir Quentin spoke to her, mostly in clumsy jokes. Miss Ballingall, likewise, only picked at her food, carefully switching between knife and fork with her left hand, the pale, fleshy right hand balled in her lap. Had she suffered an injury of some kind, or had she always had the condition? It must be a dreadful inconvenience, and yet it didn't seem to bother her much.

Still, it more or less ruled her out as a suspect in the murder. It would take a great deal of strength to jam a pair of scissors into somebody's back with enough power to kill in a single blow.

Strength and *luck*—or exceptional skill. I skirted my gaze along the table, reflecting on this. It wasn't actually all that easy to kill someone by stabbing them in the back. (I had discussed this very matter only a few weeks ago with Dr. Munjal, my friend Caroline's father and our local Police Surgeon. Hypothetically, of course!) All the vulnerable organs are up front, after all. The back is mostly muscle and bone, and there aren't many lethal places to strike: the kidneys (which would leave much more blood than we'd seen at the scene), the lungs, or a blow that severed the spinal column at exactly the right—or wrong, depending on your perspective—spot. I polished off my egg-and-cress. Mrs. Bloom's killer had either got extremely lucky or had known exactly what he was doing.

Who in our company would know that?

Besides me, of course.

"Well, Myrtle, what do you think of our little Excursion so far?" Miss Ballingall's quavering voice barely rose above the clink of glasses and the slather of butter knives.

Miss Judson wasn't here, but I knew the proper response. "Oh, it's been thrilling." I wasn't half lying, either.

"We traveled such a lot when I was a girl," she said, with a nostalgic smile. "I loved it. New places, new faces—it's the perfect chance to escape, reinvent yourself, be somebody totally different for a bit."

I wrinkled my nose at this. Why should I want to be somebody different? Then I looked around the table, at Aunt Helena and the Bird Ladies, and Cicely, and Miss Ballingall—proper Ladies of Quality, all of them. Father had sent me on holiday with these people—was it in the hopes that I might stop being Morbid Myrtle and turn into an ordinary girl? The kind who didn't think about sharp-force trauma at the dinner table or get herself involved in other people's murders? I sighed and kicked my chair legs. Was that what Miss Judson was doing right now? Perhaps she'd seen her chance to escape and be somebody besides my governess, someone mysterious and elegant, who took tea (and cakes—*lots* of cakes) with strange Swedish gentlemen. It all gave me an unpleasant, unsettled feeling, and I pushed my plate away.

"This menu is splendid," declared Miss Causton, serving herself a second helping of tongue sandwich. "Quite as good as we've had anywhere on the Continent."

"Quite," confirmed Miss Cabot. "You must be so proud, Miss Ballingall."

Miss Ballingall started. "Oh, it's all Father's doing, I assure you. I'm hopeless at that sort of thing. Well, you saw how it's all turned out."

"Nonsense," Aunt Helena said. "You've been a perfect hostess, Temperance, dear. No one could blame you for what's happened."

"No one," cooed the Bird Ladies in soothing tones.

I'd had enough of being somebody else for one day. "I do hope the *unpleasantness* won't cause problems for the hotel. I can't think a jewel theft and murder would be good for business."

There. I'd managed to work three Entirely Unsuitable Topics into one sentence.

"You'd be surprised." All eyes swung toward Cicely. "We were in Brighton this summer. The hotel there was robbed, and nobody batted an eye."

"That's enough of that talk!" Aunt Helena's voice was harsh. "We are all here on holiday. We should—" She didn't get a chance to finish, for Miss Ballingall suddenly burst from the table and fled the room.

For a stunned moment we all just sat there.

"Goodness, Sir Quentin," said Aunt Helena, "I don't recall Temperance being so excitable. What do you suppose has got into her?"

"Can't imagine," he huffed. "Steady girl. Always has been."

I'll remind the Reader that Miss Judson wasn't there to stop me. "Maybe it was Mrs. Bloom being murdered."

"Honestly, Helena Myrtle, the things you say. And That Woman. It was bad enough that she had to go and get herself killed on our train. I don't see why she has to keep disrupting *our* holiday."

"Why do people keep saying that?" I said. "She didn't get herself killed. Someone *killed her*—"

"Helena Myrtle."

"—and with *your* scissors. How did *that* happen, Aunt?"

"Helena Myrtle!"

Before anyone could scold me further, I shoved away from the table.

"Oh, never mind," I snapped at everyone and no one. "Something unimaginable must have got into *me*, too."

8

FRUSTRATION
OF PURPOSE

Paris, France: No visit to the city would be complete without a stop at the Île de la Cité, where visitors may partake in the lively French pastime of viewing unidentified bodies at the public morgue. Open seven days a week, dawn until six p.m. Free.

—*Hardcastle's Practical Travel Companion*

I stormed out of that ridiculous dining room and was immediately attacked by—I wasn't sure what, precisely: something like a great, hot, unexpectedly *solid* fog, which tumbled me to the floor and licked me.

"Nicky! For shame!" an unfamiliar voice exclaimed, and the steamy wetness was dispatched from my face. As I came to my senses, I realized I was looking into the white, slobbering maw of the sheepdog from the train. Behind him, hand gripping his collar, loomed Nurse Temby—and the voice imploring "Nicky" to behave was Poor Maudie, waving from her bath chair.

"Oh, I'm so sorry. Did he hurt you?"

I shook my head, wiping canine salivary emissions from my face.

"Perhaps I should take him back to the room, Miss." That voice, like dead leaves crumbling, belonged to Nurse Temby.

"He's been cooped up on the train for days. Let him out to run on the beach. Copernicus! Sit!" Poor Maudie snapped her fingers, and the sheepdog dropped his massive curly hindquarters to the tile floor, stub of a tail wagging, somewhere, amid the fluff.

I found my voice. "Copernicus?" I myself was a great admirer of the Polish Renaissance astronomer, whose discoveries had rearranged the solar system, though I had yet to name a family member after him.*

This, naturally, encouraged the dog to renew his acquaintance with my face and hat and collar, and I found myself once more buried in a shaggy, wriggling mountain. It was exhilarating, actually, once I got my

---

* I made a mental note to mention it to Miss Judson and Father, should the time come when they might welcome such a suggestion. *Copernicus Hardcastle* had a nice ring to it. I was likewise fond of *Mycroft Hardcastle* and *Abberline Hardcastle*.

breath back, and I couldn't help giggling, although Nurse Temby was Not Amused.

Poor Maudie drew in her lip, chagrined—but a laugh hid in her eyes. "Outside, please, Temby, before he smothers this child."

Grim-faced, Nurse Temby held her ground for a long, cold moment, and I had a sense that these two often faced off in silent stalemate.

"Very well," the dry leaves rattled. "But you're due for your tincture." She dragged Copernicus—plainly reluctant to leave his mistress—toward the great doors, black skirts swishing ominously.

Miss Penrose waved me over. "Oh, dear. Your hat's ruined, I'm afraid."

"No, it looked like that already."

Her father had been right about the sea air—she was quite a different person than we'd seen on the train. Everything about her (except perhaps her choice of pets) spoke of wealth and refinement, from the elaborate pile of her brittle auburn hair to the delicate lace of her afternoon dress, to the fine craftsmanship of the wicker bath chair. I could easily see the resemblance to her father. If she recovered from her illness, she'd no doubt also become the sort of person quietly accustomed to getting her own way.

Now she cast a furtive look toward the great lobby doors. "Quick, she'll be back to fetch me soon enough. What do you know?"

"Er—?"

"About the robbery and murder! They won't tell me anything. I have a Delicate Constitution, you know." (This was accompanied by a resigned eye roll.) "But I saw you in the Ladies' Lounge, and Father told me that you were there, too, last night, with the woman who was killed. Do you know what happened?" Her wide eyes shone, their pupils tiny pinpricks in a sea of grey-green, and I wondered what, exactly, was ailing her. "It must have been some madman on the loose."

I tried to catch up. Miss Penrose was unquestionably a Young Lady of Quality, so she was breaking all sorts of rules—written and unwritten*—by discussing this.

"Or the thief," I managed. "That's the theory, anyway."

Even as I said this, I could not shake the image of Aunt Helena, brandishing those scissors at Mrs. Bloom in the darkened sleeping carriage. I twisted my fingers together, trying to convince myself that I was ridiculous to even contemplate the notion. "My aunt thinks it was a vagrant."

But Miss Penrose dismissed that. "That tiara is going to be the most famous piece of jewelry in Europe tomorrow. What would a vagrant do with it? You can't possibly sell it, and you couldn't wear it, either."

* No, really, they write them down: see *Girl's Own Paper,* page 9.

She wore a pearl brooch at her throat, and her red tresses were caught up by jeweled pins. Clearly she knew her jewelry. I turned her words over in my mind. "Because it would be recognized as stolen?"

"Exactly," she said. "You'd *have* to be mad to steal it."

Mrs. Bloom hadn't mentioned that, but Miss Penrose's theory made sense. "The tiara's probably lost forever, then." It was the least of what was wrong, but I hated to think that not only had Mrs. Bloom been killed, she'd also *failed.* "It's so unfair," I said aloud, not meaning to.

Miss Penrose sighed with me. "I know. And it was looking like such a lovely holiday, too. My mother died six months ago," she explained. "I've been—unwell—ever since." She gestured at the bath chair. "Father keeps sending for doctors and specialists. He threatened to send me to a sanatorium for a Rest Cure,* but then Sir Quentin's Brochure arrived, and I knew that was the answer. Fairhaven would make me well again." She mustered up a brave smile that would do the Ballingalls proud. "But everything's going wrong. First Father and Temby insisted on coming along, and then all this business with robbery and murder . . . They'll never let me out of their sight again."

"You're out of their sight *now*," I said slyly.

* a questionable American invention, not nearly as restful as it sounds, involving being strapped to a bed and force-fed. I suppose it would encourage the patient to improve in a hurry, though.

Poor Maudie's laugh rang out, clear and unexpected. She had a pretty smile, with a streak of mischief to it, and I had the feeling that, if ever given the chance, Maud Penrose might turn out to be Irrepressible, too.

"For all the good it does me!" she said. "Oh, here's Father now." The lift gate had rattled open, and Mr. Penrose came striding across the lobby, long-legged and vigorous. "He's probably dreaming up some ghastly new cure for Temby to try. Can't they understand, I just want to be left alone?"

This *I* certainly understood. Of the many things Young Ladies of Quality were not permitted to be or do, *alone* was chief on the list. From nursemaid to governess to companion, unless we were in a group, we were bound to run astray.

Mr. Penrose recognized me. "Green wallpaper," he said, by way of greeting.

"Yes, sir. Miss Penrose seems to be improving already."

Mr. Penrose seized the handles of the bath chair. "Do you think you might manage some tea, darling?" Before she could respond, he wheeled Maud toward the dining room, without a word of farewell.

I watched them go with a growing pang, thinking instead of Mrs. Bloom. Bold, irrepressible, gloriously unaccompanied, *independent* Mrs. Bloom. Who'd been murdered.

Perhaps Copernicus (the scientist, not the dog) had

been wrong, after all, and the shape of the universe could never change.

☙

When I got back to our Nile Rooms, Peony greeted me with languorous meows, flinging herself to the floor in an elaborate stretch.* I threw my hat onto the sarcophagus bed with a frustrated sigh. It landed beside Mrs. Bloom's carpetbag, over which Peony had been standing guard. Well, sleeping guard.

Now that Peony and I were alone in the quiet, thoughts of the day bubbled up like a vile soup. I lay back on the bed, staring at the painted ceiling. Poor Maudie was right: everything *was* going wrong. There was no satisfaction to the thought that I'd been right about how awful the holiday would be. Mrs. Bloom was dead, I'd lost my books and magnifier, and now Miss Judson had abandoned me, preferring tea with a stranger—a strange, non-Father *man*—to sticking by my side and solving our case.

Miss Judson's insistence that we Not Get Involved troubled me. Was she just parroting Father, or was that what she really wanted, too? I hated to disappoint Miss Judson, but we'd always been on the same side before. Now I wasn't so sure.

I touched the worn tapestry of the carpetbag. There was so much more I'd wanted to know about Mrs.

---

* n.b., this was *not*, as I had discovered to my regret, an invitation to stroke her white belly.

Bloom—not just her work, but *her.* Aunt Helena didn't deem her respectable, but I'd thought she was marvelous. Now an ominous shadow had fallen over my picture of her, and it was hard to shake the creeping sense that maybe everyone else was right, and Ladies of Quality really were better off sitting demurely in a tearoom than Investigating crimes and getting murdered for it.

Peony bumped my hand with her forehead. *"No."*

I'd allowed myself to fancy that Mrs. Bloom and I might even grow to be friends, or at least see this Investigation through together. I wondered again about Mr. Bloom—Bertram—and her curious words about him. Was he waiting somewhere for her to come home? Were there little Blooms who'd lost their mum, or even their grandmum? It was all too much, and I had to press my fists against my eyes and take a shaky breath, to keep it in. Peony climbed onto my lap to knead my knees with her white paws, trying to chase away my gloom.

I gave a sloppy sniff, pondering the bag. Surely Mrs. Bloom must have left some clue behind—for someone who ought to be told what had happened. If only I *knew* what had happened. Peony's ministrations could not distract me from the image of Mrs. Bloom in the railway carriage with Aunt Helena. What had really happened after I left her there? Why had I been such a coward!

"Mrow." Peony rubbed her chin against the bag's latch. It was a dubious prospect, taking her advice. I nibbled at my thumb.

"We promised we wouldn't."

"No."

Maybe she was right. There was a murderer on the loose, after all. And I wouldn't disturb anything; I'd put it all back exactly as I'd found it. Besides, I reasoned, the bag was nowhere near her when she was killed, so it wasn't *really* disturbing evidence. I grabbed my gloves and flipped the latches on Mrs. Bloom's bag.

It was a jumbled mess. I regarded it grimly, trying to decide if I was looking at a habitual untidy state or the result of someone tampering with the contents. There was no way to tell. Notebook at the ready, I took a careful inventory, recording each item as I removed it from the carpetbag. First was the ledger, which I myself had put inside (further argument for continuing the search: this evidence had *already* been tampered with). Beneath that was the heap of knitting, which looked even sadder up close (I was certain there were too many needles—or perhaps not enough), and under that, a thick bellows file stuffed with papers. I tugged that out, an ephemeral scrap fluttering to the coverlet.

It was an old ticket stub, printing too blurry to make out more than "... *owell Steamer* ..." A souvenir from a long-ago boat trip? Ink pooled out from the letters in a hazy halo, like the ticket had been soaked in water, then pressed in a book for safekeeping. I tucked it carefully back inside.

That left nothing in the bag but the packet of sweets, a card case, and a battered little coin purse, containing some money, housekeys, and spare hairpins. Somehow these personal items didn't feel nearly as much like Mrs. Bloom as her thick red ledger did. Gripping that made me feel like she was almost still in the room with me, guiding the Investigation.

I opened it hopefully, but instead of revelations about her killer, it was full of inky doodles, random lines and dots, as if she'd been trying to get the right balance of ink on her pen nib.

"What is this?" I said aloud. It definitely wasn't Greek, and it didn't look like any *other* language, either. It seemed like gibberish, but there was entirely too much of it. I sighed. Perhaps Mrs. Bloom wasn't going to help me solve her murder, after all.

I turned back to the file. Inside was a small sheaf of papers with the mountain watermark from Mrs. Bloom's card. It read:

Albion Casualty Insurance Co. guarantees and secures the *"NORTHERN LIGHTS" TIARA, CORONET OF WHITE GOLD, DIAMOND, AND ALEXANDRITE*, against loss, damage, or theft, up to the amount of

£5000. Policy subject to the following terms and conditions . . .

The insurance policy on the tiara! Running my finger down the page, I found the security arrangements Sir Quentin had agreed to provide. Mrs. Bloom was right: the tiara was supposed to have been locked in the train's safe until its arrival in Fairhaven. Sir Quentin had been in clear violation of the policy just having it on display, let alone letting Temperance wear the thing.

"What do you think?" I asked Peony. "Mrs. Bloom said she was going to deny Sir Quentin's claim *before* anything happened to the tiara, and he was mad then." How much madder would he be when there was actually a claim to be filed? Five thousand pounds was an almost inconceivable sum—a queen's ransom, so to speak. Even an Excursion Impresario probably wouldn't have that much money.

Was it enough to kill for?

I chewed my thumb, troubled. I didn't like to picture Sir Quentin chasing after Mrs. Bloom with Aunt Helena's scissors. The idea of some unknown thief was oddly preferable.

With a start, I realized that something was missing. *Passenger manifests and employee rolls*, she'd told me—how she'd known everything about everyone on the train.

But where were they now? I shook the empty bag, then dumped the file onto the bed and shuffled through the papers, but they weren't here. My pulse quickened. Could the killer have taken them to hide his identity? But was it an employee or a passenger? I'd bumped into Mr. Coogan on his way out of the passenger carriage, and he'd acted oddly, afterward, when the stationmaster questioned him. Was it possible he'd got there before me, to remove the evidence?

"*Brrrrb*," Peony warned, ears pricking. I froze and heard the click of the Nile Rooms' grand double doors. Hastily, I shoved everything back into the carpetbag (so much for custodial procedure) and tried to look innocent. Too late, I realized I'd missed one scrap of paper. A telegram receipt! I had just enough time to slip it beneath my scarab-beetle pillow before Miss Judson returned.

9
PROMENADE

The centerpiece of any Seaside Holiday is a Promenade along the Pier, a clever innovation which permits holiday-makers to enjoy the sense of being at sea without the inconvenience of actually setting foot aboard a boat.

—Hardcastle's Practical Travel Companion

The next morning, our errand to surrender Mrs. Bloom's carpetbag to the Proper Authorities was delayed by the arrival of breakfast, served in the fashionable "continental" style of dainty baked goods and fruit. As Miss Judson piled her plate with pastries, lemon curd, and strawberries, thoughtfully regarding the tea service, I settled down with the most toast-like thing and the newspaper, eager to see what the *Times* had to say on the theft of the Northern Lights and Mrs. Bloom's death. There was nothing on the front page. Or the second. Or anywhere else—not even buried in the darkest recesses of the dull final pages, where news-not-of-note was consigned.

"There's no mention of the robbery or the murder!"

Miss Judson was unperturbed. "It just happened yesterday."

"Do you know how often people are murdered on English railways?"

She calmly applied clotted cream to a scone. "I expect you're about to tell me."

"Twice! Ever! In all the history of English train travel, there have only ever been two murders before this—Thomas Briggs in 1864, and Frederick Gold in 1881. Those caused media *sensations.* You remember, the Briggs case was the one with the telegram, and the detectives sailed to America to arrest the suspect."

"It had escaped my recollection," she said drily.

"It was a huge case! The *Illustrated London News* are still talking about it, thirty years later. That's how noteworthy a murder on a train is. So where's the coverage of Mrs. Bloom's death?" I waved the paper at her. "By my reckoning, she's the first *woman* murdered on an English train—and you know how the press love it when women are killed."

"I wish you could hear what you sound like." Miss Judson gave the newspaper a calculating look. "Eelscombe is rather remote. Perhaps no one noticed?"

"There's a telegraph signal box at the station, and there were dozens of witnesses on the platform," I said.

"Not to mention everyone working on the train. And not *one* of them got word to a curious reporter?"

She contemplated this. "Don't they sometimes offer rewards?" She peered at the newspaper, in case such a notice might spontaneously appear. "Especially with something like the Northern Lights gone missing, should it turn up at your neighborhood pawnbroker."

Families and businesses *were* encouraged to offer such incentives. Albion Casualty, or the tiara's owner, at least, would definitely be wanting it back.

Unless they didn't know it was missing. I recalled the telegraph receipt I'd found. Mrs. Bloom would have needed to wire the news of the robbery to her company, as well as notify the police. If Miss Penrose was correct, the tiara would be unsellable just as soon as word got out about the robbery. What if someone had tried to put a stop to that news getting out—by killing Mrs. Bloom?

I tapped the newspaper with a pointed finger. "Someone's covered up the story."

She did not look up from her croissant. Croissants. "I suppose you have a suspect in mind."

I didn't, besides the thief. But that didn't make any sense. "How *could* you keep a story like that quiet? Like you said, you couldn't stop the witnesses from talking. You'd have to pay the newspapers not to cover it instead."

Miss Judson looked skeptical. "That would take an awful lot of money. And influence." Slowly, her eyes lifted to the room around us, its gilded furniture and exotic fixtures, the rich breakfast with its expensive delicacies. I could tell exactly what she was thinking by the way she didn't say anything.

"Sir Quentin?"

She poured herself another (silver-rimmed) cup of (imported Russian) tea. (With milk. And honey.) "We're not having this conversation."

Seeing as we were already knee-deep in the subject, I ignored that. "He can't keep it quiet forever. Someone's bound to notice when Mrs. Bloom doesn't come back to work, and the tiara's owners probably want to know how its trip went."

"We *are not* having this conversation. You are not getting involved in this case. *We* are not getting involved in the case."

"But—"

"No." She yanked the newspaper from my hand and replaced it with the Brochure, Sir Quentin's bewhiskered face gloating all over it.

I tossed it to the tea table. "Are you defending him? I noticed you were out awfully late last night."

She rose, deep green skirts falling smoothly into place. "You're being ridiculous. Finish your breakfast so we can begin our holiday."

"You've already *started* yours," I said sourly. "What was that business yesterday, anyway, with Mr. Strand?"

Her answer was superseded by a knock at the door,

which I opened to find Clive, the young photographer from the railway station.

"Is Scotland Yard here yet?" I asked eagerly, but he just blinked at me.

"Morning, Miss, and—erm, Miss." He gave us both a nod. "Me dad—that is, the Manager's sent me up to see if you lot—er, ladies needed a tour guide. Take you round the sights an' what." He rocked back on his heels, thumbs in his bracers.

Miss Judson looked us over. "What an excellent idea," she said. "I was headed to the beach to sketch—"

"I could show you the best spots," Clive volunteered. "There's a view from Eel's Head that'll knock yer—take your breath away, ma'am. Miss."

Miss Judson's gaze fell on me with a critical weight that made me tug on my skirts. "That's a very kind offer, Master Roberts," she said. "The others are expecting me. But Myrtle would be delighted to accompany you."

Dear Reader, I don't believe I had ever been *delighted* in all my twelve years, three months, and six days. But the prospect of spending the morning with Clive was far more appealing than enduring another moment with my fellow Excursionists.

"Yes, let's." I grabbed my coat and practically mowed him down on my way out of the room, Peony at our heels.

We ran into Cicely on the way to the lift, wheeling a tea cart toward Aunt Helena's room, head down. She didn't seem to see us as we passed. When we ducked round the corner, Clive tugged me furtively aside.

"I'm not supposed to know this, mind," he said. "But I overheard Dad tell Sir Quentin that the feller that's coming down to investigate the murder is due to arrive on the afternoon train."

At last! Now we'd finally get somewhere. "Did you see the papers this morning? Not a word about what happened!"

This piqued Clive's journalistic spirit, I could tell. "That's strange, innit?" Thoughtful, he rubbed at his chin. "What do you reckon it means?"

Here I recalled just in time that he and his father worked for Sir Quentin, so I managed not to voice the idea Miss Judson had hinted. Instead I asked, "Do you like working for Sir Quentin?"

"He's all right," Clive said. "He does like to put on airs, but on the whole I reckon he's a good sort. Offered Mum and Dad a partial ownership share in the Ballingall Arms, you know."

I took in the wide hallway with its ornate ceiling and flocked wallpaper and electric chandeliers and managed not to whistle. "You *own* this?"

Clive laughed. "About five percent. Plus a share of the takings, Dad's wages, and my studio." His chest puffed out a bit, and I couldn't blame him at all. Nobody I knew back home owned part of a hotel, let alone part of a hotel as grand as the Ballingall Arms (and its terraces and indoor fishpond) *and* another whole hotel in Brighton.

Peony, vastly impressed, looked around with large eyes and said, "*Mine.*"

On the lift, the operator kept turning to Peony and giving her slow, catlike blinks. Peony leaned close and bunted him in the hand, earning a broad smile. "She likes me," he said, with confidence.

"Brrrrw," Peony agreed.

The lift lurched to a stop, and he sang out, "Ground floor: lobby, ballrooms, dining room, Orpheum. Stand clear o' the doors, ladies and gentlemen." He collapsed the elaborate iron gate so we could step out, then paused to scratch Peony's chin. "What's her name?"

"Peony."

That broad smile again. "That's a flower!"

"See you later, Tom," said Clive. "You owe me a rematch at cribbage."

"Not if I sees you first," the operator said, returning to his post.

Clive waved goodbye as we sauntered out to the lobby. "That's Tom," he said. "He's a good chap, but a bit simple, you know. Well, what do you want to see first? There's the beach, and the old Pier, the smuggler's caves, the fish market—if you like that sort of thing . . ."

We had to descend a treacherous set of wooden steps to reach the beach, which was composed entirely of millions of small round stones.

"Where's the sand?" I asked. The Brochure had plainly advertised *sand* (there was a picture), and I knew Miss Judson was expecting a proper beach.

"It's a shingle beach," Clive explained. "Just pebbles." He picked one up and handed it to me. "This here's flint—quartz, that is." It was washed smooth by thousands of years of battering its neighbors. I liked its rich ochre color, and I slipped it into my coat pocket.

Ahead of us, the Pier stretched like a stranded bridge out into Eelshead Bay. From this distance, it was clear now that it wasn't unfinished. A massive great chunk had been torn from its far end, as if some Behemoth from Below* had swallowed it, leaving behind splintered wood, sagging pavilions, and twisted beams hanging over the water.

Clive was busy snapping photographs with his beautiful camera, and Peony was busy stalking tiny crabs scurrying across the shingle, then fleeing from the slosh of waves into which they escaped. So I wandered ahead, toward the old Pier. Behind me, Clive's shutter clicked away, and overhead the lonely cry of gulls cut through the constant low *shush-shush* of the water. It was different from the ordinary suburban bustle of my neighborhood back home: the rattle of the tram and the clop-clop of hoofbeats and the insistent gnawing of squirrels eating the eaves. Now

* *Billy Garrett #10*

that the threat of calliope music and laughing holiday-makers had been stripped away, I found I rather liked it. *Austere beauty*, Miss Judson had said.

I approached the entrance of the Pier with caution. Although this part of the structure appeared sound enough, a great chain held the arched gates closed, with a strict NO TRESPASSING notice. The gates had once been painted gleaming white, but age and neglect had flaked that away, and rust bled through like a weepy scab.

I climbed up to where a strip of unkempt pavement gave way to the boardwalk. Matching towers flanked the Pier's grand entrance, like at a fairgrounds, but their ticket windows were broken, flagpoles bare. Beyond, dotting the boardwalk like shabby cottages, were the Amusement Kiosks, which had once offered everything from tintype photographs to ice cream and a concert stage for operas and symphonies. (See, Dear Reader? I *had* read the Brochure.)

Clive came up behind me. "Wouldn't you love to get inside there?"

I gave a hopeless tug at the chains as we peered through longingly.

"What do you reckon happened?" he said, readying another plate for his camera.

In answer to Clive's question, a dull bronze plaque on one of the massive stone footings beneath the gatehouse caught my eye, far more somber than the rest of

the once-cheery signage. I brushed off a bit of guano
to reveal its message:

S.S. VALKYRIE MEMORIAL

ON THE AFTERNOON OF 12 OCTOBER 1878,
THE PADDLE STEAMER *VALKYRIE* WAS DOCKED
AT EELSCOMBE PLEASURE PIER, CARRYING
HOLIDAYMAKERS FROM A LOCAL CHURCH TOUR.
AS PASSENGERS DISEMBARKED, AN EXPLOSION
RIPPED THROUGH THE *VALKYRIE*'S BOILER,
DESTROYING THE VESSEL AND SEVERELY
DAMAGING THE PIER. THE DISASTER CLAIMED
SEVENTEEN LIVES—MOSTLY CHILDREN.

———◆◆◆———

THIS PLAQUE IS DEDICATED TO THEIR MEMORY.

"There was a shipwreck," I called. "Come look."

Clive finished his photograph and came over. "The
Valkyrie? There's a painting of that at the hotel."

I instantly knew what he meant. "At the front desk,"
I said. "That steamboat."

"Paddle steamer," Clive corrected. "Say—that was
almost exactly fifteen years ago." His gaze traveled up
to the mangled wreckage at the end of the Pier. Farther
out at sea, a specimen of the same kind of vessel glided
past, a long slip of white and red against the dark water
and grimy sky. Surely none of its passengers, on their

way to a real seaside resort, had any notion they were aboard a floating incendiary.

I ran my finger down the names. There were so many of them! All Eelscombers? Or tourists—strangers—like me? I spotted a familiar name among them: *Davey Hoskiss, aged 16.*

"Hoskiss," I said. "Like the constable?"

Clive peered in. "A brother, maybe? Here, let's get a closer look." He swung himself back up onto the Pier and squeezed through the chained gates before I could say anything.

"But we can't," I protested. *"No trespassing."*

"What are you, a *girl?*" he scoffed.

Was that meant to be insulting? "Yes," I said scornfully. "But I'm not *scared.*" I wriggled through after him, my fat skirts flaking off paint and rust and . . . other substances.

Although I generally advocate obeying posted ordinances, I had to admit there was a delicious thrill creeping after Clive down Eelscombe's abandoned Pleasure Pier. It was like we'd stepped back into a faded version of the past, where just a moment ago, holiday crowds had Promenaded, taking the sunshine and sea air and Amusements. Our footfalls echoed eerily, a rime of salt on the boardwalk evidence that no one else had been here for ages.

Clive kept stopping to set up another photograph, but Peony and I wandered along, peeking in cracked windows and leaning out over the iron railings. The water was far below us, the October sky vast and grey. Abandoned kiosks with broken fretwork on their windows and missing roof tiles still looked jolly, despite their fading red-and-blue paint and peeling notices: a skating parlor, a soda fountain, a portrait artist (Sketches Whilst You Wait, 6p), a revolving stand that must have once held *cartes de visite* and stereograph cards for sale.

One tattered sign promised LATEST OPTICAL WONDERS: KALEIDOSCOPES, TELESCOPES, ZOETROPES, AND MORE! A PENNY A PEEK! But the kiosk, alas, was empty—save for a curious copper tube emerging from the boardwalk like somebody's misplaced plumbing. It was nearly as tall as I was, with an opening at the end like a trumpet's bell.

"Myrtle."

"Hmm?" I turned, but Clive was nowhere to be seen.

"Right here." Once again, Clive's voice, right beside me—but no sign of Clive. "Look up—'cross the way."

I did, casting my gaze across the Pier, to where a distant Clive at the opposite railing waved a friendly hand. "Blimey!"

I Observed Clive bend over slightly and talk into his own fixture. "Speaking tube! Like on ships. We've got 'em in Brighton, too."

At once I understood. The copper pipe had amplified his voice, allowing it to travel across the Pier and be easily overheard at great distance. "That's brilliant," I whispered, and heard Clive's ripple of laughter right by my ear. Amazing that it should still be perfectly functional after all this time.

We spent a few minutes Amusing ourselves with the speaking tube (Clive knew several spectacular Inappropriate Words, which I traded for the same in Latin and French, all shared via the clandestine acoustics) before exhausting the novelty.

The Pier was about a quarter mile long—or it had been, before the explosion tore the end off. I ventured toward the wrecked edge. Up close, it looked even more like some vast creature had taken a bite from it, leaving a great gaping wound with the sea splashing through. Abruptly I felt the whole mass shudder beneath me, like a lift slipping. I eased my way back, bumping into Clive, who let out a *whooph* of surprise.

"Sorry!" I mumbled, backing away from the weakened structure. "Don't go any farther." Peony, naturally, ignored my advice, springing across the broken beams, scaling the railings like they were ordinary tree limbs, toward the ruins of a grand Pavilion clinging stubbornly on. Faded theater posters advertised musical performances that had never happened. One featured a plump girl in a fancy dress glittering with stars and moons. The bottom half was torn away, but the top announced, INTRODUCING THE BRIGHTON NIGHTINGALE!

"The Brighton Nightingale," Clive mused, snapping a photograph. Tucking the plate back into his bag, he said, "I've seen her before."

I had, too. "That's Miss Ballingall!" The poster showed a girl, not a grown woman, but her round face and dimpled cheeks were unmistakable. "She sang on the train."

Clive peered closer. "Blimey. That *is* her."

A moment later, another alarming creak of the boards had us both scurrying for safety, the opera posters forgotten.

"We should get back," Clive said. "I'm supposed to be writing an historical essay on the charge o' the Light Brigade."

He was too old for the village school, and at my look of surprise, he uttered a dramatic groan. "There's no grammar school here, but Mum insisted I had to keep up with my lessons if I came out with Dad. She sends *exams!*"

I commiserated. "Miss Judson brought her geography primer." Then added with a grin, "It's been impounded, though, with the rest of our luggage."

"Lucky shot," he said, kicking his foot into the pebbles.

We'd scrambled down from the Pier and made our way back across the shingle toward the hotel. We were closer to the cliffs this time, and Peony was playing mountain lioness, scaling the rocks after seagulls who were utterly unafraid of her fierce little white paws.

"Look, there she is now." Clive pointed to the wrecked carousel, where Temperance Ballingall herself sat astride one of the cracked wooden steeds. She was wearing a girlish dress of salmon pink, a matching parasol propped on her shoulder. When she spotted us, she waved gaily.

The carousel must have fallen victim to the same disaster that had destroyed the Pier. It now sat at an oddly jaunty angle, striped roof half buried in pebbles, once-bright colors bleached by the elements. One of the horses had a sea serpent's tail and looked like it was about to swim free of its fellows.

"Myrtle, Clive!" Miss Ballingall seemed much improved from yesterday, when she'd fled tea in such a state. "Come join me! It's mostly still sound, despite appearances."

Clive stayed below, setting up his camera to capture the view, but I followed Miss Ballingall's example and scaled the tilted platform to a mount fashioned like a giraffe. I had to grip its wooden legs with my ankles to stay upright, and splinters dug into my knees. Behind us, the water lapped the edge of the carousel's base, which was pocked to lace by rust and decay. As I hung on, Miss Ballingall began humming, then softly singing a merry little holiday tune.

"Oh, don't mind me," she said, laughing. "That's the song this carousel played. Father used to bring me, every year." She broke off, rubbing her arm. "He has such fond memories. That's why he's so keen to fix it all up again."

"We saw your poster!" I indicated the Pavilion on the Pier.

Miss Ballingall's smile vanished. "Oh. That was so long ago, I'd almost forgotten." She gazed into the distance, lips tight. "I wasn't that much older than you two, I suppose. A different lifetime."

Clive had joined us. "You should sing in the Orpheum at the hotel! I can see it now: *The Brighton Nightingale.*" He spread his hands like a theater sign. "You'd be famous."

Clive had not actually heard Miss Ballingall perform yet, so I politely held my tongue.

She gave a carefree laugh. "Speak to my father, Master Roberts. You could be my tour manager!" Miss Ballingall slid from her steed. "Have you been beachcombing?" she asked brightly. "It's a perfect day for it."

I had a moment's daft image of hotel staff with massive great rakes tending the stones, the way Mr. Hamm back home raked the garden paths. But it turned out she just meant wandering about and looking for anything interesting that had washed ashore. Farther along the beach, a man in a battered weatherproof seemed to be enjoying the same Amusement, puttering among the rocks along the water's edge. Clive snapped a picture.

Miss Ballingall stooped for a shell, holding her voluminous skirt out of harm's way, and handed it to me. "Huzzah! Sea potato!"* It looked like a squashed American baseball, but was unquestionably the exoskeleton of some expired creature. "Don't taste it," she warned. "I made that mistake when I was your age. Take it from me: they do *not* taste like spud." She gave a merry laugh and moved along.

"You must go bathing, both of you," she continued, "when the weather's fair. The waters here are . . . usually calm."

My bathing costume had (thankfully) been impounded by the stationmaster. "Do you enjoy bathing, Miss Ballingall?"

"Me? Oh, no. No." This said with a little shudder. "I—there was an . . . accident, when I was a schoolgirl, and I—I don't really care for the water."

"That's perfectly reasonable," I said earnestly. "Drowning is a terrible way to die. It takes much longer than most people suppose."

Her invisible eyebrows drew together. "I see."

"Is that how you hurt your arm?"

She flinched, and I was instantly sorry I'd asked. We walked beside her in silence for a bit, the wet

* *Echinocardium cordatum*

pebbles shifting underfoot. Clive spotted something in the rocks, a corner of rusty metal poking out of the water. He wiggled it free of the stones and brought it over.

It appeared to be part of the iron shell of some machine. I could just make out letters stamped in the metal—an *S*; maybe a *V*. This was not nearly the find that Miss Ballingall's sea potato was, but she was staring at it like he'd unearthed Spanish doubloons.

"Is that from a ship?" I asked.

"Cor," said Clive. "Maybe it's part of the *Valkyrie*!"

"Where did you find that?" Miss Ballingall's voice was sharp. "Give it here." She held out her hand.

Clive surrendered it, and her expression soured. "Nasty rubbish," she declared, flinging it back out to sea with surprising force. "You'll get lockjaw."

Since tetanus is *also* a terrible way to die, Clive and I didn't object. But we exchanged an expression of perplexity at Miss Ballingall's strange reaction. She brushed off her hands.

"You two seem like nice young people," she said. "Don't let anyone take that away from you too soon."

10

INTER RUSTICOS

Experienced travelers do not call attention to themselves by appearing out of step with their surroundings. Subscribe to the local customs as much as possible.

—Hardcastle's Practical Travel Companion

As we drew closer to the hotel, a familiar *woof* heralded the shaggy presence of Copernicus the sheepdog, who bounded about the shallows, snapping at the surf. Some distance behind, Nurse Temby shoved Poor Maudie's bath chair admirably through the shingle—though goodness knows how she'd got it down here. Miss Penrose, bundled in rugs to her chin, gripped the armrests with white knuckles, like she'd been abducted in a runaway coach.

At the top of the stairs, the rest of the Excursion had assembled at the seawall to Admire the Vista. Aunt Helena had Sir Quentin by the arm again, and

Cicely lurked behind them, holding a superfluous fringed parasol over Aunt Helena and her gigantic hat. The Bird Ladies in their fluttery lace looked like one strong gust might sweep them right off the edge. To my alarm, Mr. Strand had Miss Judson's gloved hand, and was helping her navigate the terrace steps.

I halted midway up and blocked Clive's path. "What do you know about that Mr. Strand?"

"Him?" He nodded up the cliff. "Salesman. Motorcars, I think."

For a moment this distracted me. I had not heard of any horseless carriages in England, although the modern marvels were gaining popularity on the Continent. "He thinks Sir Quentin might want one?" Given his taste in trains and hotels and tiaras, a motorcar would fit right in.

Clive shrugged. "Maybe he's just on holiday."

Watching Mr. Strand laugh as he held Miss Judson's hand, I doubted that.

At the top, Sir Quentin had unfurled a roll of wide papers and was gesturing grandly toward the seashore. Impressive renderings of this very spot—almost as good as Miss Judson could do—depicted (per their florid captions) FAIRHAVEN-BY-SEA, but they resembled nothing of the scene now. The Ballingall Arms was the central attraction, a white castle at the tip of the promontory, overlooking a sandy shoreline of wheeled bathing machines lined up and ready to cart people into the water. Rows of tall villas flanked the hills, and the glossy blue bay was filled with pretty little sailboats. It looked just like the Brochure.

"We'll knock down those cottages to improve the view." Sir Quentin pointed toward the jumble of cliffside houses.

"But what will happen to the villagers?" I couldn't help asking, and I felt Miss Judson's approval.

Sir Quentin and Aunt Helena looked like I'd asked what would happen to all of the sand they'd dug out of the bay, or the air displaced by the hotel.

Miss Judson spoke up. "Is everyone in the village in favor of this development?"

"Course they are, of course they are!" Sir Quentin boomed. "How could they not be? Progress, that's what it is—progress! Can't stand in its way."

I bit my lip and considered the map of Fairhaven-that-was-once-Eelscombe, and wondered what happened to people who *did* stand in Sir Quentin's way.

&

That afternoon, we made our way to the railway station to return Mrs. Bloom's bag. Winding back up Eelscombe's twisty main thoroughfare was even more challenging than the precipitous descent. Young Ladies of Quality are not ever intended to Exert Themselves, lest they do something so unforgivable as perspire or breathe deeply, but it was plain that Eelscombe had not been built with the convenience of

Young Ladies of Quality in mind. Or anyone, for that matter. Whitewashed cottages were crammed onto the hillsides like an overcrowded pantry, facing every which way, sagging front porches and crumbling stone steps evidence of the town's age and constant battle against the wind and sea.

Villagers as cramped and weatherbeaten as their houses went about their business—which appeared, this Monday afternoon, to be Gawking at Strangers. They lined the streets, arms folded over their chests, or glared out from narrow windows, and a decided air of *Unwelcome* emanated from them, like the invisible Miasma once thought to cause disease. Perhaps Eelscombe wasn't as keen on Sir Quentin's plans for Fairhaven as he thought.

I tugged my rotting-meadow hat down lower on my head and soldiered on.

Miss Judson strode up the hillside like a born mountaineer, Peony trotting ahead, tail held high. I struggled in their wake, hauling the weight of Mrs. Bloom's bag, which seemed to have doubled overnight. I couldn't believe Miss Judson was making me hand it over. Wasn't she even curious? Where was her Investigative Esprit de Corps? I tried to console myself with the fact that I'd at least preserved the evidence for Scotland Yard, but it was a hollow victory.

A flock of ducks blocked our path, stranding us before a cluster of shops, Eelscombe's high street, evidently. A public house called The Revenue was all but obscured by its neighbor, a squat, slate-roofed building covered in painted notices announcing its business . . . es: POST OFFICE, TELEGRAPH, TEA-SHOP, PIES & POND PUDDING, FISH—FRESH DRIED SMOKED—TOBACCO, and NEWSAGENT. It sported a round red postbox outside, so it seemed to be official. As I watched, a dour face at the window pulled inside, slamming the shutter closed.

With encouragement from Peony, the ducks finally moved along, although their owner was nowhere in sight (they'd apparently been released on their own recognizance and were free to wander at large). We continued on toward the station, and the faraway wail of a whistle.

"That's Scotland Yard!" I quickened my pace, Mrs. Bloom's bag swinging at my side.

In truth, I hoped to arrive before Miss Judson, in order to conduct my Investigation with a minimum of gubernatorial interference. I hated to go behind her back like this, but she wasn't leaving me much choice.

Mrs. Bloom had a telegram receipt from the railway, yet she'd already been dead when we arrived in Eelscombe, so she obviously hadn't sent a telegram then. But she might have arranged for it while she was still aboard the train—indeed, that could explain her errand to the baggage carriage, which also typically housed a train's signaling device and postal service.

The more important question, though, was what had been in that message? Had she simply notified the police of the robbery, or had she sent word to Albion Casualty canceling Sir Quentin's insurance policy? That telegram might even be the killer's motive!

I arrived at the station breathless and damp,* but—mindful of Miss Judson swiftly bringing up the rear—took a moment to compose myself. The impounded baggage car sat in a shed off on a siding, diverted away from the main tracks, and the shed had been transformed into a makeshift memorial, surrounded by heaps of autumn flowers—chrysanthemum, bittersweet, and Michaelmas daisy—candles, cards, and other offerings. Mrs. Bloom's body would have been moved by now, to a local mortuary (or whatever passed for one in Eelscombe—probably the pie shop) for the district Coroner to examine. But somebody—lots of somebodies—had remembered her where she'd fallen, with gifts and tributes.

My gaze carried down the hill, where the angry villagers still glowered at us. What had been Mrs. Bloom's connection to Eelscombe? *Visiting old friends*, she'd said. From the looks of things, she must have been friends with the whole village. I felt a fierce stab of determination. Mrs. Bloom, and all the people touched by her death, must get justice.

* See "exert themselves," above.

Inside the station, Stationmaster Clark was busy at the telegraph unit, so I waited for him to finish before tapping on the glass.

He looked up, squinting over his spectacles with bleary eyes. "Yes?"

"Myrtle Hardcastle, sir. I was on the train yesterday."

"I remember," he said drily.

"Do you have any telegrams from Mrs. Bloom?" I showed him the receipt. "The victim? She must have been sending word to someone about the robbery."

The train's whistle was joined by the distant-thunder rumble of its engine.

"Come inside here," Mr. Clark said. I squeezed round the green turnstile into the cramped little office, barely more than a façade, a window, and a stool to perch upon. "I had several telegrams delivered from the train yesterday morning." He shuffled through them. "But I don't see one that matches that receipt."

"What happened to it?"

Mr. Clark fiddled with his empty teacup and neatened the pile of telegrams. I eyed him warily. Was he *nervous*? "Is something wrong? Is it lost?"

His bespectacled eyes flew to my face. "No, nothing like that. I just didn't have a chance to go through them all yesterday morning, given the, erm, excitement." (Why wouldn't anyone say *murder*? Avoiding the word didn't make Mrs. Bloom any less dead.)

"But afterward, one of the guards came by, asking to examine them. It was all highly irregular, but he insisted Sir Quentin himself had given the order." He rubbed his face again and stared in dismay at the teacup. "He—he might have taken one or two of them out of the stack."

My heart took an energetic leap. "Which guard was it? Did he do anything else?"

Mr. Clark's expression turned distasteful. "Big feller. Cooley, or something?"

My breath caught. "Coogan?"

"Coulda been, at that." Mr. Clark was nodding warily. "Didn't like the looks of 'im."

I hadn't either—and nor had Mrs. Bloom. "How do you mean? Was he acting suspiciously?"

Mr. Clark seemed reluctant to answer. "No particular reason."

I changed tactics. "Is there any other way to find out what was in that telegram?"

"Not unless you find the original slip. Sorry, Miss."

Vaguely I thanked Mr. Clark for his help and wandered back to the platform, trying to make sense of this. Had Sir Quentin really sent Mr. Coogan to retrieve the message—or had Mr. Coogan done that on his own? Someone had taken the passenger manifest and employee records from Mrs. Bloom's bag, *and* someone had stopped her telegram from being sent.

And someone had killed her.

It seemed probable that all those Someones were the same person. *Strength and skill*—Mrs. Bloom's murder had required both of those things. Mr. Coogan was a big man, and he had a history of violence—that brawl with another employee (which he was evidently eager to cover up). And not only that, Mrs. Bloom had threatened Mr. Coogan's job. Could he have hurt her, just to stop her from reporting his behavior to the railway?

That was an ugly thought, and I was grateful for the piercing squall of the arriving train's brakes that cut it off. The bright light of the locomotive was like a great fierce eye, and I fancied it belonged to Scotland Yard, training its keen gaze on Eelscombe and Mrs. Bloom's murderer. I gripped Mrs. Bloom's bag more firmly and joined Miss Judson on the platform to greet the arriving Competent Authority Figure.

"Calm down," Miss Judson said in a low voice. "You look like a schoolboy outside a sweetshop."

The train had barely eased to a stop, the doors squealing open, when a smallish man in a deep red uniform, very smart with its black trim and gold braid, sprang out. He was about Father's age, with a sharp pale face and a dark moustache, and he was scowling—exactly as if he'd come for Fairhaven and discovered Eelscombe, instead.

"Don't Scotland Yard wear blue uniforms?" Miss Judson Observed.

As we waited, a figure emerged from the train shed where they'd parked the baggage car, kicking aside the flowers: Sir Quentin, wearing a khaki campaign jacket, as if he were off to tame lions in the savannah.

"Arkwright!" he boomed—loud enough for all of Eelscombe, and every village from here to France, to hear. "What the devil took you so long?"

Inspector Arkwright brushed some invisible dust from his fastidious uniform. "The train from Bristol was four minutes late." He had a brusque, businesslike voice I quite respected. "Your lines are in disrepair, and this 'station,' if that's what you're calling it, is a disgrace."

Sir Quentin's ruddy face turned a deeper shade of red, and he shifted his bulk over Mr. Arkwright's smaller form. Mr. Arkwright did not flinch. "Nothin' wrong with the lines, laddie, and this station's just undergone renovations that cost me a pretty penny. Now, are you going to sign off on this here report or not so we can all get back to business?" He waved a document in the man's face.

Inspector Arkwright eyed him, up the length of his nose. "I hope you're not implying that the Eastern Coastal Railway Police intend to give this case any less than its proper attention."

"Railway police!" I groaned. "What happened to Scotland Yard? I *knew* we should never have left yesterday."

Before Scotland Yard was established as England's national police force, every railway company had its own private police service, charged with protecting the trains and cargo. Many still did—but they didn't generally investigate grievous crimes like murder.

"It's obvious what happened," Sir Quentin was saying.

"Let *me* be the judge of that," the Inspector said.

Railway police aside, I liked this Arkwright fellow immediately. He was coming our way, and I mentally prepared my statement. I'd been rehearsing it all night: Sir Quentin's argument with Mrs. Bloom about the insurance policy, the robbery, and now the missing telegram and Mr. Coogan's suspicious behavior. I'd let the Inspector draw his own conclusions.

"Let me have a look at the carriage, and then I want to talk to your local man." Inspector Arkwright brushed past Sir Quentin, nearly plowing right into Miss Judson.

"Good afternoon, Inspector." Her voice was crisp. "I'm Miss Judson, and this is Miss Myrtle Hardcastle. We were passengers aboard the *Empress Express*. We'd like to speak to you about yesterday's events."

Mr. Arkwright barely paused. "I am not here to satisfy the curiosity of every nosy miss who thinks I owe her an explanation just because she paid the price of a ticket." He sidestepped Miss Judson and continued up the platform, barking impatient orders at Sir Quentin.

"Nosy miss!" I exclaimed. "We're *witnesses*!"

Without waiting for Miss Judson, I abandoned all pretense of Ladylike Restraint and broke into a run, Mrs. Bloom's bag thumping against my leg. I heard the determined sound of a telegraph behind me—Miss Judson, doggedly bringing up the rear. Sir Quentin looked as though he'd like to swat me like a fly but didn't dare with Inspector Arkwright there. Inspector Arkwright finally turned around, and the look he gave me made Sir Quentin's expression seem positively benevolent.

"Why are you still here?" he demanded.

"Aren't you supposed to interview witnesses?" I demanded back.

He gave a long-suffering sigh. "I have already spoken to the railway staff who were on duty when the Incidents occurred. I don't imagine mere passengers have much to contribute." He said *passengers*, but I could tell he really meant something else. "Fine. Can you add anything?" And he stood there, looking at us impatiently.

"Well," Miss Judson said with dangerous precision, "Miss Hardcastle *did* discover the body."

This finally caught Mr. Arkwright's attention. "You disturbed a crime scene? Dear God Almighty." He took off his red cap and shoved an exasperated hand through his black hair. "Ballingall, what were you thinking, letting children run wild through a murder scene?"

"I wasn't running wild!" I said indignantly—then recalled that in fact I (not to mention Clive) had been in hot pursuit of Peony, who *could* be accused of the same. I bit my lip, wondering if I looked contrite.

Miss Judson had produced her sketchbook. "Perhaps this will be of help." I caught a glimpse of the sketched interior of the baggage car, showing the position of Mrs. Bloom's body. Inspector Arkwright's gaze focused sharply, and he snatched the book from her hands, flipping through the pages and muttering.

"There are also several views of the missing tiara—" She didn't get to finish.

The Inspector clapped the sketchbook shut and shoved it beneath his arm.

"What are you doing?" I cried. "Give that back."

"Not a chance," he growled. "Think I don't recognize your work, *Mlle A. Judson*? I read the papers. I'm not taking the chance you'll be selling these little drawings to the press. I'm confiscating this as evidence in my investigation."

Miss Judson seemed too stunned to reply.

"You can't do that," I said. "You need a subpoena." I reached for the sketchbook—and he smacked my hand with a sharp rap that made me cry out loud. "Ow!"

"How dare you?" Miss Judson had gone livid,

blood flooding her tan face. "Striking *a child*? What sort of policeman are you?"

"A very busy one." Inspector Arkwright gave us one more look of contempt. "Was there anything else? Do you have any other 'evidence' you'd like to contribute?"

I felt the weight of Mrs. Bloom's carpetbag but was too shocked to say anything. My hand stung. No adult had ever struck me before, not like that.

Miss Judson held me fast. "No," she said, voice as tight as her grip on my arm. "We haven't found anything else, *have we, Myrtle*?"

My eyes flew to her face, still taut with fury, and I saw that she was pointedly *not* looking at Mrs. Bloom's bag. I felt a surge of warmth from her loyalty. "No, Miss. Nothing at all."

Inspector Arkwright looked at us like we were a pair of ninnies, and he sighed yet again. "Excellent. Ballingall, see to it that these . . . people get . . . wherever they're going." Shaking his head, he stalked off toward the train shed, Miss Judson's sketchbook disappearing with him.

As Inspector Arkwright commandeered the baggage car, literally and figuratively slamming the door of the Investigation right in our faces, I turned to Miss Judson, unable to speak. How could he take her book like that? I wasn't sure what to do. I was incensed, but Miss Judson was practically incandescent.

She grabbed my arm—nearly as rough as Inspector Arkwright had been—and shoved my sleeve up. "Did he injure you? When your father learns of this—"

I yanked my hand back. "Never mind that! He stole your sketchbook!"

For a moment, we regarded each other in mutual resentment on each other's behalf. "The *nerve* of that little man," she fumed. This statement was followed up by some impressive (and *expressive*) French which is not suitable to print herein. Even untranslated.

"We'll get it back," I said, trying to sound more confident than I was. "Somehow."

Lips still tight, she drew up the cuffs of her gloves and forced a grim smile. "Well. So much for the Proper Authorities."

"You never said the 'nice' authorities," I pointed out, and she let out a high, surprised laugh.

"If he didn't like my drawings before," she said, and a wicked spark lit her cool eyes, "he'll *love* the next one I have planned." Snapping her fingers for Peony, she turned back toward the village. "I certainly hope you found something useful in that carpetbag," she added, leaving me gaping at her as she set off.

❧

I clutched Mrs. Bloom's bag in a death grip (no grim humor intended) all the way back to the hotel. As soon as we were back in our rooms, I ventured my tentative question.

"What do we do with this, then? Wait for the next policeman to disappoint us?"

Miss Judson was still in high humor, so this made her smile. "No, indeed. We shall take a proper inventory." Eyeing me sidelong, she added, "Due diligence. Naturally."

Having done so already, I reviewed my findings for Miss Judson, who Observed the untidy jumble of Mrs. Bloom's files with mild disapproval. (I have seen that same look, Dear Reader, given to my own drawers and wardrobe, and felt another wave of kinship with Mrs. Bloom. Clearly even disorganized people still managed to make successes of themselves, despite all parental claims to the contrary.)

"Are you sure *she* made this mess, or could someone else have been searching for something?"

"Well, it wasn't me, if that's what you're implying."

"I would never." The tone of her voice suggested that Mrs. Bloom's untidiness must somehow have contributed to her unfortunate demise, and I nearly carried the carpetbag off for good. But harnessing all my Exceptional Forbearance, I Forbore. Exceptionally.

"It could have been Mr. Coogan." I explained how I'd run into him on my way to Mrs. Bloom's compartment. "Mrs. Bloom had passenger manifests and employee records, but they're not here. She threatened to report Mr. Coogan to Sir Quentin for drinking on duty."

"Interesting. So we're missing a telegram receipt, the passenger list, and the employee rolls. Not to mention a priceless tiara." She continued with my list. "*Item: one notebook full of gibberish*.' Clarify."

I presented Mrs. Bloom's red ledger, with its pages of loopy nonsense. Was it no more than just poor penmanship? Miss Judson cracked it open and laughed aloud.

"Oh, well, I can see where I've left gaps in my tutelage," she said.

"Wait, you can read that? It's not French."

"No, *ma râleuse*, it's shorthand."

It took me a moment to catch up. "You mean like what clerks and secretaries use?" It was a code, of sorts, meant to speed up the taking of dictation from impatient employers the world over, from the ancient Greeks to the Japanese to harried English clerks.[*]

"Can you read it?"

Miss Judson contemplated the notebook's mystifying inscriptions. "Sadly, no." She held the ledger with tight fingers. "So close! What if it says something useful, like *Aunt Helena, in the baggage car, with the scissors*?"

"That's not funny." It was really too much to hope, I supposed, that Mrs. Bloom would simply have left us a note naming her killer. I took the book from Miss Judson and thumbed through it glumly.

[*] not all the *same* shorthand, naturally. Although that would improve efficiency.

"Mrs. Bloom would have known how to handle Inspector Arkwright," I said. "She probably faced down lots of men like that in her Investigations."

"And worse." Miss Judson sounded solemn. "Exceptional Forbearance, no doubt."

Even without giving us any answers, holding Mrs. Bloom's book still made me feel better. I had that sense of her guiding presence again, warm and solid and steady, instead of the wild muddle of my thoughts since we found her body. I held the book tightly. Keeping a murder victim's notebook would be tampering with evidence, well beyond the offense of just looking through her things, and went against every principle of criminology I believed in. But even *knowing* it was wrong, somehow it still *felt* right.

Miss Judson knew what I was thinking. She put a firm hand on the book, fingertips touching mine. "I don't think she'd mind," she said.

"*No*," Peony agreed, rubbing her chin against the binding, claiming it.

We still hadn't decided what to do, but at least we were all united. I slipped Mrs. Bloom's notebook into my coat pocket, so she'd be with me through the whole Investigation, too.

11
PRIMA FACIE

However well-prepared an excursion may be, expect
detours, delays, and changes of plan.

—Hardcastle's Practical Travel Companion

I was still angry over Inspector Arkwright's treatment
of us hours later. It was hard not to rant about it all
through dinner in the hotel's lavish dining room. We
sat with the Penroses, Poor Maudie's father scrutinizing every bite of food she didn't eat, until she looked
like she wanted to stab him with her oyster fork. The
Ballingalls had not joined us this time, but Cicely
was bubbling over with a nervous energy I'd not seen
before.

"Is it true you saw the Inspector who's come to find
the tiara?"

Aunt Helena interrupted before I could launch
into my tirade against the man.

"Cicely, gossip is a most unbecoming habit in a young lady. Have some more liver—you're looking peaky."

"Yes, Miss Hardcastle." Cicely picked at the limp, slimy dish, and I sent her telepathic waves of sympathy. She glanced up and met my eyes with a wan smile.

Aunt Helena told Miss Judson and me what to eat as well. Miss Judson was *not* looking peaky; Aunt Helena's prescription for her was milk, to "cool" her constitution.* Instead, Miss Judson took three rolls and the entire dish of butter and flagged down the server for extra jam.

Mr. Penrose spoke with soothing confidence. "I'm sure yesterday's unpleasantness will be wrapped up very soon, and we shall all be able to rest easy." He smiled reassuringly at his daughter. "The railway has sent their best man down. Acton, or something."

"Arkwright," Miss Judson muttered, sawing violently at a roll until her knife squealed on her plate. Cicely's eyes flew to Miss Judson's but dropped again an instant later.

Aunt Helena's attention turned to Miss Judson. "Judson, I saw you were quite in the company of that charming Mr. Strand yesterday." She sounded approving. "Will he be joining us for dinner, I wonder?"

* I got Brussels sprouts. With no explanation.

Miss Judson did not have a chance to answer, as Poor Maudie was suddenly overcome by a fit of coughing, and six servers, her father, and Aunt Helena all sprang to her aid.

I barely attended to any of this. I was stirring at my gravy, trying to put together a picture of Mr. Coogan stalking Mrs. Bloom to the baggage car, surprising her and stabbing her with Aunt Helena's scissors, then stealing her records and telegram. It fit what I'd uncovered so far, but I still couldn't shake the image of Aunt Helena arguing with Mrs. Bloom, or the way Sir Quentin had kept it all out of the press. I sighed. I supposed Inspector Arkwright would have to figure it out without our help. It served him right.

I was still stewing when the dining room doors flew open with a bang. We all looked up in surprise, and Mr. Penrose was instantly on his feet. "I say, what's the meaning of this?"

In strode Inspector Arkwright, beady eyes and slash of a mouth looking even more disagreeable than they had this afternoon. Following on his heels like a lovesick puppy was Constable Hoskiss—and bringing up the rear, a rather harried Mr. Roberts.

"I'm so sorry, ladies and gentlemen," Mr. Roberts said. "They just barged in. Constable, Inspector—if you'll please wait in the lobby—"

The Inspector ignored him and made straight for our table.

"Hoskiss, round them all up. And find the Ballingalls. *Both* of them. Maybe we can wrap this up in one go."

The Inspector waved an impatient hand toward the side of the room, a seating area of wicker settees and potted palms.

Mr. Penrose was perfectly polite. "Inspector, surely you won't need to question my daughter. She was not present for any of the events and cannot be of any help to you."

Everyone else was looking at Mr. Penrose, but I caught Poor Maudie's eye, and her look of frustration at being shut out, yet again, of the most interesting Family Amusement in Fairhaven. I recognized that thwarted expression all too well. But Maud was far too much a Young Lady of Quality to put up a fuss. When Nurse Temby appeared out of nowhere to wheel her away, pausing long enough to give Mr. Penrose a deep and unreadable look, Maud just bowed her head and sighed.

Constable Hoskiss reminded me of a collie, vainly trying to herd us together when all we did was mill about in nervous disarray. Finally Miss Judson took pity on him. With a look of seething contempt at the Inspector, she clapped her hands and steered us into place. To my surprise, she didn't pull me away, but planted us squarely in the midst of the assemblage. If Inspector Arkwright didn't want us here, he'd have to pry us out with a lever and carry us away.

"I'd like to see him try." I only fancied I'd heard Miss Judson's reply, but it bolstered me. I settled in more firmly.

Mr. Roberts had fetched Sir Quentin, who huffed in, tugging his waistcoat over his paunch as he sat down on a spindly wicker settee that looked fit to crumble beneath him. "Get on with it, then, man. Haven't got all day. Hotel to run, you know."

"Father." Miss Ballingall's voice was pleading as she took the seat opposite, looking fretful and worrying at her bad arm.

"Now, then, Inspector," Aunt Helena said, like the grande dame of a fancy salon holding court. "What was it you wished to know?"

The Inspector pulled out his little notebook and flipped furiously for a clean page. "Start by telling me where you all were during the robbery."

Over the next several minutes, he took down our recollections of that night—which I had to admit was quite a feat. Only Miss Judson and I made any effort to present them in an orderly fashion. The others tripped over one another in their attempts to tell the story. Even Miss Ballingall, who'd been unconscious most of the time. I Observed that the Inspector ignored Cicely, except for one brief question to ascertain her whereabouts.

"Playing the piano," she mumbled into her lap, dark eyes downcast. She hunched into her shoulders as if trying to disappear. Any minute, I expected Aunt Helena to tell her to stop slouching.

Mr. Penrose watched the questioning unfold with interest, fingers in a neat pyramid before his face. "And do you believe that the crimes are connected?" His voice was quiet but keen. "The same culprit who stole the tiara also killed that poor woman?"

Irritation flashed across the Inspector's face. Mr. Penrose's question had interrupted his efficient, mechanical inquiry, like a stick jamming up a wheel. Sir Quentin answered for him.

"Course they're connected. What else could it be?"

I felt Miss Judson's hand on my wrist, forestalling any contributions I might feel compelled to offer. She needn't have worried. I wasn't giving *anything* to Inspector Arkwright!

Mr. Penrose sank back into his chair, looking thoughtful. "Then the rest of us need not fear for our lives."

"I shouldn't think so, sir—" Constable Hoskiss tried to break in, but Inspector Arkwright cut him off.

"We're not in the business of *speculation*," he said coldly. "But we are pursuing all avenues of investigation."

I doubted that. Did he even know about Mr. Coogan and the missing telegram? What about how the story had been kept from the newspapers? Or the other information Mrs. Bloom and I had uncovered together, Investigating the robbery? I fidgeted, torn between trying to share what I knew and the knowledge of how Inspector Arkwright would shut me down.

Eventually I realized (with the assistance of a none-too-subtle pinch of my arm by Miss Judson) that I'd lost track of Inspector Arkwright's questions. I pulled my attention back to the interrogation.

"What happened later that night? Where were you two after the robbery?" This was directed at the Ballingalls.

"Went to bed, of course," said Sir Quentin. "Private car. Temperance overset. Needed rest." His answers sounded like the train's wheels clipping round and round.

"And were you there all night?"

"Course we were. Where else?"

But Miss Ballingall looked uncomfortable. "I wasn't," she admitted. "I stepped out to get some air." She gulped. "I think that was about—about midnight, I suppose? I'm afraid I didn't check, Inspector." Her watery smile didn't melt the Inspector's heart.

"And did you happen to see anything out of the ordinary?"

Twisting her fingers, she replied, "I'm afraid so. I should have said something at the time—I know that now, but I just didn't realize—"

"What?" I said, ignoring propriety. "What did you see?"

Even Inspector Arkwright forgot to glare at me.

"It might have been a man," she admitted. "Running away from the tracks."

Stunned silence followed. Unfortunately, I recovered first.

"Why didn't you say anything?"

"I–" Miss Ballingall looked helplessly from me to her father, whose lionlike face had drooped in a deep frown. "I didn't think it was important."

"You knew we were looking for the thief! You should have alerted the guards."

"Myrtle."

I managed to heed Miss Judson and held my tongue.

"I'm sorry, Inspector," Miss Ballingall said. "In all the excitement, it just slipped my mind. Until now."

He held her in his stony glare. "And the murdered woman didn't jog your memory?"

"How dare you, sir!" Aunt Helena rapped the floor with her stick.

The Inspector turned on her, wheeling slowly like a toy soldier come hideously to life. "Ah. Helen Hardcastle, is it?"

She stared him down. "It most certainly is not."

"Er"—Constable Hoskiss leaned in—"I believe it's Helen*a*, sir."

Holding the bridge of his nose, the Inspector forged ahead. "And what was your relationship to the victim?"

"*Relationship?*" Aunt Helena sounded appalled by the very notion. "I'd never met the woman before in my life."

"Hmm." The Inspector studied his notebook. "And yet witnesses report that you quarreled with her."

"What witnesses?" Aunt Helena's withering glare took in the rest of us, ferreting out who had betrayed her. "What quarrel?"

"I *mean*, you did not care for how she was treating Miss Ballingall after the robbery."

"No, I did not. She was treating Temperance—the victim, mind you—like a common criminal. All of us! That vulgar woman had no refinement at all. *And* she was a disruptive influence on my niece, who is very impressionable."

I couldn't believe what Aunt Helena was saying. Besides impeaching my character, she was making Mrs. Bloom sound like the villain!

"I see. And you owned the murder weapon, is that correct? Gold scissors—Disher-something?"

"*Die Schere.* German. And I'll kindly have those back," she said. "They were a gift, and they're quite valuable."

Inspector Arkwright held her in a stunted, stupefied gaze. He must not have encountered very many

Aunt Helenas in his Investigatory Career. Lucky him. "And where were you at midnight on the night of October the seventh?"

Instead of answering, Aunt Helena rose to her feet, like a mastodon hauling itself from the tar pit.

"Young man, I have had enough of your questions. Good day."

"We're not finished here, Miss *Helena* Hardcastle."

She lifted a bare inch of skirt, ready to step out. "Miss Ballingall has described the culprit to you. I am certain you have better things to do right now than pester upstanding people on their holidays." And with that she swept past him, the tidal force of her exit pulling the rest of us along with her.

The last thing we saw, as we all decamped, was the Bird Ladies arriving in the dining room doorway. "Oh," squeaked Miss Causton, voice thick with disappointment. "Did we miss it?"

☙

The next morning, I pounced on Miss Judson, hoping to catch her off guard. It was a tactic used by skilled professional Investigators, albeit not generally upon their governesses.

"We need to know more about the man Miss Ballingall saw."

She barely looked up from her tea (honey, lemon, *and* sugar). "The *police* do, you mean."

Not this again. Last night she'd been eager to go through Mrs. Bloom's bag with me, but now she'd reverted to her Holiday Self. I waited a moment before saying, "You wouldn't sic Inspector Arkwright on poor Miss Ballingall."

Finally, she sighed. "I suppose you're right." She rose in a graceful column of deep green skirt, looking utterly unruffled at being worn for three—now four—straight days, and we set off to find Miss Ballingall.

She was in an airy parlor on the seaward side of the hotel, standing at the tall windows, looking out over the roiling, unsettled water. At our greeting, she turned her stricken face to us, seeming to know why we'd come. "If only I'd said something earlier . . ."

"It wasn't your fault," I said. "He'd probably already killed Mrs. Bloom by the time you saw him. You couldn't have stopped it."

She nodded faintly. Miss Judson spoke in a calming voice. "If you think you can describe him to me, I might be able to produce a sketch of the man you saw."

Miss Ballingall shuddered. "I don't know," she said. "I don't like to think of him."

"It might help catch the killer," I stressed. "Your father may be able to identify him, and the Inspector can circulate the image to other constabularies. He'll soon be apprehended."

Finally, rubbing her elbow, she nodded. "All right. If you think it will help. What do I need to do?"

"Have a seat." Miss Judson led her to a settee by the windows. "Tell me what you remember."

Miss Ballingall was still anxious, but she relaxed as she described the man she'd seen leaving the train. "I didn't get a good look at him," she said. "And it was dark."

Miss Judson focused on her drawing paper. "Just do your best. We'll see what we come up with."

"Very well. He was . . ." She trailed off, gazing out the windows, remembering. "Older. He was an older man—perhaps sixty-something?"

So far that described Sir Quentin, although I supposed even the least Observant witness would recognize her own father if she saw him hop off a train after ripping a tiara from her head. I chewed on my lip and listened.

"With a long grey beard."

Alas.

"Can you remember anything of his clothes?" Miss Judson never looked up, charcoal scuffing along her paper as Miss Ballingall spoke. "Was he wearing a uniform? Workman's clothes? A suit?"

"A—an overcoat, I think. Dark. A bit shabby, actually," she admitted, almost apologetically. "I suppose he must have been a tramp."

Aunt Helena's words came back to me: *It must have*

been a vagrant. Perhaps he'd sneaked aboard the train at Upton Station. Or even earlier.

Miss Judson never faltered, but I felt her eyes flick to me briefly. As Miss Penrose had noted earlier, why would a tramp steal a priceless tiara? The robbery was well planned, not a spur-of-the-moment crime of opportunity. Perhaps the two crimes weren't connected after all; perhaps Mrs. Bloom had surprised a tramp in the baggage car while searching for the thief, and he'd panicked and stabbed her.

With Aunt Helena's scissors.

The whisper of charcoal on paper continued– along with Miss Judson's questions: *How long was his beard? How tall was he? Was he wearing a hat? What kind? Carrying a bag?* I had questions of my own (How had she seen him so clearly, in the dark, from a moving train?), but did not wish to interrupt. They went on, until Miss Ballingall seemed exhausted, and Miss Judson held the sketchbook at arm's length, nodded, then blew across the page to rid it of loose dust. She turned the book to Miss Ballingall, who paled.

"Yes," she whispered, trembling hand to her breast. "That's exactly the man I saw."

Miss Judson turned the sketch to me, and I took in the details: the long gaunt face, the thicket of grey beard, a thatch of unkempt hair, the shapeless work coat. I felt my heart thump with recognition.

"I've seen that man, too," I said. Everything about him tugged at my memory, but I could not place him. It must have been on the train, or at the station . . . Try as I might, I couldn't remember.

Miss Judson's expression was unreadable as she put a few last polishing touches on the sketch. "We'd best turn this over to Inspector Arkwright straightaway." She sounded reluctant, but it was the correct course of action.

She gathered up her things, and we made our way to the doors, only to run into the Bird Ladies, bright eyes glittering.

"Oh," said Miss Causton, peering at Miss Judson's sketchbook. "Is that The Man Temperance Saw?" She sounded breathless, fluttery fingers at her throat. "We saw him too, you know."

"*I* saw him, Nettie," Miss Cabot said. "You were in the compartment."

"We both saw him." Miss Causton was firm. "Perhaps we could help with the sketch!"

Miss Judson hesitated. "Yes, well—"

But I was eager. "What did he look like?"

Miss Cabot's eyes grew even wider. "Well, a *bit* like that," she critiqued Miss Judson's drawing. "But his eyebrows were bushier. And his eyes"—she gave a shudder—"much darker. More . . . menacing."

"Menacing," echoed Miss Judson. She held her charcoal motionless above the page. "What else?"

"And his beard was longer," Miss Causton added. "He had . . . rather clawlike fingers." She demonstrated, holding her hands diabolically—just as she'd done when reenacting the robbery over breakfast. I tugged on my hat ribbon, uncertain.

"Hmm." Miss Judson made a motion like she was drawing, but I could see she was only rubbing charcoal on an already smudged background shadow. "Perhaps an eye patch? Or a snaggletooth?"

The Bird Ladies blinked at her, but then Miss Cabot broke out in a high, twittering giggle. "Oh, you're having us on, Miss Judson! But we *did* see him," she insisted. "He was horrible."

"Just horrible," Miss Causton added, with a sigh of relish.

"Well, this has been very—" Miss Judson did not get the chance to finish. A commotion from the beach below carried up through the terrace doors: raised voices, scuffling, and, very distinctly, an affronted bellow.

"Unhand me at once, young man!"

"Aunt Helena!"

We all rushed to the terrace doors—Miss Judson, the Bird Ladies, Miss Ballingall, everyone. Miss Judson flung them open, and we charged outside. On the beach below were Aunt Helena, Cicely (dragging the parasol and a folding beach chair), and two dark uniforms: blue and red. The police were back.

"Ooh, how exciting!" Miss Cabot squealed.

"What can they want with Aunt Helena?" I scurried in Miss Judson's wake down the endless steps to the pebble-strewn beach, where Constable Hoskiss was drooping like a wet dog and Aunt Helena was bawling at Inspector Arkwright.

"Get away, you villains!" She beat them off with her walking stick.

"Well, get on with it, man!" snapped Inspector Arkwright.

"Er, I'm sorry, ma'am," the constable said, edging toward my aunt like a nervous matador. He held something in his hand. I could see what it was but could not make myself believe it.

Constable Hoskiss shook out the handcuffs. "Helena Hardcastle, I'm arresting you on suspicion of murder."

12

PERVERTING THE
COURSE OF JUSTICE

Polstead, Suffolk: Site of the 1827 murder of Maria Marten.
Little remains of the notorious "Red Barn" where her body
was discovered, having been largely destroyed by souvenir
hunters, but artifacts from killer Robert Corder (including
death mask and a book bound supposedly in his skin) are
on view at a local hospital.

−Hardcastle's Practical Travel Companion

I had to hand it to Aunt Helena. She didn't crack.

The constable wouldn't let us in while Inspector
Arkwright was questioning her, so we spent the next
three hours in the Eelscombe police station, if you
could call it that. It was an old country gaolhouse,*
barely more than a dungeon of weepy stone walls,

---

* This older spelling of *jailhouse* certainly applied to the
Eelscombe station!

rusty iron bars for windows, and damp. Big new desks, filing cabinets, and a typewriter had been moved in to modernize the space, but they only made the rest seem even older. The gas lamps were fitted into *torches*. Miss Judson and I waited on a bench carved from a stone alcove, and I half expected an Inquisitor to come marching out with a black hood and thumbscrews.

"The Inquisition was Spain," Miss Judson murmured.

"The Tudors then. Who did they have?"

"Hush."

Poor Constable Hoskiss twitched about nervously, worrying a teakettle suspended in the fireplace. He'd been all but usurped from his own office; the stacks of paperwork on his desk surely belonged to Inspector Arkwright, leaving the constable like an old rocking chair someone had stuck up in the attic and forgotten about.

Outside, it had started to rain, and the ducks were lying in wait like an angry mob. I could hear their sinister quacking even through the thick stone walls.

None of it felt real. Aunt Helena, arrested for *murder*? It was too fanciful to be believed.

Constable Hoskiss managed to produce three mismatched cups of steaming tea and a tin of biscuits. "Me sister's best," he offered gently. "Jam-filled."

Miss Judson accepted them graciously. "When do you suppose we might be allowed to see Miss

Hardcastle?" Her voice was pitched exactly on the edge between question and command, and it made the constable fidget.

"Well, erm, that's not up to me, I'm afraid, Miss."

"But it is," I said, encouragingly. "Inspector Arkwright's jurisdiction extends only to the premises and properties of Eastern Coastal Railways–unless this station has been officially impressed for their investigation. Has it?"

"Er–"

"So *you* have control over prisoners in your jail, Constable. And English law requires that a prisoner be allowed access to legal counsel."

"Er–"

"Or the clergy," I added helpfully.

Miss Judson gave the constable a shattering smile and rose to her feet. I joined her. "Well, there you go, Constable," she said. "We won't take up much of your time." Holding her new sketchbook as officially as possible, she brushed past him, straight back to the barred interior door, before Constable Hoskiss entirely understood what was happening.

"But the Inspector–" he protested, hastening to catch up.

"Can eat my hat," invited Miss Judson, bobbing the same to the man in question, who had just appeared in the threshold, the old door groaning open like it was exhausted.

Inspector Arkwright's hard gaze landed on me. "Hoskiss, are you half-witted? Get these people out of here."

"Yes, sir," said the beleaguered constable. He shuffled forward, unsuccessfully dodging a heap of files that careened off the desk.

"Hoskiss!" The Inspector's face turned a shade of scarlet nearly as dark as his uniform.

"Sorry, sir." He dived for the papers, upsetting his tea all over them.

"Get them *out*!"

"My good sir," Miss Judson said. "Your behavior is untoward, uncalled for, and entirely unbecoming a gentleman in uniform. I can't imagine how you have any business in an official capacity at all, if this is the way you treat your fellow law enforcement professionals."

For a moment Inspector Arkwright merely stared at her, as if he could not comprehend how we could still be here, let alone *speaking* to him. Then he recovered himself. "You have exactly fifteen seconds to find the door and let yourselves out."

"Or what? You'll lock us up with Aunt Helena?" Miss Judson's spirit had made me bold. "What'll you charge *us* with, High Treason?" (Maybe a little too bold.)

Inspector Arkwright took a step toward us. For such a small man, he was surprisingly imposing. "Obstructing an official investigation," he snapped.

"Hindering prosecution. Interfering with an officer of Eastern Coastal Railways and his duly sworn duties. Making a nuisance. Wasting my time. Whistling in public! I don't much care, as long as it gets you out of my sight!"

"Perhaps you'd care to add mail fraud," Miss Judson said coolly.

"Don't encourage him," I muttered.

"You cannot keep us from Miss Hardcastle. She's in your custody only as a courtesy. No formal charges have been filed against her."

"Don't *encourage* him!"

"In fact." Miss Judson's voice grew sweeter with every word. "You should know, we'll be filing a grievance with Eastern Coastal Railways, the Magistrate's Office, and the local constabulary. Constable Hoskiss, would you take down my complaint?"

"Don't you move." Inspector Arkwright's voice was a snarl. "I will not be intimidated by a flock of females! A spinster, a nanny, and a little girl?" He shook his head in contempt.

"Furthermore," Miss Judson said, "you haven't the authority to hold Miss Hardcastle here."

"That's where you're wrong," Arkwright said. "*I* didn't arrest her. Hoskiss here did."

"On the flimsiest of evidence!" Miss Judson continued.

"She owned the murder weapon."

She dismissed this with a wave of her hand. "Your theory is that the sixty-two-year-old gentlewoman in there orchestrated a high-stakes jewel heist aboard a moving train, and then murdered someone to cover it up?"

Arkwright glared at her from beady eyes, like a fly's. "Stranger things have been known to happen."

Drawn up to her full height (plus hair, plus hat), Miss Judson towered over him. "Case in point," she said, "the notion that *you* were ever promoted to the rank of Inspector!"

It was like watching someone fire a trebuchet–the winding up of the counterweight and the release of the flaming stone to smash through the enemy's defenses. She was *glorious.*

Inspector Arkwright's jaw clenched, the corner of his eye twitching. "Ten minutes," he finally spat. "Hoskiss!"

Miss Judson's expression was cold. "Wise choice," she said, and glided into the cell block.

Disappointingly, they hadn't locked Aunt Helena into one of the dungeon's dank, heartless cells. "We've put her in the staff tearoom," Constable Hoskiss explained. "On account of her being, er–"

"Old?" I volunteered.

"A *lady*," he said.

"We're *very* appreciative, Constable," Miss Judson said. "Thank you for your help."

"No problem, Miss." He wasn't wearing his domed helmet, but he touched its phantom brim nonetheless, and unless I was very much mistaken, he was blushing. He pushed the door open into the room where they were keeping Aunt Helena. It might not have been a cell, but that wasn't saying much in the Eelscombe police station.

Aunt Helena sat rigidly upright, filling the entire space. In her mushroom-colored traveling suit, she resembled a lumpy fungus that had grown out of the dungeon walls. She had her feet planted and hands folded atop her walking stick (oughtn't they have at least *disarmed* her?), as though she were merely await-ing the arrival of the connecting train.

"Well?" Her voice was hard. "What are you two doing here?"

No one seemed to know what to say. Miss Judson was taking in the scene with alarm, and Constable Hoskiss looked hunched and embarrassed. I took charge.

"Did you kill Mrs. Bloom?"

"Myrtle!" cried three people at once. Well, Constable Hoskiss didn't know my given name, but still.

Aunt Helena glared at me. "What an impertinent question."

"Well, did you?" I pressed. "Those were your scis-sors, and you don't have an alibi. You had means and opportunity. All Arkwright needs is a motive, and you're done for." And at the rate he was going, drumming up charges and evidence out of thin air, that wouldn't take him long, either.

"What are you blathering on about, girl?" Aunt Helena snapped. "Judson, my niece should not even *be* in this godforsaken place." She betrayed the ghost of a shudder.

"Nor should you, ma'am," Miss Judson said gently. Aunt Helena gave her a strange look, like she'd never really seen her before. "We'll notify Arthur—Mr. Hardcastle straightaway, and—"

"You will do no such thing!" Aunt Helena said. "I will *not* disturb him for such a trivial, ridiculous matter—"

"We need him!" I said. "You've been arrested. Father can help."

She went on as if I hadn't spoken. "This is all a silly mistake, and it will be rectified immediately. There is certainly no need to disturb Arthur on his holiday—"

"It's not a *holiday*," I said. "He's working."

"All the more reason not to bother him. Sir Quentin will have this nonsense straightened up right away."

"I'm afraid it might be rather more serious than that," Miss Judson said. "The Inspector seems to be building a case against you." But Aunt Helena brushed her comments away, too.

"Send for Sir Quentin. He'll take care of it. I'll be having tea at the Ballingall Arms this very afternoon.

Now get Helena Myrtle out of the police station before someone sees her. I don't know how we'd live that down." She sat back upon her bench with a harrumph. "Daniel, won't you see my niece and her governess out? There's a dear boy."

I gazed around, baffled. *Daniel?* Apparently she meant Constable Hoskiss, who was nodding deferentially. "Yes, ma'am, I'll see to it. Don't worry, ladies. I'm sure this will be sorted soon."

And before Miss Judson could raise a protest, let alone stop him, we found ourselves back out in the street once more, staring at each other.

I marched straight out of the police station and made an abrupt southerly turn, plowing through the ducks like an icebreaker toward the pie shop–and–post office.

"Wait! Myrtle! Where are you going?"

"To wire Father, of course."

"I just promised Aunt Helena we *wouldn't* do that!"

I spun round. "You were serious? I thought you were humoring her!"

She looked strangely uncomfortable. "Well, she made a good point. We don't want to bother your father, do we? He'll only want to cut short his own trip."

"Exactly! He'll rush here straightaway and put it all to rights."

Miss Judson glanced up and down the street, as though concerned someone might be listening.

Perhaps the ducks, who were currently engaged in a competition to see which might leave the most odious duck mess in our path. "Well, it would be a shame to call him home, if everything is straightened up immediately, as Aunt Helena said."

I tried to make sense of this. It wasn't like Miss Judson to take the "don't tell Father" side of an issue. "Wait!" I startled a duck taking its round in the contest. "You don't want to interrupt *our* holiday!"

She didn't answer, exactly, but she did gesture helplessly about the village, and in the general direction of the shore.

"Call me eccentric," I snapped, "but I rather thought *a murder* seemed a good reason to put off our Family Amusements!"

"Now, that's not fair—" she began, but I wasn't finished.

"And don't you think he ought to hear this from us first? Paris gets newspapers, too, you know. Sir Quentin can't keep this covered up forever. The murder of an Insurance Investigator aboard the *Ballingall Empress Express* is bound to attract attention eventually. Particularly at a conference of forensics experts!"

"Well, it's certainly attracting attention here," Miss Judson said mildly. A few shop doors and cottage windows had opened, the better to overhear our argument. She pulled me aside, out of the rush of traffic (a fellow was hauling a recalcitrant donkey and a cart of pilchard barrels up the hill, and at the rate they were going, might actually arrive by Guy Fawkes Day).

As if on cue, the police station door creaked open, too, and Constable Hoskiss squeezed outside.

"Beggin' your pardon, ladies." The rain had evolved into profuse splattery drops, and he'd be soaked in an instant. The domed helmet might be good protection in a fight, but it did little against the rain. "Might I walk you back to your hotel?"

"No, that's quite all right." Miss Judson led us beneath a slate eave that kept the worst of the deluge off. "No sense in you getting wet, as well."

"I just wanted to say how sorry I am for how the Inspector spoke to you both."

To my mind, *he'd* taken the brunt of it, but Miss Judson was not inclined to be forgiving. "That man has no business investigating a murder."

"Well, I've not either, you see," he said. "And that's who's been sent here to do the job. What can I do?"

"You may not wish to ask," Miss Judson advised, but I leaped in.

"Actually, there's quite a lot you can do, Constable," I said eagerly. "Someone should contact Albion Casualty about the other robbery cases Mrs. Bloom was working on. They might know if she had a suspect in mind."

"Er, all right then—" The constable searched his pockets and found a notepad and a pencil. They looked frightfully new.

". . . And since it's possible the thief *didn't* kill her, Mr. Coogan should be questioned. He's the guard who removed the telegrams. Not to mention Sir Quentin—ascertain *his* motive and alibi—" I stopped at the sound of Miss Judson coughing lightly. Constable Hoskiss had gone pale again.

"I don't know, Miss." He looked uncomfortable. "I didn't sign on for investigating a murder."

I stared at him. "Of course you did. You're a policeman."

"Not for murders! This is Eelscombe. Nobody gets murdered here."

"But—why did you join up, then?" As far as I was concerned, investigating serious crimes was the whole point of becoming a constable to begin with. I couldn't imagine *not* leaping at the first opportunity that arose.

"Ah, you know," he said. "Maintainin' the peace, barroom scuffles, the odd domestic. Keepin' Old Man McGuffin's ducks oot of the 'ighway."

"You became a police officer to Investigate *ducks*?" My voice hit an unnatural pitch. He seemed to be falling short even of his avowed mission. The ducks had over-run a neighboring cottage's stoop and were splashing in the window boxes. A dog had retreated in intimidation.

Constable Hoskiss's gaze was lost in the distance, somewhere out to sea, unspoken thoughts shadowing his long face. "Nay," he said at last. "I became a copper because of *her*. Mrs. Bloom."

Everything seemed to have gone very still and hushed. Even the rain quieted. "She come down 'ere, after the *Valkyrie* explosion—we lost our Davey, you know—an' was like nothing I'd ever seen. Fierce an' sharp, protectin' folk. A fine thing to watch. I were just a lad, then, but we'd see her, off and on through the years. She allus made it seem so noble, findin' the truth, keepin' folk safe."

I knew what he meant—she'd been just like that. I felt a catch in my throat, and another surge of loyalty, this time toward Constable Hoskiss.

Miss Judson was softening, too. She put a hand on the constable's arm. "We didn't realize you'd known her. I'm so sorry."

The constable gave a brave sniff. "Aye. Well, she'd want us to find her killer. I owe her that."

"I believe the Inspector cares more about closing the case than finding the truth." Miss Judson's voice was gentle, but the words were heavy.

"You've met my aunt," I added. "Does she seem like a murderer to you?"

He shuffled his feet and looked even more uncomfortable. "No," he admitted. "But, then, I've never met any murderers."

"We have. And she's not one. Can you help us? We just want to know what happened to Mrs. Bloom. I want to be like her, too." I hadn't meant to say that part aloud.

Constable Hoskiss stood up straighter. He contemplated his notebook, now wet and rippled, and scribbled down some hasty but determined notes. "All right, then, Miss. I'll see what I can do." He paused before returning to the station, a kindly (and very policeman-like) look of concern on his face. "An' what about you two? How'll you manage?"

Miss Judson started to make up some comforting answer, but I was looking at Constable Hoskiss's notebook, a quiver of an idea tugging at me. My fingers searched my own pocket and found Mrs. Bloom's ledger, full of the mysterious code known only by clerks and secretaries.

"Miss!" I broke into their conversation. "We need to send that telegram!" That was exactly what we needed: a law clerk. And I knew just where to get one.

❧

Two minutes later Miss Judson and I presented our soaking wet selves before the little whitewashed storefront midway down the hill. Its plastered notices were barely legible in the downpour, but the round red postbox outside suggested we were at the right place. Making our way through the gate and up the rocky front garden, we spotted the word PETTIGREW'S stenciled among the other signs.

The door swung open with the jangle of a bell, and a plump woman draped in shawls bustled out, bearing a stack of pies nearly as tall as I was. She grunted a wary greeting as Miss Judson held the door for her. We stepped inside, blinking against the dim light and the scent of hot apple and cinnamon, plus the inevitable overtones of fish.

"We're closed!"

I whirled toward the voice—sending an unfortunate spray of rain from the brim of my hat, which spattered a handful of waiting customers and a gaggle of small children.

Miss Judson looked round evenly, taking in the crowded common room, and the steady flow of money coming in and pies going out (a young lad in an oilskin jacket left with a tin as another squat fishwife planted herself at the counter).

"We need to send a telegram," she said, as though the shopkeeper hadn't spoken.

"I *said*, we're closed!" The woman was a few years older than Miss Judson and seemed to be regarding us with a particularly suspicious air. It turned out she *was*, at that—but part of what gave that impression was that the skin on one side of her face was red and twisted, causing her left eye to droop. I swiftly averted my gaze, although I suspect that was just as obvious and rude as staring. I bit my lip, ready to back out before we offended the woman any more, but Miss Judson planted herself behind me.

"Don't let us be a bother, Mistress." Miss Judson steered me to an unobtrusive corner. "We'll just wait until the lunch crush is over."

Mrs. Pettigrew shooed her customers out with practiced efficiency (which explained how she'd crammed everything from a small pie empire to the whole post office into her single shop), then leaned on her elbows and scowled at us. "I can't stop you sendin' a telegram," she said. "But you'll be on your way after that. I don't truck wiv the likes of you."

"What have we done?" I asked, and Mrs. Pettigrew's expression grew even colder.

"We all know what happened on the train. You're related to that murderess."

"She didn't murder anyone!" I said, before Miss Judson could shush me. But Miss Judson's attention was elsewhere. She had weaved her way through a labyrinth of mismatched tables and benches, display cases, and fish barrels* and was inspecting a framed picture on the far wall of the post-office section. I joined her.

My mouth dropped open in surprise. It was a newspaper article, with an immediately recognizable half-tone photo dead center. "You knew Mrs. Bloom, too?"

Mrs. Pettigrew's cold gaze was still on us, but she let us read the article with no further haranguing.

* FRESH DRIED SMOKED

SETTLEMENT FOR
VALKYRIE VICTIMS

Thanks to the ongoing noble and persistent efforts of Mrs. Isidora Bloom (pictured), Investigator for Albion Casualty Insurance, the Victims of the recent steamship explosion at Eelscombe Pleasure Pier will receive their Fair and Due Recompense for Pain and Suffering from October's tragic and deadly mishap. Fault has been placed where it belongs: with Lowell Steamer Lines and owner Harold Lowell, for their negligence in maintaining their vessel.

My gaze swept back to Mrs. Pettigrew, who was tucking her hair self-consciously into her cotton cap, fingers brushing her disfigured—her *burnt* skin. I felt guilty for no reason I could understand but met her eyes.

"I were on the Pier that day," she affirmed. "Wiv me big brother Davey. Little Daniel were there, too, but he weren't hurt, thank the Lord."

"Hoskiss," I breathed, everything clicking into place at last. The name from the memorial plaque. "You're Constable Hoskiss's sister?"

The resemblance was obvious now, as was the fact that she'd got married and had a new last name.

"An' Mrs. Bloom, she were a *hero* to us, here in Eelscombe," she said. "Made the insurance and steamship companies pay us what they owed. Enough to bury our dead and cover the doctors, and a little extra, too."

"Oh," I said softly. I could see why we weren't exactly welcome.

It seemed foolish and inadequate to protest that Aunt Helena hadn't killed her, and that Miss Judson and I would find the real murderer. I returned to the newspaper article, my own outrage simmering. Poor Mrs. Bloom. It might have been fifteen years ago, but it was clear that no one had forgotten the accident, *or* her role in the recovery. The flowers and offerings left at the railway station made even more sense now. Mrs. Bloom hadn't forgotten, either: she'd even saved the steamer ticket, that water-stained memento of her work here in Eelscombe. *Visiting old friends.* That's why she'd been coming back here—not just for the tiara.

Miss Judson turned back solemnly. "The telegram?"

Mrs. Pettigrew drew her distant gaze from the framed newspaper and bustled through to the caged-off section for the post office and telegraph. She handed me the message pad, scowling at my sleeves dripping on her counter. I swiftly composed my brief, urgent plea before we took our apologetic leave. I could only hope it would do the trick.

"Now be off wiv yourselves," Mrs. Pettigrew commanded. "You're stabblin' my clean floors wiv your wet shoes."

13
ROOM SERVICE

No holiday is complete without that most enduring of
Souvenirs: a photograph capturing the journey for posterity. From tintypes by beach photographers to *cartes de
visite* of Notable Sites and three-dimensional stereographic Views, there are travel photographs to suit every
taste and budget.

—*Hardcastle's Practical Travel Companion*

We were hoping to find Sir Quentin and send him
straight off to Inspector Arkwright to clear everything
up, but when we finally squelched back inside the
hotel, to "stabble" the tiled lobby floor, Mr. Roberts
couldn't tell us where he was. Not betraying her impatience, Miss Judson composed a terse note requesting
his attention at his earliest convenience (the words
were far politer than their connotation, Dear Reader,
an art I had yet to master), while I paused to study
the painting of the *Valkyrie*. There was no date, so it

was impossible to know whether it had been painted before or after the accident.

"Why would Sir Quentin want a painting of it here? It seems"—I groped for a word—"morbid." Miss Judson was a great admirer of William Turner, who'd made a whole career out of painting shipwrecks, but even so. He probably didn't hang them up right where the victims could walk by.

Mr. Roberts smiled. "Miss Temperance would agree with you," he said. "She hates the thing. I'm surprised the villagers told you about it, in fact. Eelscombers don't talk about it much, especially to outsiders." I realized he was including himself in that description. "I remember when it happened, though. You couldn't help but hear about it, anywhere on the coast, really. Everyone knew somebody affected. We even sent aid in from Brighton." He fell silent, remembering.

A moment later, he shook himself back to his good spirits and handed me a thick cardstock folder of gilt-edged paper fastened with a gold Ballingall Arms seal. "Clive's finished your photographs." He nodded toward the tiger, where Clive lifted his hand in a half-hearted wave.

While Miss Judson chatted to Mr. Roberts, I split the folder's seal apart with my fingernail and wandered over to Clive. He seemed nervous—had the picture turned out that badly?

"I only got the two shots," Clive mumbled, so softly

I hardly heard him. "Himself doesn't know about them."

I snapped my attention to him. *Himself* might have meant his father—but I had a feeling he was talking about Sir Quentin. Inside the folder was a sturdy cabinet card of Peony and me posed jauntily before the *Empress Express*—not too unflattering, despite the hat. But behind that were two others, and my heart slowed, blood pounding in my ears, as I took them in.

They showed the inside of the baggage car, in shocking black-and-white detail.

The baggage car—and Mrs. Bloom's body.

Clive had taken photographs of the crime scene.

My eyes flew to Clive's over the edge of the album folder. His own were wide with—What? Fear? I clapped the folder shut and said, somewhat louder than necessary, "This is brilliant. I've never had a photograph of Peony before. Can I show Miss Judson?"

He took a calculated look at her, still talking with his father, and nodded. The force of our joint Telepathic *Stare* finally made her turn. Her face was a question, taut with concern.

"Can Clive come up and show us the pictures he took?" I wasn't sure about the propriety of inviting a boy to a private hotel room, but I cracked the folder for her.

She drew in a sharp breath. "If it's all right with his father," she said firmly. Whereupon the necessary permissions were secured and we hastened into the lift. With Tom the operator there, we couldn't discuss anything (although he inquired after Peony), and I forced myself to relax my grip so I didn't crush this precious evidence.

Finally we made it inside the Nile Rooms, where Clive seemed relieved to have something else to Observe. "Blimey," he breathed. "Lookit that. Sir Quentin had that shipped from Egypt for real. I've seen the crates."

Peony peeled herself from her position as part of the room's regal décor and strode straight up to Clive, giving him an appraising look. "*No*," she decided, then rubbed her entire self shamelessly against his legs.

Clive sneezed.

I was dimly aware of this, having carefully laid the photographs on the tea table. I knelt, bending closer, heedless of my wet dress and (only pair of) wet stockings.

"I wish I had my magnifying glass!" I exclaimed, trying to take in every detail of the shot, yet not sure what to look at first. It brought back the horrible, heart-pounding memory of the moment we'd found her—how helpless and stupid I'd felt then. I was determined not to repeat those mistakes, now that I had a second chance at examining the scene. Was it inappropriate to hug a boy for delivering unexpected evidence of a murder? The *Girl's Own Paper* hadn't specified.

"I've got one." Clive dug through his kit and produced it, a nice little lens like a jeweler's loupe. "You can put it right on the picture, see?" And demonstrated—although I Observed that he did not look through it himself.

"I wasn't sure what to do with them," he was saying. "On account of—" He faltered, but we all knew what he meant: *on account of Aunt Helena being arrested.* I looked up sharply, trying to read his expression. Did this mean he thought she was innocent? He could easily have sold these pictures to any newspaper. Or turned them over to Constable Hoskiss. Or given them to Sir Quentin, to quietly bury. But he'd brought them to us instead.

"We'll take very good care of them," Miss Judson assured him.

"Oughtn't they go to the police, though?" He sounded doubtful, and Miss Judson agreed.

"Ordinarily, I'd say yes. But there's a railway inspector who's taken over the constabulary, and . . ." She trailed off, evidently undecided on how to finish that sentence.

"But *you* lot know what to do?"

"Of course," I said, more cavalierly than was perhaps warranted. "We're experienced Investigators. We've already solved one murder back home."

Clive issued another long whistle. "You never did! For real?"

Miss Judson sighed. "Yes, we seem to have a Knack for stumbling into them."

I returned to the photographs. The gloomy afternoon didn't offer much light, but Clive's loupe made it easier to focus on the details without getting distracted by the big picture. The grisly big picture. Literally. There were two photographs, one of the whole baggage car—Clive had backed toward the doors to get the best view (my skirts were in the frame)—and a closeup of Mrs. Bloom's body. I couldn't immediately see anything new in the longer view, so I set it aside to focus on Mrs. Bloom. The shot was so clear I could make out every little floret and cherub on the scissor handles, the dark spread of blood on her bodice.

"These are *really* good," I said. But Clive seemed uncertain.

"Seeing it was bad enough," he said. "Having pictures makes it worse, somehow. Like I can't ever forget it."

I didn't *want* to forget it—I wanted to recall each detail with perfect clarity, make sure I didn't miss anything that might solve Mrs. Bloom's murder. Thanks to Clive, now I could.

Mrs. Bloom's face was not clearly visible in the picture, with her arm flung overhead, but I could see a bit of exposed neck and a strange sort of shadow above the lace of her collar. I studied it with the magnifier, pulled back to see with my naked eye, and then looked close again.

"What does this look like to you?" I meant Miss Judson, but Clive gave it a cursory glance.

"Those aren't smudges," he said, with a hint of defensive pride. "Those were on—on her neck, I guess." His voice slowed down as he realized what he was saying.

Miss Judson realized it, too. "It's not a shadow," she said, very softly. "There's nothing to cast it."

And it wasn't just shadows, smudges, dark finger-shaped bruises on the side of Mrs. Bloom's neck, but a smattering of tiny pinprick dark dots.

"Tardieu spots," I breathed. The blood vessels burst, leaving behind telltale hemorrhaging on the skin. "She wasn't just stabbed," I said. "She was *strangled.*"

ംര

After that Clive didn't linger. I tried not to be disappointed—the study of post-mortem lividity really isn't to everybody's taste—but I'd been hoping for a bit more scientific camaraderie. They were *his* photographs, after all. Still, even if he didn't wish to stay and grapple with the implications, I was glad he'd brought them. Clive Roberts was *definitely* an ally on the side of Justice.

That didn't make it much easier to do what came next, however. After Clive decamped, making some hasty excuse about getting home for tea, Miss Judson and I sat down for a Frank Discussion of the Case. It was a relief to talk about it openly now, even if it was happening at Aunt Helena's expense.

"I don't like this," Miss Judson said. "Stabbed with Aunt Helena's scissors was bad enough, but strangled? That's a bit much."

I didn't exactly see how being stabbed or strangled—or stabbed *and* strangled—was any worse than being poisoned, or anything else for that matter, but I didn't belabor the point.

Miss Judson had rung for tea, and we'd hung up our wet things and changed into dressing gowns. (Well, Miss Judson had, having sensibly packed hers in her valise. I had to make do with bundling into a spare coverlet from the bed. I knew Miss Judson was waiting for me to admit I'd been overhasty in insisting upon the securing of the baggage car. But wet petticoats and squelchy stockings were nothing compared to the pursuit of Justice. Although just now I could do with both more justice *and* dry underclothes.) I'd carefully put up Clive's pictures so we wouldn't get jam on them. Peony was Investigating the food, and she regarded a crustless sandwich with some sort of fish filling with an approving eye. And paw.

"Never mind that," I said, dragging the sandwiches away from Peony. "How can they *possibly* think Aunt Helena killed anybody?" I heard the challenge in my voice—daring Miss Judson to prove me wrong, to tell me that the scene I'd witnessed, Aunt Helena threatening Mrs. Bloom, didn't mean anything. That it was the thief, or Mr. Coogan, or The Man Temperance Saw. Or Sir Quentin. Or anybody else.

She didn't. Not at first. She sat fiddling with her teacup, stirring more and more sugar into it until it was little more than syrup.

"Miss! You can't think she's guilty!"

"Of course not," she said, forcing briskness into her voice. "But Inspector Arkwright clearly does, so we must understand the case he has—thinks he has—against her."

I glared at her, trying to figure out what she was really thinking, but Miss Judson is a deep well. I sighed. "Very well, Miss Prosecutor," I said. "Proceed."

She nodded crisply. "Exhibit One," she said. "The scissors. They belonged to the accused, and were last seen in her possession."

I had nothing to refute this, so I crossed my legs and grudgingly said, "Fine. So she had *means*. But so did everybody else on the train. Anything could have happened to those scissors after Aunt Helena had them. Perhaps Mrs. Bloom took them from her, and the killer used them on her later."

"Before or after he strangled her?" Her voice was wry. "Next, we have motive. Aunt Helena was seen—on more than one occasion—arguing with the victim."

"So was Sir Quentin," I countered. "And his motive—five thousand pounds' worth of insurance money—is much stronger. So is Mr. Coogan's—she threatened his job. Plus, Sir Quentin and Mr. Coogan each had means *and* opportunity. They had access to every inch of that train. Why should Aunt Helena go to the baggage car, anyway? And don't say to get her scissors." I took a breath. "Also, Mr. Coogan has a history of violence, and he's a big man. He could easily have strangled someone."

"*And* stabbed her."

"Why do you keep saying that?"

"Well, because it's so odd." Making a novel switch from tradition, Miss Judson got up to pace. "Why not just stab her *or* strangle her? Why do both? She wasn't a large woman. *One* of those wounds would have been enough to stop her."

I pondered this. "So it was someone very determined."

She gazed back at me grimly. "Or someone who truly hated her."

And who did that best describe? I was afraid I knew the answer. Setting that aside for the moment, I turned to Miss Judson's sketch. "What about The Man Temperance Saw? I'm certain I've seen him before."

"Yes, there's a lot of that going around." I knew she was talking about the Bird Ladies.

"Do you think Miss Causton and Miss Cabot lied about having seen him?"

"Not exactly. I think they just wanted to be part of the excitement, poor dears." She stirred a new cup of tea without looking at me. "I'm sure you can understand that."

"I don't make things up!" The idea was inconceivable. "Besides, this man is real. I've seen him, too. I just can't think where."

"Well, try to remember fast," she said. She paused before Clive's photos, head tilted, as if a different angle might nudge loose the memory. "Poor Mrs. Bloom. Who could have hated you enough to kill you?"

I sorted through what we knew about her—which was, regrettably, not all that much. That wave of disappointment and unfairness washed over me again. I'd only known her for a few hours; the people of Eelscombe had known her for years. "It wasn't anybody local," I said confidently. "They *adored* her."

Miss Judson looked at me thoughtfully, stirring, stirring. "Maybe not all of them." Her voice was dark with meaning.

ↁ

Wednesday morning, I rolled out of my sarcophagus, full of a vague excitement I could not immediately pinpoint. And then I remembered: Aunt Helena had spent the night in jail! I managed to tamp down the Decidedly Uncharitable Impulse to laugh by envisioning what *her* reaction was likely to be next time we saw her.

"Now?" Peony had pinpointed the source of her own agitation—the disgraceful lack of kippers and cream—so as Miss Judson padded about getting ready, I rang the bell for breakfast. Miss Judson had sent no

fewer than *four* Strongly Worded notes to Sir Quentin regarding his plans to save Aunt Helena from the noose, with no reply. I could only hope he was already at the police station, talking sense into Inspector Arkwright.

He was not.

When the knock came, I swung wide the doors, not onto a maid with a tea cart but upon a small army of footmen and housemaids, laden down with parcels. Behind them all, booming jolly orders, was Sir Quentin.

"What's all this?" Miss Judson wandered out—she'd had the foresight to finish dressing, fortunately—only to be caught up in the tide. Porters flowed past her.

"Miss Judson!" Sir Quentin caught her by both hands, and kissed them. "Myrtle, my girl! No, no, that won't do at all," he said to a maid holding a huge frilly dress up to me. "Can't you see she's only the size of a minute? Find her something that fits. I told you, spare no expense!"

"Sir Quentin, perhaps you'd better explain things." Miss Judson put a hand to her forehead as a footman began unpacking a crate full of canvases and easels.

"My dear girls." Sir Quentin wrapped a fatherly arm around her, squeezing me in too. "This business with the luggage is *such* an inconvenience—not at all the sort of service Ballingall Excursions pride themselves on, no, not at all! Can't have you running about in this beastly weather with just the clothes on your backs! It's taken some doing, I don't mind telling you, but I think I've pulled off quite a feat."

"Sir Quentin!" Miss Judson had to shout to be heard above the bustle of maids unwrapping clothes and decanting them onto the beds. "Kindly explain, *what feat?*"

"Why, all this, of course." He waved an expansive arm. "Sent for everything from Brighton. Arrived this morning on the train. Look—" He snatched a gown from a passing maid and draped it over his arm, stroking its delicate sleeve. "Finest French lace and bombazine. No idea what bombazine is, but Temperance tells me it's all the fashion."

Dear Reader, I hadn't the foggiest idea what bombazine was, either.

Miss Judson glanced around the room, nearly overwhelmed. "I'm sure this is very appreciated," she finally managed. I wrestled my way through the maids to find Peony being fitted for a new leather collar (purple, of course) with a shiny brass bell. She was looking awfully proud of herself. I surveyed the scene with growing dismay. The notion of at least one pair of dry stockings was not unwelcome, particularly as mine were still dripping *yesterday's* rain. But the rest of it, the fancy dresses and—good grief, was that striped-and-ruffled thing another bathing costume?—the stack of art supplies for Miss Judson and a growing heap of sand pails and fishing nets and model boats . . . It seemed like more than mere generosity to make up for our being "inconvenienced." I felt a quiver of alarm. Why was he doing all of this?

I worked my way back through to Sir Quentin. "Are you going to help Aunt Helena?" I asked.

I'd caught him off guard. He paused in petting a velvet dressing gown and turned an entirely new shade of red.

"Well, of course, I am, my dear!"

"How?"

He tried to chuckle. "Well, now, how do you mean?"

Mindful of Miss Judson, not to mention the small battalion of innocent maids and footmen, I drew in my breath and said, in my sweetest voice, "Thank you ever so much for all this, Sir Quentin. It's frightfully generous. But what are you doing to help Aunt Helena, who has been *wrongfully arrested for murder*?" It's very possible that I did not manage to keep my voice at a ladylike volume on that last bit.

A satisfying hush fell over the room, lasting only a shocked second before the maids all scurried to look busy once more.

Sir Quentin fumbled his armful of dressing gown and appealed to Miss Judson, who merely raised a neat eyebrow at him.

"Well, er, looking into the matter, of course.

Cleared up very soon." Sir Quentin tried to sound soothing, but I interrupted him.

"She's already spent the night in jail! She's convinced you're going to help her."

"And I will, my dear! I have my best people working on it, even now."

I glanced about the room. It looked like his best people were at work showering us with fancy gifts.

"Who?" I asked. Sir Quentin hesitated, so I clarified: "Who do you have working on it? What are they going to do? Do you have a lawyer?"

Here Sir Quentin went distinctly pale. "What would I want one of them for? No, no—no need for that. I'll have a word with Arkwright, straighten everything out. Your aunt will be back out enjoying her holiday again in no time." He punctuated this with a beaming smile, making him look more than ever like a lion tamer—or the hungry lion.

Miss Judson did not appear to be convinced. She had the bombazine frock draped across her arm, inspecting the workmanship. "What did this cost, I wonder? That lace is handmade. And all the rest . . . ?"

Sir Quentin nervously shifted his weight from foot to foot. "Well, now, not to worry—on the house, you know."

"I expect that someone might consider such largesse a *bribe*," I said. "Isn't that right, Miss Judson? To keep us quiet, not raise a fuss about my aunt being arrested?"

"Oh, surely not." Miss Judson smiled brilliantly at Sir Quentin. "I'm sure Sir Quentin had no such designs. Because"—she lifted the lid on a glove box to inspect its kidskin contents—"we have *every* intention of making a fuss. Don't we, Myrtle?"

I squeezed next to her, strangling the bathing costume. "Unless you'd care to explain where *you* were when Mrs. Bloom was killed?"

Sir Quentin didn't have a chance to answer. Miss Judson abruptly handed the glove box back, saying, "I think we can manage the rest. Thank you very much. Good day." And she bustled him, along with the full complement of maids, out into the corridor, closing the doors behind them.

"What did you do that for? I was going to question him!"

"Why do you think I stopped you?" She paced through the room, momentarily distracted by a carton labeled WINSOR & NEWTON, BY APPOINTMENT TO HER MAJESTY. Probably a paint set—an elaborate one, from the size of it. "Myrtle, you have to be more careful! Look around! Do you know how much all this must have cost him? And the sort of effort it would take to silence any newspaper accounts?"

I stared at her, not understanding. "So?"

She plucked the photograph of Mrs. Bloom's body from where we'd tucked it into the mirror frame and waved the gruesome reminder in my face.

"So, he's a murder suspect! He might have killed one woman and sent another to jail for it. Let's be content he's only tried to bribe us!" She shoved the picture into my hands to make her point, then checked her watch. "Get dressed. I believe we're expecting another delivery."

And that one, Dear Reader, was welcome indeed.

14

AMICUS CURIAE

Pentonville Prison, 1842: England's first "Model Prison."
Designed after the progressive Separation System of forced
labor and strict isolation, Pentonville swiftly developed a
reputation for causing insanity in the prisoners, including
delusions, paranoia, and hallucinations. This experiment
proved so successful that a further 54 structures have
been built on its model. Caledonian Road, North London.

—Hardcastle's Practical Travel Companion

The express train from Brighton squealed into the
railway station later that morning with an ear-pierc-
ing shriek, not un-reminiscent of the sound Miss
Ballingall had made when her tiara was stolen. Miss
Judson and I huddled beneath a huge new purple
umbrella, which would have made us impossible to
miss on even the most crowded London train platform. This, however, was Eelscombe, scarcely large
enough to allow the train to stop and discharge its

passengers. Passenger, singular, today—the answer to our urgent telegram.

The train slowed just enough for the doors to clatter open. A young man juggling a valise and a briefbag and a cardboard box tied up with twine, all while trying to don his overcoat, hopped down—landing in a puddle.

"Stephen!" Mr. Blakeney called, just as his hat went sailing onto the tracks, where it was lost forever beneath the iron horse. "Humbug," he said cheerily. "That was my favorite hat."

"Hallo, Mr. Blakeney!" Miss Judson called, hastening over with the umbrella. "Welcome to scenic Fairhaven!"

Forgive me for waxing metaphorical, but Mr. Blakeney's arrival felt like the sun coming out at last. He'd proven himself a clever and resourceful ally on our last Investigation—and, due to Circumstances Beyond His Control, was now free to drop everything and come down to the seaside on a moment's notice. I was frightfully relieved to see him.

"Let me help with those." It wasn't exactly ladylike, but I was afraid he'd drop something important, so I wrestled the carton from Mr. Blakeney's tenuous grasp, then nearly buckled under its weight. "What's in here? All of *Law Reports*?"

"Of course not," he said. "We didn't need 1881. Ever, apparently, since it was not to be found in the library." Completely oblivious to the rain, Mr. Blakeney gave me a very clear-eyed look. "Stephen, I booked the fastest train I could when I got your wire. I had no idea you had a maiden aunt!"

"Well, now," Miss Judson began, "you may wish to withhold judgment—"

"Take me to her! I ride swift to the aid of the damsel in distress." He whirled dramatically, startling the lurking ducks into a volley of rather sinister squawking. "The locals seem dangerous."

"Yes, don't cross them," Miss Judson said. "I'm afraid there's no coach, and I hope you don't mind the, er, descent. The Ballingall Arms is down this way."

Mr. Blakeney's gaze followed her gesturing arm to where you could just see the barest glimpse of the hotel's green roof. Between the cliffs and the roiling black water, it looked quite lost at sea.

"Very grand. But I'm a working man. I have a room at—" He fumbled in his pockets. Or, rather, he fumbled *for* his pockets. "Well, it was here somewhere."

"Mrs. Pettigrew's?" She didn't advertise rooms, but probably only because she'd run out of wall to paint it on.

Mr. Blakeney snapped his fingers. "Pettigrew! That's the one."

I cast Miss Judson a Look. I couldn't imagine how *that* was going to go, given our reception yesterday.

"You should know that Mrs. Pettigrew is not Aunt Helena's biggest supporter."

He appeared not to hear—or heed—me. "Lead on, Stephen, and then let us go and rescue your dear sweet Auntie Helen."

"Helena," I corrected. It would take all week to correct the rest of his misapprehensions. "I'm named after her."

"You have an Aunt Stephen? Curious name for a woman."

Mr. Blakeney maintained an amusing but useful fiction that I was a boy called Stephen, brought about by my abrupt and unauthorized appearance in his offices one sweltering afternoon last summer. A Young Lady of Quality had no business calling upon young men at their workplaces, so he had voluntarily misunderstood me. I could never really tell when he was being serious, although it happened so rarely that it was generally a safe bet that he was jesting. His own legal ambitions had taken something of a stumble after the Redgraves Murder.* Notwithstanding the abrupt end to his last post, he'd kept up his studies, still going to court and, through means no one had quite identified and seemed disinclined to poke into very deeply, had kept up the law offices, despite not

* He'd clerked for Mr. Whitney Ambrose, Esq., whose name you no doubt recognize from that misadventure.

being officially qualified as a solicitor yet or having any apparent source of income to support himself.

It's not every Investigator who can avail herself of the *pro bono publica* services of an expert in the law, particularly criminal defense. "If this goes well, I expect Aunt Helena can pay you," I said uncertainly.

"Nonsense!" declared Mr. Blakeney. "I am sustained only by my noble pursuit of justice! I need no monetary remuneration! Although," he added, "lunch is much appreciated."

"Good idea," Miss Judson said. "We can recommend a pie shop."

I wondered how Mrs. Pettigrew would like having her premises turned into the headquarters for Aunt Helena's defense team, let alone giving aid and comfort to the enemy, but it did seem safer than doing it all right under Sir Quentin's nose back at the Ballingall Arms.

❧

That afternoon, we presented our (more or less refreshed, thanks to clean underthings, but no thanks to the hike up the hill) selves, with no small sense of trepidation, to collect Mr. Blakeney from the pie shop. But when we swung the jangly door open onto an unusually empty common room, Mrs. Pettigrew was all smiles.

"He do clean up nicely, your lawyer," she said.

Mr. Blakeney emerged, looking surprisingly, well, *professional*. He seemed like a silly boy most of the time, with his fair curly hair, ruddy cheeks, and ready grin, but now he was clad in a fine dark suit that must have cost more than his rent, with his hair oiled back as neatly as it would go. Noticing Miss Judson and me staring, he halted in Mrs. Pettigrew's stooped threshold and patted awkwardly at his head. "Er, I haven't another hat," he said, destroying the illusion entirely.

"You can borrow my Jake's." Mrs. Pettigrew was already retrieving what was obviously Mr. Pettigrew's Sunday best from a hatbox stowed among the other wares crammed onto the shop shelves. She blew a layer of dust from the lid as thick as the icing on her buns. Opening it released a powerful blast of mothball, but the smart black felt top hat looked quite dashing on Mr. Blakeney. Or it would, as soon as he was somewhere he could stand up straight with it on.

"Do you have a spare brolly? He's going to ruin it," I said.

"I say, that's rather rum, Stephen! Mrs. Pettigrew, I assure you, my record for hats is *nearly* unimpeachable. That last one escaped my custody through no wrongdoing on my part whatsoever. I will take excellent care of Mr. Pettigrew's fine, fine hat. I thank you, milady."

Mrs. Pettigrew let out a girlish giggle and swatted at him with her dust cloth. "Oh, get on wiv you, then." I turned to gape at Miss Judson, who appeared as wonderstruck as I.

"What did you do to her?" I burst out, as soon as we were out of earshot. "She *hates* us! On account of Aunt Helena having murdered her favorite person in the world, you know."

Mr. Blakeney looked sheepish. "Oh, nothing, really. Played with her children, fixed her water pump, ate my weight in apple dumplings. And I might have mentioned that I was here to help the finest Investigative Minds in England solve the murder of Mrs. Bloom."

Miss Judson watched him with a most curious expression. "You know how to fix a water pump?" was all she said.

As we headed up the hill, the rain drummed down, thunder humming in the distance.

"Capital day for a legal battle!" Mr. Blakeney said. "Ready to enter the arena?"

"*Morituri te salutamus*,"* I muttered.

"That's the spirit! But what's this?" Mr. Blakeney's stride slowed as the police station came in view, and we realized it wasn't just thunder we'd been hearing. The avian mob which habitually slowed our progression had been displaced by humans—a great crush of them,

* the traditional greeting of Roman gladiators: "We who are about to die salute you."

braving the weather and no more welcoming than the ducks. Angry chants rose from the crowd, who toted signs demanding JUSTICE FOR MRS. BLOOM! and DOWN WITH HARDCAST—(evidently they'd run out of room).

I meant to keep walking, but my feet grew roots and tethered me to the spot.

"Oh, dear." Miss Judson covered her mouth with a gloved hand.

"Well," Mr. Blakeney said, flagging a measure, "never underestimate the English mob. Fine old tradition, mob justice." His fine old words were belied by the ghost of doubt in his voice.

Outraged, I stared at the crowd. A girl about my age held aloft a pole bearing a scarecrow figure in black petticoats and a grotesque hat. For a moment I could scarcely take it in, but my stunned brain finally worked it out.

"They're going to burn Aunt Helena in effigy!"

"Of course they aren't," Miss Judson said. "Not in this weather."

"It's not funny!"

"I would never suggest it," she said in a strained voice. "Not a bit. Not in the slightest. It's—I wish your father could see this."

"Don't you *dare* draw this." I forced myself through the angry Eelscombers. Someone had brought a basket of ammunition, and my borrowed coat caught a splat of day-old pilchard right in the shoulder.

"Justice for Mrs. Bloom!" they roared.

I whirled around. "That's what we're *trying* to do!" I cried—just in time to have Mr. Blakeney step in to deflect another volley of fish guts.

"Cricket fielding," he huffed, shuffling me and Miss Judson into the dubious safety of the stationhouse. He heaved the door shut behind us, sagging against it. "I hope they don't have a battering ram. I don't think this old place could withstand a siege."

"Well." Miss Judson tugged off her gloves. "That was . . . unfortunate." She pressed the back of one hand to her face, which had flooded with color. A peal of laughter escaped anyway. "Oh, my heavens."

It was all very well for her, not having been pelted with piscine projectiles by a mob determined to see her only aunt burned at the stake. Why couldn't Aunt Helena have managed to get herself arrested for killing somebody no one *liked*? She really was most inconveniently disagreeable.

Constable Hoskiss was monitoring the situation with worried eyes. "They've been at it all morning," he said. "They're calling for—well, you saw." He took in the stain (or the stink) on my coat, and produced a crumpled handkerchief. "Sorry aboot that. Mum can get carried away."

"That's your *mother* out there?" I couldn't decide whether to laugh or cry. Miss Judson hiccoughed.

Constable Hoskiss grimaced. "Well, she has strong feelings about our Mrs. B., you understand."

I sighed. Mrs. Hoskiss had every right to be angry. Mrs. Bloom had stood up for her when she'd lost her son and her daughter was injured. But couldn't she see that her *other* son was working hard to solve the murder? How was hanging about haranguing him with an angry mob supposed to help matters?

We could still hear them chanting outside. "Any chance they might let up?" Mr. Blakeney's voice was hopeful.

Constable Hoskiss gave an apologetic shrug. "Can't fish in this rain," he said. "I reckon they'll be at it all day."

Miss Judson recovered first. Of Inspector Arkwright there was no sign. Was it too much to hope that he'd get caught in the same gauntlet? Perhaps they'd burn *him* in effigy. The thought was almost enough to raise my spirits.

As Mr. Blakeney hung up his coat, Miss Judson produced the sketch of The Man Temperance Saw for the constable, along with our carefully composed notes about Mr. Coogan, his quarrel with Mrs. Bloom, the missing telegram and other paperwork—everything we had, so far, to exculpate Aunt Helena. I'd copied it all out the night before, in my most refined penmanship, wishing for the use of the typewriter in Mr. Roberts's tidy office.

"Coogan, eh? Guard on the *Empress* . . . Should be easy enough to check out." Constable Hoskiss scratched his head, though, over Miss Judson's drawing of the bearded tramp. "Miss Ballingall says she saw *him* on the train? You're sure?"

"Running away from the train," I clarified. "Do you have a copying machine? Can you distribute that to other constabularies?"

He was studying the sketch. "Er—certainly. I'll look into this, you can be sure of it." He folded everything carefully and tucked it into his uniform jacket, just as Inspector Arkwright returned.

To Miss Judson's particular annoyance, Mr. Blakeney made all the difference with Inspector Arkwright, too. I would like to say it was the top hat, but I very much suspect the real factor was the Incontrovertible Biology of the situation: he was *a man*.

As soon as the inspector arrived, he strode forward and thrust out his hand. "Good day, sir. I'm here to see Miss Helena Hardcastle. Robert Blakeney, Esquire." (*Almost*, I added mentally.)

Inspector Arkwright gazed up and down Mr. Blakeney's fine suit and very official-looking brief-bag and evidently decided he was legitimate. "Fine," he snapped. "But the girls stay here."

Miss Judson regarded him coolly. "Here?" Her voice was sweet. "With you?"

Inspector Arkwright reconsidered.

A moment later Constable Hoskiss led us back to the station's tearoom, where they had installed Aunt Helena in her makeshift cell, but his expression grew peculiar as we approached.

"What's wrong?" I asked, alarmed.

"Er," he said. "Well, nothing. Not exactly. Just–" He unlocked the door. "See for yourselves."

The little room was transformed. Aunt Helena sat upright on her hard bench, which was now liberally padded with plush cushions, the entire space draped about with beaded velvet shawls, like her parlor back home. Someone had brought in a pleasant oil lamp with an etched glass globe, which gave off a homey glow. A blackboard had been installed at one end of the room–I shot Miss Judson a Look of stabbing envy.

"Ah, Daniel." Aunt Helena still wore her fungus-colored traveling skirt, but had somehow conjured up a fresh shirtwaist of fine black cambric. She'd doffed the jacket and hat and rolled up her shirtsleeves. "That is quite satisfactory. Will you bring my guests some tea, and some of young Molly's lovely biscuits?"

"Yes'm," he said.

"She knows you're a policeman, right?" I said. "Not an under-butler or something?"

The constable had adopted an expression Miss Judson and I recognized instantly. "It's just easier to do as she says," he murmured, then made his escape.

Aunt Helena turned on us. "It's about time you two showed up. There's work to be done. And who are you, young man?" She subjected Mr. Blakeney to an examination with her lorgnette, which he bore well. They had not chanced to meet on our previous case, which Mr. Blakeney acknowledged.

"Robert Blakeney, at your service." He set his bag on one of the hard chairs and looked about the room. "I say, this is . . . something."

I thought Mr. Blakeney showed Exceptional Forbearance. As he made a cautious exploration of Aunt Helena's tiny empire, I took in the scribbles on the blackboard and the paperwork spread about the room, pinned to every surface not already covered by a scarf. Was—was Aunt Helena *Investigating*?

"What exactly are you working on here, Miss Hardcastle?" Mr. Blakeney's voice was tentative, and I could hardly blame him. It was like a penny dreadful scene depicting Broadmoor, the asylum for criminal lunatics, the way she'd covered her cell with fevered notes and sat here grandly, as if hosting a dinner party. But as I flipped through Aunt Helena's papers, it wasn't *madness* I saw, or that gave me such a queer, off-kilter feeling. She was trying to get to the bottom of what was happening to her. Trying to solve—

"The case, of course," Aunt Helena snapped. "Obviously, they're trying to frame me. This is all a plot to discredit Sir Quentin."

I sat down with a heavy thump. Maybe a little madness.

"And who would 'they' be, Miss Hardcastle?" Mr. Blakeney had taken out his own notebook, holding it before him like a shield.

"Well, isn't it obvious? The insurance company, jealous rivals, his creditors . . . Look. I have everything written down." She handed Mr. Blakeney a stack of papers. "And here"—she produced a thin folder and slapped it atop the table before us—"are their so-called charges against me."

She'd somehow got her hands on Inspector Arkwright's file of the case. "He *gave* this to you?" I was dumbfounded. "He doesn't have to show that to you."

The Look Aunt Helena bestowed upon me said everything necessary about her Opinion of *that* silly law—not to mention how skillfully she'd circumvented it. I eyed her in an alarming new light.

As Mr. Blakeney read through the file, Miss Judson and I tackled Aunt Helena's notes. There was a full page of speculation on Sir Quentin's financial prospects, which Miss Judson studied with a growing frown.

"You gave Sir Quentin money, Aunt Helena?"

Aunt Helena drew back, affronted. "Don't make it sound so vulgar. I *invested* in his Excursion Company. He's an old friend, and his other contacts had turned their backs on him in his time of need."

"Time of need? Clarify."

"Well, I wouldn't expect *you* to understand. His business affairs are very complicated."

Not that complicated, apparently; Miss Judson's frown intensified as she read. "Sir Quentin's in debt?"

Another dismissive wave. "He's explained that to me. There were all sorts of delays in getting the hotel built—suppliers not delivering on time, contractors taking longer than promised. You have no idea the trials he suffered, just installing the drains. And then, several *dishonorable* investors cheated Sir Quentin out of what they owed him! Scoundrels and blackguards, the lot of them."

Her Defense Team exchanged glances, but we continued to study her notes, sorting them into organized stacks, and asking her questions. Her volumes of vitriol against Mrs. Bloom and Sir Quentin's other "enemies"—everyone from the jewelers who made the tiara to the driver on the *Empress Express*—poured out upon the page in florid, convoluted prose, weren't exactly reassuring.

"They've done it before, you know."

Miss Judson eyed her carefully. "Aunt Helena, are you feeling quite well?"

Mr. Blakeney put in, "*Who's* done *what* before?"

"Tried to ruin Sir Quentin." She glared at us. "For heaven's sakes, I thought you lot were supposed to be clever! What have you been *doing* all this time?"

Since it had barely been a day, and she'd forbidden us from doing anything but sit on our hands and wait for Sir Quentin, this seemed rather unfair to me. I had my mouth open to protest, but Aunt Helena didn't give me a chance.

"I can see I was wise to take this on myself. As I was saying, that insurance company has been trying to ruin him for years. It almost destroyed Temperance the last time. The poor dear has Never Been the Same Since. That was before I knew them, of course. They don't like to talk about it, but one picks things up."

I swung my feet, trying to make sense of this. Was it possible she was on to something, there in her Sir Quentin–addled brain? The clues she'd uncovered did make a compelling picture. I just wasn't sure it was the same one Aunt Helena was looking at.

"Are you saying Sir Quentin had a grudge against Mrs. Bloom?"

"Helena Myrtle! Have you listened to a *word* I've said?" Impatience flashed across her creased face. "This is clearly a conspiracy—"

"All right, Aunt." Miss Judson was soothing. "What do you think?" She turned to Mr. Blakeney. "Can you help us?"

He looked up from the Inspector's file, serious for once. "I'm afraid his case is fairly solid. It's entirely circumstantial—there's no physical evidence placing you at the crime scene, Miss Hardcastle, such as blood on your clothes—but they have enough here to bring charges against you."

Aunt Helena's eyes had grown narrow, but she listened to every word he said. "And what does that mean?"

He was solemn. "Magistrate's court, to start. And I doubt they have one locally, not for a crime as serious as murder, so they'll commit you to trial at the county assizes. Those would be"—he paused, thinking—"in Lewes, probably." From Mr. Blakeney's remarks, I Deduced that Lewes was the county town of Sussex, where major trials took place.

"I see." Aunt Helena's voice was quiet. "Thank you."

I was not so composed. "That's it then? Just like that? She's going on trial for murder? Don't you realize that three-quarters of all defendants *are found guilty*?"

"Stephen! You wound me!" Mr. Blakeney clapped a hand to his chest. "You seem to have underestimated the services of Blakeney and Self, Solicitor-*almost*. Nor can I believe that the Hardcastles would give up so easily."

Miss Judson said, cautiously, "What are you proposing?"

He produced his brief-bag. "Well, until *some better evidence turns up*"—this was uttered with considerable emphasis, and I fidgeted, realizing what he was saying—"I think our best recourse is going to be creative legal wrangling."

Aunt Helena leaned forward to see into his files. "Meaning?" She sounded intrigued.

"Stalling. I have writs! I have motions! I have briefs!" With each item, he heaped another stack of papers onto the table. "I have read *Bleak House** sixteen times, and by the time I'm done with Crown against Hardcastle, Jarndyce and Jarndyce will look like a cakewalk!"

And unless I was going a little bit mad myself, Dear Reader, I thought Aunt Helena laughed.

As we turned to leave, her hand lingered just a little too long in Mr. Blakeney's. "Are you married yet, young man?"

---

* Charles Dickens, 1853. A cracking good novel with *several* excellent murders. Famous for the aforementioned neverending legal battle, it also features the clever and resourceful Inspector Bucket (inspired by Scotland Yard's Charles Field). Not to mention the spontaneous human combustion.

15
SIDE TRIPS

Some of the most interesting Experiences in travel occur on unexpected and unplanned jaunts. Be open to diverting from your Itinerary.

–Hardcastle's Practical Travel Companion

When we emerged from Aunt Helena's cell, it was to find Inspector Arkwright glowering over a gloomy-looking girl huddled miserably near the station's ancient fireplace. She was soaking wet, with a mud-splattered hem, and looked like she'd been wrestling the mob *and* the ducks.

"Cicely!" Miss Judson marched over to them. "What is going on here? Have you not arrested enough of the Hardcastle family already? You're moving on to staff?"

Cicely sprang to her feet like a hare, looking for an avenue of flight, but her path was blocked by Inspector Arkwright on one side and Miss Judson on the other.

"I'm not arresting her," the Inspector spat. "She came here on her own."

"What for?" I cried. Had she come to inform on Aunt Helena? What could she know?

"I was only—I wanted to know about the luggage," Cicely mumbled. "I've run out of all Miss Hardcastle's fresh things, and I tried to tell the stationmaster, but he just slammed the window in my face and said I had to take it up with the police, and when I came down here—" She took a gaspy breath, dark eyes brimming with tears.

"There, now," said Constable Hoskiss, materializing with a cup of tea, which he pressed into her shaking hands. "I'm afraid she ran afoul of the, erm . . ." He waved a hand toward the lane outside.

"Your mother?" I couldn't decide who I felt sorrier for, Cicely or Constable Hoskiss.

"Miss, are you hurt?" Mr. Blakeney broke in sensibly.

"I'm fine." Cicely set down the tea undrunk. Before we could say anything else, she squeezed through the press of people surrounding her and shot for the door and out into the rain.

"But won't they catch her again?" Miss Judson said.

"I sent them on home," said the constable. "Told Mum they were disturbing the peace, and threatened to lock the lot of 'em up if they didn't clear out."

Miss Judson rewarded Constable Hoskiss with a look of pure admiration.

Mr. Blakeney interrupted us once more. "What's this about the luggage?" Whereupon we had to explain the situation to him, as his expression grew colder. He addressed Inspector Arkwright. "And you haven't released it yet? These ladies have no clothing, my good man."

"They look perfectly all right to me," growled the Inspector.

"Well, I'm sure *you* think so." Mr. Blakeney's voice was deep and theatrical. "But Miss Judson here is wearing a traveling frock instead of the proper walking suit that a visit to a police station occasions. And I cannot account for the atrocity on Young Miss Hardcastle's head, there." He shuddered. "Furthermore, my client is entitled to full access to her possessions, until such time as formal charges have been filed against her. Replevin!" he finished, quite grandly.

"Re–*what*?"

I was baffled, too, but Mr. Blakeney sailed full steam ahead. "Replevin! From the Old French *replevy*, meaning–replevy. The return of illegally seized goods. I'll be filing an action of replevin, unless Eastern Coastal Railways release the belongings of the Hardcastle family forthwith."

"Including my sketchbook," Miss Judson added.

"And the sketchbook," Mr. Blakeney said.

Inspector Arkwright glared at us. "File whatever

you want," he said. "I've not finished my formal examination of the baggage car yet."

Mr. Blakeney did not look sorrowful at this news. "Unfortunate. You seem to have missed your chance." He whisked a sheaf of papers from his brief-bag and thrust it at the Inspector. "Good day."

I followed Mr. Blakeney and Miss Judson out of the station, staring at Mr. Blakeney in dazed wonder. He grinned at us.

"Don't look so surprised," he said. "How do you think Old Ambrose made all his money? I can stall with the best of them." He sobered. "I'm afraid this does mean, however, that it will probably take a day or so before you'll actually get your luggage back. Do you think that poor girl can wait that long?" He glanced about for Cicely, but she had vanished into the warren of streets.

∾

Now that Mr. Blakeney was here, there was little for me to do but fret about what would happen if his legal scheming didn't work and Aunt Helena was committed to another town for trial. It would bring her one step closer to being convicted, for one thing. But more than that, we'd lose access to the Investigation—there was no way we could avoid telling Father if things went that far, which meant Miss Judson and I would be whisked away from Eelscombe and all the clues and suspects. Everything would be scattered to the winds—all of us, all the evidence, and all our hopes for saving Aunt Helena and finding out what had happened to Mrs. Bloom.

My fretting took me through the rest of Wednesday evening and past breakfast on Thursday. Miss Judson had found plenty to occupy herself. She'd set up her new easel before the terrace doors and was attempting to capture the rainy view of Eelshead Bay. Right now the piece was looking frightfully Modern: nothing but a great swath of black and grey on the canvas.

Or perhaps it was my mood she was painting.

With a sigh, Miss Judson set down her palette and wiped her hands on one of the hotel towels.* "You're driving me crazy with your pacing. We won't know anything for a while. Find something to do." When I responded with a blank look, inviting suggestions, she produced a horrible one:

"Perhaps Cicely would like to play cards."

"More Family Amusements?" I groaned.

"Exactly. Run along before I lose the light."

The light, if you ask me, had gone out sometime around July and wasn't likely to return before spring, if not the twentieth century—but I was smart enough to keep that thought to myself.

"And take Peony!" My feline sidekick was engaged in testing the new paintbrushes for readiness or perfidy,

* Sir Quentin's order of fancy new clothes and supplies had failed to include aprons or smocks.

and had already stalked one to oblivion beneath the radiator.

With a grumble, I gathered Peony up and headed for the corridor. When we approached the suite Cicely had been sharing with Aunt Helena, I Observed that the door was cracked. Low, tense voices filtered into the hallway. Naturally, we drew closer, hovering just out of sight of the open door—but it was not difficult to identify the quarreling parties.

"I've done my job." That voice, low and thready, must be Cicely. "Now I want to be paid so I can clear out."

"Your job's not finished here, my girl." That leonine growl was undoubtedly Sir Quentin. What was he doing in Cicely's—and Aunt Helena's!—rooms? "Don't you dare run away so soon."

"What am I supposed to do now? The old bird's been locked up!"

I was startled to hear her speak so coarsely about Aunt Helena, but who could blame her?

Sir Quentin said, "You'll put a smile on that pretty face and get to work. Remember where I found you, Miss Highsmith. One word from me and it's back where you came from—or worse."

If Cicely responded to this, I didn't catch it. When Sir Quentin spoke again, his voice was its normal jolly timbre. "There we go! Is that so hard? You're a Ballingall now, my dear, and don't you forget it."

I could not make sense of this odd scrap of conversation—why should Sir Quentin care if Cicely stayed to be Aunt Helena's companion or found a better post where people weren't getting robbed and murdered and arrested by the minute?—but there was no time to hear more. I heard heavy footsteps approach the suite's door, so I squeezed Peony closer and dashed around the corner, toward the lift—and ran straight into Clive, coming the other way.

"Come up to the attic," he said, voice low. "I have to show you something."

I was distracted, glancing back behind me toward the main hallway, wondering what I'd just overheard—and if I ought to have stayed to check on Cicely, as Miss Judson would expect. But Clive's oddly urgent tone and Peony's cross meows finally commanded my attention.

"The attic? What's up there?"

"My workshop. C'mon." He glanced down the hallway as if someone might be listening, and I scurried after him toward the servants' staircase. We scaled several narrow flights, finally arriving at a landing with a freshly painted white door.

"You go up all these stairs every day?" I asked with admiration.

"Aye," he said. "Doesn't make you half breathless, though. Here." He unlocked the door and led me across a bright, airy space of high ceilings and glass skylights. One corner was decorated like a little parlor, with wallpaper, a swagged curtain, and a faded velvet settee. A potted fern perched on a marble stand, and one wall featured a scenic backdrop, painted with stone pillars and misty trees in the distance.

Peony was enchanted. After poking her head hopefully into several corners, she climbed atop the settee and started eating the fern. One long wall served as a gallery of photographic work, and I stepped closer, admiring the framed pictures and cabinet cards, many of exotic locations: islands of sandy beaches, blazing skies, and coconut palms; a forest of thick, dark, unfamiliar trees; an iceberg, desolately adrift in a bleak, black seascape. I put my fingers to a polished frame, the domed glass sealing the image inside. "Did you take all these?"

Clive laughed. "No, silly. Those are my granddad's." One picture was of a massive sailing vessel, her proud crew assembled on deck, *Rainha Estefânia* stenciled on the hull. "He was an able seaman on a Portuguese merchant ship. This was taken in Brazil." The photograph captured a wide, unpaved lane in a village of white buildings with delicate verandas, soft mountains in the background. It looked a bit like Miss Judson's drawings of her own homeland.

"There was a Dutch science expedition on that voyage, with a photographer aboard. Taught Granddad the trade, and when his commission was up, he came back to Brighton and opened a studio."

He stepped to the end of the gallery, where the travel pictures gave way to posed portraits of well-dressed families and wedding couples. The last in the row showed a stately man with curly grey hair and Clive's dark skin posing among his camera equipment and a sign reading BURTON'S FINE PHOTOGRAPHIC PORTRAITURE.

"That's him. One of the first pictures *I* ever took," Clive added proudly. "He died last year. This is everything he left me."

We were both quiet for a long moment. "My mum died when I was seven," I said softly. "She was going to be a doctor. I have her microscope and her books."

Clive shook his head. "Rough," he said. "Is that when you got your Miss Judson?"

"That's when I got Aunt Helena! She lived with us when Mum was sick." I didn't like to remember that time, and not just because of Aunt Helena. "She hired Miss Judson, though, thank goodness."

Clive gave me a sly look. "She can't be all bad, then, I reckon."

"You can have her! I'll trade you some sisters."

With a grin, Clive grabbed my hand and shook it firmly. "Deal! You want Bossy Elise or Bratty Sarah?"

Here Peony offered her opinion on the subject of sisters. "*No*," she said, earning a laugh from Clive.

"What's going to happen to your aunt, then?" Clive's question pulled me back to the moment.

"I don't know." I explained how Inspector Arkwright

wanted to send her away for trial, and Clive scowled sympathetically.

"And your dad could help, but your Miss Judson won't let you send for him?"

"It's really Aunt Helena that won't let us," I said. "But Miss Judson doesn't want the holiday to end, either." Said aloud, however, to an Impartial Observer, that sounded foolish and petulant.

He fiddled with a lens, pondering this. "They probably don't want him to know it hasn't turned out like they hoped."

I turned to him, uncertain, and he elaborated. "Well, you were saying how he wanted them to take you away after that last murder. On a holiday, right? So how's it look for *them* if they land you in another one straightaway?" He shrugged. "Like as not, they just don't want to admit to him it's happened again."

I sat down heavily on the settee, a broken spring jabbing me in the thigh. "Maybe you're right." If Father had charged Miss Judson and Aunt Helena with keeping me away from Unpleasantness, the events of this week *would* appear like an impressive failure. "But it's not their fault!"

Clive politely refrained from noting that the blame for said murder *was* in fact currently resting squarely on Aunt Helena's shoulders. "Well," he said cheerfully, "you just gotta solve the case before your father gets back."

I grinned—then sighed. If only it were that simple.

"Here," Clive said. "This is what I wanted to show you." He took me to the working section of the studio, where his equipment and chemicals were set up, along with several more cameras of every configuration, including a double-lensed one for reproducing three-dimensional stereographic images.

For a moment I was lost in all the fascinating paraphernalia, the beautiful wooden cameras with their clever moving parts, the glass plates coated with silver bromide and hardened gelatin, all waiting to capture light and turn it into pictures through the modern magic of chemistry, technology, and Clive's skill. The trays for developing the plates and printing the pictures looked more like a laboratory than an artist's studio, but Clive's photographs, pinned up to dry, were as beautiful as anything Miss Judson had painted. The haunting picture of the abandoned Pier looked just like you could step right onto the rickety boardwalk and vanish.

"I think someone's been going through my things."

"What?" I jerked my gaze back to him. "Are you serious?" I took in the space with new eyes—the neat bottles of chemicals arranged, labels-out, on the shelf; a specialized rack for storing the glass photographic plates; a crate of paper for printing on. "It doesn't look as though anything's been disturbed."

"I know," Clive said. "That's what made me suspicious. It's like they tidied up after." There was no logic to this assertion, but in my (theoretical) understanding, thirteen-year-old boys were not generally known for their organization. "The pictures I gave you—the plates are missing."

I gaped at him. "The pictures of the crime scene? Someone *stole* them?"

"Well, they're not here. They took the one of you and Peony, too." He gestured to the filed plates. "You're the *only* folks I showed those pictures to. Not even Dad."

It took me a brief, affronted moment to realize Clive wasn't accusing me or Miss Judson of the theft. Which left a darker, more ominous possibility. "There must be something in those pictures that implicates a suspect!" My voice rose, excitement growing.

Clive had his own theories. "At first I reckoned it must be the jewel thief, right, the Brighton Bandit that's been in all the papers all summer, robbing hotels. Who else could slip in and out without leaving a trace?"

"You might have taken a picture of the thief?" I said, heart banging. "Has anything else gone missing from the hotel?"

"Dunno. But there's more. Look here." He took me to a crowded corner of old trunks and covered clothes racks. "This is all their old stuff—the Ballingalls. Remember when I told you I'd seen that opera poster before, the Brighton Nightingale one from the Pier?"

"The one of Miss Ballingall."

"Right. It was up here, hung on the wall."

Clive pushed aside the old clothes, revealing the

bare attic wall, nails holding torn corners of paper in place. On the floor, a few more scraps lay sprinkled about like fallen flower petals. I stooped and picked one up. Splashy colors—red, yellow, blue—and part of a swirly *Br* were all that remained. I swept the bits into my hand, but there weren't enough for the poster to be pieced together into anything recognizable.

We were equally baffled. "Why would a jewel thief tear up an opera poster?" Something else was going on here, and I was missing it. "Those photographs are *evidence*," I said slowly. "Who knew they existed?"

"And what about the poster? Was there something suspicious in *that* picture, too?"

"Just Miss Ballingall," I said, trying to remember. Chest thrumming with tension, I gazed about the attic, willing it to give up its secrets. What did a priceless tiara, a missing telegram, stolen crime scene photographs, and a ripped-up opera poster all add up to?

Aunt Helena's head in the noose, if I couldn't figure it out.

"You'd better make sure the rest of your plates are safe," I said.

For the first time Clive looked alarmed. "Do you think they might come back?"

I couldn't give him an answer. Until we understood exactly what was in the pictures he'd taken—or who swiped them—I didn't know what to think.

And that was a disturbing sensation, indeed.

16

CUI BONO?

Rugeley, Staffordshire: This historic market town is best
known as the home of Dr. William Palmer, "The Rugeley
Poisoner," who in 1855 murdered his friend John Cook
with strychnine, and was suspected of likewise poisoning
at least six members of his own family. Several points of
interest in the crimes are viewable in and around town.

—Hardcastle's Practical Travel Companion

After leaving Clive's studio, I hurried back to the Nile
Rooms to make sure the printed photographs were
safe. Without the original plates, those prints were
our only proof of how Mrs. Bloom had really died.
Perhaps it was time to turn them over to the custody
of Constable Hoskiss.

I didn't quite make it. When Peony and I emerged
from the servants' stair, I nearly stumbled headlong
into Maud Penrose. For a stunned moment I didn't
recognize her.

"Brrrb?" said Peony.

"You can walk," I blurted, stupidly. She was standing in the corridor, one frail hand braced against the wallpaper, the other twitching nervously at her skirts. Peony halted beside me, tail swishing.

"So I keep telling Temby," Miss Penrose said, but she sounded faint and breathless, and despite her protests, looked like she might fall over at any instant. "But she makes me stay in that horrid bath chair because I sometimes have some trouble with my legs."

"What are you doing out here? Where's Copernicus?" She was seldom without the dog, let alone the bath chair. Solitary and pale, she lurched down the corridor like a wraith, ghostly and foreboding (not that I believed in such things, of course).

"Temby's walking him." She didn't answer my first question. "Why are you looking at me like that?"

I had not seen much of the Penroses since Aunt Helena's arrest, and now my doubts about Mr. Penrose's behavior the other night came trickling back—how intent he was on keeping Maud from the police, how he'd kept pressing the matter of the robbery and murder being connected. About Poor Maudie's strange symptoms, the hovering nurse with her "tincture," and Maud's desperation to be free of their attentions.

"What kind of trouble with your legs?" I couldn't help myself. The questions just tumbled out. "Weakness?" Maud nodded. "Numbness and tingling?" (The very same feelings now crawling up my spine. I tried to tell myself I was Being Fanciful and Getting Carried Away, but it didn't help.)

"Yes," she said slowly. "Why? What is it?"

I didn't wish to alarm her unduly—or without any way to test my supposition—but she was watching me, sea-green eyes so intent they seemed to look right into my bones.*

"You were asking my father about my wallpaper—I heard him talking." She took a stumbling step toward me and caught my shoulders with surprising strength. She weighed scarcely more than Peony. "Do you know what's wrong with me?"

"No." I shook my head firmly, then took a breath and forged onward. "But you have the symptoms of chronic arsenic poisoning."

Maud stared at me, like she hadn't quite heard. "How could I?" But she wasn't really asking me. She had a hand to her forehead, searching her memory. "Confusion?" she asked, and this time I nodded. "Memory lapses? But arsenic makes you *sick*," she insisted.

"In large doses—acute poisoning. Chronic exposure is more insidious." I was not sure where the word *insidious* popped into my head from, but it was appropriate. Arsenic gradually affected every organ, quietly

* which would be a scientific feat, indeed, Dear Reader—think of the medical implications of such a power!

destroying the skin, the hair . . . the nerves and the brain.

"I think I should like to sit down," Maud said. She leaned on me, and I helped her back toward her room—across the hall from Cicely and Aunt Helena's, I noticed vaguely. She had the key out, and steadied herself long enough to unlock the door. "I'm all right now," she said, taking a few halting steps toward a bench.

Maud's room was done up, improbably, in a scene from the American West—the walls hung with woven blankets, a steer's skull above the door, rug of some indeterminate fur by the hearth, painted scenes around the room of red-and-orange hillsides beneath a faded yellow sky. Delicate, refined Maud Penrose, in her lavender and lace, could not have looked more incongruous.

The bench she sank onto was made from discarded cart wheels. "Could I trouble you for some water? There's a carafe on the dressing table." Peony sprang into Maud's lap, heedless of her delicate dress, to administer a Therapeutic Massage to her troubled legs. Maud stroked Peony's sleek fur with absent fingers, and Peony, focused on her work, issued a low, rumbly purr.

The dressing table was covered in tooled leather, with silver charms dangling from the drawer pulls. But what caught my eye was Miss Penrose's jewelry box, sitting open with a strand of pearls pulled half out, as though she'd been rummaging desperately through its contents when she abruptly decided to flee her rooms on foot.

"Am I going to die?"

Her question made me spin round. "I–" What could I possibly say?

"My mother died," she said simply. "She had these very same symptoms. She was sick for a year."

My mind was whirring, and I could hardly sort it all out. First the curious argument between Sir Quentin and Cicely, then Clive's stolen crime scene photographs. And now Maud Penrose asking me if she was going to die.

She was watching me with those wide, alarming eyes, so I pulled my attention back to her. "What happened?" I asked.

"She fell off a boat," Maud said. "Father and Temby had taken her yachting, for some air. But she was so weak by then–she fell constantly." She put a hand to her mouth, realizing something. "When she died, Temby moved me into her rooms."

I felt like I needed to sit, too. "Green wallpaper?" I asked faintly. Arsenic dyes weren't used as much anymore–I mean, they've known it's toxic *forever*–and surely old wallpaper would eventually stop giving off fumes. But that wasn't what I was really worried about. *Insidious.*

Nor, it seemed, was Maud. "Temby got an insurance settlement when Mother died. It was only fifteen hundred pounds, but . . ." She turned her stricken face to me. "I inherited all my mother's fortune. I'm *very* rich."

I found a place to sit and handed Maud the water. She fell silent, as if nervous about the unintended confidences she'd shared. I stared helplessly at Peony, until she found her voice once more. "Father thought he would inherit everything. But it was in some sort of trust, or entailment. It came down from Mother's family, so now it's mine."

I met her eyes and said softly, "Unless you die."

She gazed back at me, huge eyes very clear, and nodded.

Poor Maudie looked terrified—and it was all my fault. Miss Judson and Aunt Helena were right: a seaside holiday was no place for talk like this. I took a deep breath and assumed Miss Judson's role (if I *had* to be Somebody Else, there was no better choice). "We have no evidence that anything untoward is happening. You could have any number of illnesses—" *Not exactly reassuring, Myrtle.* "We can't assume your father is a murderer."

The word didn't shock her. "But you don't know that he's *not*," she said. "You don't know him. Or Temby."

I went even deeper into my Miss Judson impression. I caught her free hand, squeezing firmly. "But you do. Can you see them murdering anyone? Your mother? Or you?"

Maud wouldn't answer that. I searched for some way to distract her. My glance landed on her open jewelry box, and I rose to tidy it up. "What were you doing out in the hallway?" I asked.

"Oh." Here she looked guilty, and put fingers to her throat. "My cameo is missing," she said. "And the coral beads. I thought perhaps Temby had . . . borrowed them. So when she took Nicky out, I meant to look for them."

Now I stared at her, an even wilder and more improbable theory registering. "You think Nurse Temby is a jewel thief?"

❧

After that, I broke all Rules of Feminine Decorum and fairly sprinted out of Poor Maudie's suite and down the hall to the Nile Rooms, where I banged like mad on the door. Peony reached her paws up my skirts with an urgent "Mrrow!"

The door flew open before we were done knocking, revealing Miss Judson, looking unusually animated, her color high. She had changed from her painting clothes, but her hair was damp, with curling tendrils about her forehead she hadn't tucked back in yet. (It was quite fetching—yet another thing Father should be here to see.)

We regarded each other scarcely a moment, and then said in the same breath, "I have something to tell you!"

Miss Judson stepped back half a pace, half a smile on her lips. "You go first."

I squeezed inside the room and instantly set about looking for the photographs. I could talk and search at the same time. Peony took the low places: under the tea table, beneath the hippopotamus, behind the fender. "I might have—accidentally—convinced Maud Penrose that her father and Nurse Temby are plotting to kill her."

There was no response from Miss Judson. I looked up, now searching her face. She did not seem nearly as shocked as I'd expected. Instead she said, "What are you looking for?"

"Clive's pictures." They were not among our paltry collection of case notes, so I yanked out Mrs. Bloom's bag and dug through the knitting. "Why aren't you *surprised*?" Why wasn't she scolding me for planting ideas in that poor woman's head?

She was slow to reply, and careful. "I have been thinking something seems . . . odd, about that group."

I abandoned Mrs. Bloom's bag to gape at Miss Judson. "Why didn't you say something? Never mind." That would lead to a lecture about Not Getting Involved and Enjoying Our Holiday, and we hadn't time for that right now. Rushing over the specifics, I summarized my encounter with Miss Penrose: her mother's death, the insurance settlement, the symptoms of arsenic poisoning, how she'd attempted (and failed) to escape their clutches by coming to Fairhaven alone.

"Escape their clutches?"

I ignored that, concluding with: "She thinks Nurse Temby stole the tiara!"

This, at last, gave Miss Judson pause. Her mouth set as she worked backward through this supposition, reviewing the events of the night of the robbery—how Nurse Temby and Maud had made such a fuss of leaving early, putting themselves above suspicion this whole time. "And murdered Mrs. Bloom?"

"She didn't say."

"But that's what her father was getting at the other night, wasn't it?"

I let out all my breath, relieved that I wasn't leaping to conclusions. Or nonsensical ones, at least. Miss Judson had clearly been pondering all of the details of the case, as well. It had never left her thoughts, even when she'd pretended to be distracted by Holiday Amusements. For a rash moment I wanted to fling my arms around her, reassured that she was still herself—still *My* Miss Judson.

"They *could* have done it," I said slowly. "Everyone on the train had opportunity. Miss Penrose's fortune provided their motive, and Nurse Temby is strong enough to strangle someone." I pictured her hauling Maud about in the bath chair, or keeping control of the tornadic mop that was Copernicus, and could all too easily imagine her—small as she was—overpowering another woman. Or three. She had the means. "Or stab her."

After a thoughtful moment, Miss Judson said, "It's possible that Nurse Temby has done everything—if indeed she *has* done anything—on her own. All of the—I hesitate to say *evidence*—points to her, and her alone. Perhaps Mr. Penrose also suspects her."

That ought to have been reassuring, but I couldn't find the feeling. Like the photographs.

"This insurance settlement," mused Miss Judson, "it was awfully modest, wasn't it? Perhaps the late Mrs. Penrose's 'accident' was a trial run."

"Miss! That's dreadful!"

"We *are* talking about murder," she reminded me. "As we were saying: Nurse Temby and Mr. Penrose both share a motive."

"For killing Maud. Not for Mrs. Bloom!"

"Yes, but where there's an insurance settlement, there's an insurance *Investigator.*"

"They paid out the settlement, though," I countered. "The insurance company must not have suspected foul play."

"But Miss Penrose did. Or does. Perhaps the Conspiring Parties worried that Miss Penrose might take her concerns to Mrs. Bloom, before they could carry out the rest of their plan."

"Wait—Mr. Penrose and Mrs. Bloom only just met on the train," I said, recalling that night in the Smoking Carriage. "He didn't know who she was."

"Because murderers would obviously *never* lie."

Her theory was dizzying—but made too much sense to dismiss as coincidence. I set it aside for a moment, to simmer into something thick and substantial, while I turned my attentions to the Other Urgent Matter.

"*Where* are Clive's pictures? Did you hide them? Tell me they're safe."

"Of course I didn't, and of course they are. Why, what's the matter? Did he happen to capture Nurse Temby stealing the scissors, too?"

Breathlessly, I stood up from the carpetbag. "The plates are missing. Stolen. Someone came into his studio and took them—or destroyed them—and also tore up— Wait. What do you mean, *too?*"

"Curious. And he's certain he didn't misplace them?" Clearly Miss Judson was still laboring under the misapprehension that tidiness was a sure defense against misfortune. "Without the plates, he can't print more copies?"

"Exactly. What did you mean, *too?*"

"Well, we'd best secure them, then." She was obviously stalling for Dramatic Effect. She beckoned me toward the terrace doors, where her easel stood. "Which brings me to what *I* wanted to show *you*. *Voilà!*"

I finally realized what she'd been painting.

"I thought your father might like a souvenir. Something besides Aunt Helena's arrest warrant."

It *was* a picture of me—or it would be, eventually (she'd only just started): the scene Clive had captured of me and Peony posed in front of the *Empress Express.*

"But *look!*"

I peered closer, taking in the singular detail Miss Judson had picked out from the photograph and sketched in—very lightly—on the canvas. Now I could see exactly why someone had stolen the photographic plates from Clive's workshop. And *who.* Because he hadn't just caught my jaunty pose, or the gleaming glory of Sir Quentin's new train. In the background, Clive had captured a figure mounting one of the distant passenger cars, well away from the crowd on the platform. She must have thought everyone's attention was elsewhere. It was Temperance Ballingall in her floppy plaid cape, hanging firmly on to the stair rails with both hands.

Miss Ballingall could use her right arm, after all.

"I saw Maud Penrose walking, too," I said. "We assumed she was paralyzed because we only ever saw her in the bath chair. Just like we assumed Miss Ballingall's arm was lame."

"There's one significant difference, though," Miss Judson pointed out. "Miss Penrose didn't try to hide the truth."

I looked at the canvas and the picture clipped beside it with dismay. "*Everyone's* a suspect. Mr. Coogan, The

Man Temperance Saw, Aunt Helena . . . and now Mr. Penrose, Nurse Temby, and Miss Ballingall?" My voice was thin and shrill by the end of that. "They can't have *all* done it!"

"That defies imagination," Miss Judson agreed. "Let's think through this sensibly, starting with the missing photographs."

She plucked the canvas from the easel, rotating it to reveal its back side—whereupon was scribed, in her neat schoolteacher hand, a list of the names I'd just rattled off, to which she now added PENROSE/NURSE T. and MISS B'GALL. I was too distracted to be incensed that she'd continued the Investigation without me. I just gritted my teeth and dived right in with her.

"The *stolen* photographs," I said.

"Missing. This could be an explanation—*if* Miss Ballingall had any reason to suspect this image of her existed. How could she?"

"Sir Quentin was right here yesterday morning. He could have told her about it." Although the pictures of Mrs. Bloom's body had been tucked away, this particular photograph had been on display, prominently perched upon our mantelpiece.

Miss Judson looked doubtful. "Possible," she said. "Assuming that Miss Ballingall took the photographs, we must assume she did so to conceal the fact that her arm is not as weak as it seems."

"So she *could* stab someone. Or strangle her."

Her charcoal paused in midair. "It's quite a leap to go from *could stab* to *did stab*. What's her motive?"

"She's protecting her father—Aunt Helena has it all backward. Sir Quentin has plenty of motive for killing Mrs. Bloom over the insurance on the tiara. Or, skip the middleman. Woman. Sir Quentin swiped the crime scene pictures himself." As my brain caught up with my mouth, I stopped. "Do you think Clive's in danger?"

"No more than the rest of us," she said, back to her crisp self. "And somewhat less, at the moment, than Miss Penrose."

"We should present our findings to Mr. Blakeney and Constable Hoskiss before something happens." Something *worse*, I meant, but didn't say it out loud.

"Mr. Blakeney first. You do that," she decided. "I shall spend the afternoon taking tea with Miss Maud Penrose, textile heiress, and not letting her out of my sight. She seems like *exactly* the sort of association I should cultivate, don't you think?" She sounded so much like Aunt Helena that I managed a faint laugh.

"Find some evidence against Nurse Temby while you're at it," I suggested.

17
SALVAGE OPERATIONS

England's southern coast was once a haven for smugglers, and artifacts of these lawless days still wash ashore, waiting to be discovered.

—Hardcastle's Practical Travel Companion

I met Mr. Blakeney in his makeshift office at Mrs. Pettigrew's shop, which was even more crowded than usual, as he'd taken over half the common room with files, law books, and cartons stamped with the Albion Casualty mountain peak. I felt a flutter of excitement. Mrs. Bloom's own case files? Constable Hoskiss had managed the impossible! We were fortunate to live in an age when the postal service and railways were so swift and efficient.

"Aha, Stephen! Just in time." Mr. Blakeney rose and shifted aside a heap of papers on a bench, uncovering a plate with his half-eaten lunch on it. I squeezed in, finding room at my feet for Mrs. Bloom's bag, wherein were safely stored Clive's pictures, which were even more precious now.

"Do you really think there's anything in there that might help?" It seemed an overwhelming prospect, but also an oddly comforting one. Once again, I felt surrounded by Mrs. Bloom's steady, guiding presence. I reached into my pocket for her ledger book. "I have some more of her things. Can you read this?"

"Shorthand, eh?" He took the book from my hands and flipped through a few pages. "Nothing I recognize, I'm afraid. I learnt Pitman as a wee clerkling. Not sure what this is."

I gave a heavy sigh. That ledger book got more hopeless every time I looked at it. I showed Mr. Blakeney the other contents of Mrs. Bloom's bag, including Clive's photographs and the insurance policy. He now knew everything we did. Or thought we did.

"We should turn this over to the police, shouldn't we?"

"I'd say it belongs right here with the rest of it," Mr. Blakeney said firmly, tucking the carpetbag in among the boxes. "Mrs. Pettigrew will take good care of it."

Reassured, I yanked the top off a carton. Maybe I'd get lucky and trip over Mrs. Bloom's shorthand manual. As we looked through the files, Mrs. Pettigrew hovered about, bringing Mr. Blakeney fresh refills of tea before he'd had a chance to finish his first cup, a biscuit for me, wiping down already clean tables. Her sleeves were rolled up, her scars a mottled map of the injuries from the explosion, as if she'd been reaching into the boiler—or for her little brother—when it went up.

I nudged Mr. Blakeney, but he just blinked at me blankly.

Finally, I said to her, "Would you like a go?"

She pretended to hesitate, but dried her hands on her towel and tossed it over her shoulder before slipping onto the bench opposite. Mrs. Pettigrew turned out to be just as efficient a legal clerk as she was a postmistress, baker, and shopkeeper. In minutes, she had worked through Mrs. Bloom's files, plucking out anything that might be pertinent, and neatly sorted them into alphabetical stacks. Among O–Q, I spotted the name *Penrose*.

Inside were a brief policy for a Mrs. Frances Penrose, stamped PAID, and a check for £1,500 made out to Eliza Temby. Mrs. Bloom hadn't added any incriminating notations, not even little shorthand squiggles that, once deciphered, might say, "Probably poisoned with arsenic then thrown overboard. No proof." I put it aside, just in case.

As Mrs. Pettigrew's stacks got taller, her expression grew grimmer. "Ain't right what happened," she muttered. "Someone killing Mrs. B.? Ain't right at all."

I knew exactly how she felt. "Constable Hoskiss told us she inspired him to become a policeman," I said. "She must have been brave."

"She were, at that." Mrs. Pettigrew rolled down her sleeves, suddenly self-conscious. "She went against her own company, you know—testified in court at the trial, made sure the owners of the steamship line paid out for all our injuries."

Mr. Blakeney, watching with admiration, gave a quiet whistle. "Quite a woman," he said. "A wrongful death suit? That's not for lightweights."

"That's not the half of it," Mrs. Pettigrew said. "Even afterward, she never forgot us." Here she got up and disappeared into the private back area of the shop, returning with a cigar box stuffed to the gills with cards and letters.

"All from Mrs. Bloom," she said proudly, fanning them out so I could see the Manchester postmark and Mrs. Bloom's untidy scrawl addressing them to *Molly Dear*. "Sent me a shilling, she did, every birthday and Christmas. Me mum, too. For Davey, you know." She gave a wistful sigh. "The anniversary's coming up. Fifteen year. Hard to believe. We knew she'd come. She came every year."

"We'll find out who killed her," I vowed. Mrs. Pettigrew looked dogged—but unconvinced. We dug through the files in silence after that.

At the bottom of my carton from Albion Casualty was another bundle of letters. "Oh, here's more." I lifted them out gingerly, tracing the illegible handwriting addressed to someone else that Mrs. Bloom had not forgotten, even after their case was resolved.

Mrs. Pettigrew leaned in. "Not sent?" she asked. "Nay—sent *back*," she said wonderingly. Then, "Oh."

"What?" Mr. Blakeney and I spoke together, breathless.

"They're to *his* gell." There was a note of distaste in her voice. "The steamship owner's daughter. She were in the wreck too, you know. Why'd she want to help *her*, then?" She dropped them back into the box like they'd burned her anew.

"Why were they returned?" Mr. Blakeney said. "Did they move around a lot?"

"In hiding, most like." Mrs. Pettigrew had crossed her arms over her chest, like she was done with the lot of us. "After what they did, they couldn't show their faces among decent folk again."

I fished the letters out again, making out the addressee, Miss Dorothea Lowell, among all the RETURN TO SENDER and DELIVERY DENIED stamps all over them. "No," I said slowly. "She sent these back. She got them, but she didn't want to hear from Mrs. Bloom."

The letters were all sealed, but after a quick

consulting glance to Mr. Blakeney, I broke the seal on one and unfolded the note.

> *6 May 1886*
> *My Dear Miss Lowell,*
> *I hope this finds you well, and that your injuries no longer trouble you so much. You are always in my thoughts, you and your father both. I like to picture you traveling together on your grand adventures. I have heard you've been overseas—America! How exciting! You're a brave girl to make the journey, and I admire how you've made your way, despite everything that's happened.*
> *If ever you need a friend, I remain,*
> *Very Truly Yours,*
> *Izzy Bloom*

"Izzy!" My voice caught. No one would ever call her that again. "But why wouldn't Dorothea accept them?"

Mr. Blakeney said, "Mrs. Bloom *did* testify against her father in court."

"But still," I argued, "Mrs. Bloom cared about her. It's not fair." I sniffed back the tears before they escaped and mortified me in front of Mr. Blakeney. Face tense, I carefully returned the letters to the carton.

Mrs. Pettigrew, refusing to waste any sympathy on the ungrateful Dorothea Lowell, was instead leafing through Mrs. Bloom's journal. "You know," she said, tapping a page, "you might bring this to Daniel. He does shorthand for his reports. He might be able to read this."

I looked at her, a spike of hope rising through the unfairness. "That's a good idea," I said. "Is he still on duty?"

She grinned. "Hardly leaves the station, that lad. Here—I'll pack some pie."

∾

A few minutes later, laden down with a tin pail stuffed with meat pie and scones, I presented myself at the Eelscombe Constabulary. Daylight was fading, but I reasoned there were few safer places than a police station. Constable Hoskiss seemed to be alone, and he jumped up when I burst in, gangly knees banging into the edge of his desk.

"Your sister sent tea." I set the pail on his desk. "And she got Mrs. Bloom's files."

"You reckon they'll help?"

"I hope so." I wrestled the ledger book from my pocket. "She also thought maybe you could decipher this. It's Mrs. Bloom's. She had it the night of the robbery—it might tell us something about what she saw that night. Who—she might have met with." Who might have been lying in wait for her in the baggage carriage.

I Observed that Constable Hoskiss was exercising Exceptional Forbearance by not inquiring where I had come by such an extraordinary piece of evidence, or why it had taken so long to turn it over to the police. With studious concentration, he opened the book upon his desk and bent over it, slowly turning pages and mouthing silent words.

Finally, he looked up. "Nay. It's Greek to me," he said, with his apologetic smile. "But I reckon your aunt could manage it."

For a moment I was certain I hadn't heard him properly. "Aunt Helena?" I said, as if I might have *another* shorthand-reading aunt on hand to choose from instead. "Why would you think that?" What I really meant was, whatever had given him the impression that Aunt Helena would be inclined to help me at all, with anything, but I confined my question to the shorthand.

"She's been makin' all sort of notes in it, hasn't she? Or very like. If anyone hereabout knows, it'll be Miss Hardcastle. Let's ask."

I'd really only wanted to see the constable. But Miss Judson would undoubtedly expect a report on how Aunt Helena fared, and if Aunt Helena *could* be any use, I supposed I had to find out.

But first I had another question. "Have you had any luck identifying The Man Temperance Ballingall Saw?" I didn't see the sketch posted on the notice board, where anyone wandering into the station to report on the latest Malfeasance of Ducks might recognize him.

"Er, well." The constable scratched his head. "Still looking into that one. Strange, though . . ."

I pounced. "Strange? How?"

"Oh, no reason. Let's see your auntie, then." I had a feeling there was more he could tell me, but the police *were* entitled to pursue leads without sharing their findings with the public—particularly twelve-year-old members of the public—so I bit back my sigh, nodded professionally, and followed him to the cells.

He took me back to the room where they'd installed Aunt Helena. I didn't give her a chance to criticize my appearance—either my appearing *or* how I appeared—but plunked myself down at the table. It was stained with centuries' of constables' teas and fish, and the ceiling was blotchy with damp. The glow from the borrowed lamp didn't seem quite so cozy now. Deep, sinister shadows filled every corner. Aunt Helena was seated on the bench, gazing into their depths.

"Helena Myrtle, I trust you have an excellent reason for barging in here like a herd of elephants."

Dear Reader, it was *maybe* one elephant. A small one.

"Has Sir Quentin been in to see you yet?" I asked, but Aunt Helena looked away with (ladylike) disdain.

"I'm sure he's far too busy to bother with my little inconveniences."

"Aren't your little inconveniences his *business*?" I retorted. "He's supposed to be catering to our every holiday need." Of course, as long as Inspector Arkwright wasted time Investigating Aunt Helena, Sir Quentin was free to swan about his new little kingdom, playing the benevolent emperor. There was nobody left to stand in his way.

I needed Aunt Helena's help, and had no idea how to go about getting it. She seemed weary, lips pinched more than usual, and the timetable of lines on her face had increased overnight. Under my scrutiny, a clawed hand came up and patted her silvery hair.

People were generally too polite to remark upon it, but I took after Aunt Helena somewhat. She didn't look like Father—her nephew—much at all, with her dark eyes and sour expression. I didn't fancy the notion that I resembled her in more than name and appearance. Was it possible that Aunt Helena had once (centuries and centuries ago) been Irrepressible? What had happened to her?

Maybe she'd come on this holiday to be someone else, too, and it had all gone horribly wrong.

I didn't—I *couldn't* feel sorry for her. I wouldn't.

"Don't bite your lip, Helena Myrtle. It's not refined."

I took a deep breath. There were bound to be Uncooperative Witnesses in my Investigatory Career—and there was no way they could get less cooperative than Aunt Helena. This might be my only opportunity to question her freely about the crime. Like it or not, she *was* still a suspect. She had it all: mens rea, motive, means, and opportunity.

And I couldn't forget that the last time I'd seen Mrs. Bloom, Aunt Helena was threatening her with the murder weapon. That's what I really needed her to explain. Criminal Justice aside, I *had* to know what had happened between Mrs. Bloom and Aunt Helena after I left them that night in the train car.

"Don't sigh, Helena Myrtle."

Really, it was a wonder things hadn't gone the other way, and I wasn't sitting here cooking up a defense for Mrs. Bloom, instead.

"You didn't like Mrs. Bloom, did you?" I began.

"No, I did not. I thought she was an interfering busybody, always meddling in other people's affairs."

"What do you mean, *always*? You lied to Inspector Arkwright—you *had* met her before, hadn't you?"

Her gaze was cold. "Hardly. But I had a letter from her once, trying to warn me off associating with the Ballingalls. I told you, that woman had it in for them. They never should have let her aboard."

Much as I hated to, I had to agree with that. "What did you say to her that night on the train? I *saw* you, with the scissors."

"Fiddle-faddle. I merely suggested that she stop interfering in Sir Quentin's business, and that if she knew what was good for her, she'd leave my niece and family alone, too."

I wanted to put my head down on the table. *If she knew what was good for her?* Aunt Helena made a terrible witness on her own behalf. She'd only have to open her mouth, and the jurors would trip over one another to cart her to the gallows.

"So you had to stop her? You killed her?" How would I ever explain this to Father? I could picture his reaction now—somehow, this would be all my fault. She really was Father's only family, and I was about to make sure she was hanged for murder.

"Oh, for heaven's sakes, child. I don't like a great many people. But I have never disliked someone enough to go to the effort of *killing* them. What do you take me for?"

I didn't answer that. The Right to Silence of a criminal defendant was well established; she couldn't make me respond. Recognizing that my interrogation had somewhat jumped the rails, I changed the subject.

Gesturing toward the blackboard, I said, "You know shorthand, is that right?" If that came out a bit like a cross-examination, I couldn't help it.

"Of course," she said stiffly. "Unlike Some People, I learned something useful in school. Why?" A spark of interest had lit her eyes, making me feel all unsettled again.

I passed the ledger to her. Since it had Mrs. Bloom's name on it, Aunt Helena could hardly miss its significance. "Can you read this? We can't find anyone to decipher it."

She opened it, gesturing to me. "Bring the lamp closer, girl."

I did as she bade, shifting the heavy thing onto the table, nearly toppling its glass globe. But Aunt Helena was absorbed in the ledger and didn't scold me. Unlike the others, she didn't merely flip through the pages, but studied them—*read* them. Hope and fear clenched my chest, and I squeezed my fingers together while I waited, half mad with anticipation. Could I trust Aunt Helena to tell me the truth about what Mrs. Bloom had written?

I didn't have any choice.

"Are you going to sit there sulking all night, or are you going to let me do this in peace?"

Exceptional Forbearance. I stood up to go—but could not resist one final plea.

"You know it looks bad, right? If we can't find exculpatory evidence to clear you—and fast—Inspector Arkwright *will* commit you to Lewes for trial."

For the first time, I saw a ghost of concern darken Aunt Helena's face, but she flicked it away like a bothersome gnat.

"*Please* let me wire Father." I gripped my fingers together so I didn't do something lunatic like grab her hands. "He can help you."

"Absolutely not."

I glared back at her. "Is it because you don't want

to bother him—or because you don't want him to know you're guilty?"

"That is *enough*! I have nothing more to say on this matter."

And at that moment, the door creaked open, and another voice put in, "I quite agree." Inspector Arkwright's shadow was larger than he was, filling up the threshold. "You, out." He was pointing his level finger at me. Obviously.

I cast one last look at Aunt Helena, but she'd turned away from me, sullenly staring into the corner. "What's the use? She doesn't want my help." I pushed past him out of the room, but paused. "Sir Quentin's not coming to save you. He's too busy saving *himself*."

Inspector Arkwright took his time locking up Aunt Helena's door. I could tell he was thinking about something, and I was determined to ferret it out of him. But how? He was even less cooperative than Aunt Helena.

I needn't have worried. It seemed the man took an especial glee in tormenting my family. He was whistling, a glint in his dark eye.

"What is it?" I demanded. "If you have evidence against Aunt Helena, you have to disclose it."

The whistling stopped. "Parliament has yet to conceive of a statute requiring the Railway Police to tell *anything* to meddlesome little girls."

I was determined not to let him beat me. "Have you Investigated the other suspects? The Man Temperance

Saw? Or Mr. Coogan? Or Sir Quentin? My aunt's not the only person with motive, means, and opportunity, you know."

"We looked into Coogan, and there's nothing to him. His alibi checks out. He was helping repair the broken electrical system in the Lounge Carriage." There was a strange note in his voice. It sounded like disappointment.

"Oh. You're sure?"

"Six men can vouch for him, including Driver Urquhart. Believe me, I liked him as a suspect too. Always been a troublemaker. But his alibi's good for the time of the murder."

I sighed. If he hadn't killed Mrs. Bloom, all Mr. Coogan's other actions looked much less suspicious. "The man in the sketch?" Somehow, I wasn't hopeful.

"The constable's looking into that. Keeps him out of my hair, at least."

It seemed to me that Inspector Arkwright was in the *constable's* hair—but I was smart enough to keep my mouth shut about it.

"And Sir Quentin?"

"What about him?" He was losing interest in me.

"He has a motive worth five thousand pounds, he quarreled with the victim, she threatened to deny the insurance policy on the tiara, and he's certainly strong enough to strangle someone. He's also engineered matters to keep the news out of the papers, he prevented

Mrs. Bloom from telegraphing her company about the robbery, and he's framed my aunt for murder!"

Inspector Arkwright took in this speech with a cold silence that made me fidget. At last he said, "How do you know about the strangulation? Did your aunt say something? Who told you?"

"No one told me. I found the body, remember?"

"And?" The Inspector's voice was loaded with skepticism.

"And there were Tardieu spots."

He looked nonplussed. "Tar—"

"*Tardieu spots.*"* I gestured toward my own face. "Hemorrhaging? The little blood vessels in the face burst when pressure cuts off the circulation. They're bluish, because of the lack of oxygen."

The Inspector was staring now. "Why do you know this?" Not *how*, I noticed.

"I *read*. And she had finger-marks on her neck. That's hard to get any other way."

He rubbed at his moustache. "A woman could do this?"

I shrugged. "It takes a long time, though.† You have to be strong."

"Easier if your victim's already incapacitated with a stab wound."

---

* for the late Dr. Auguste Ambroise Tardieu, who first described them

† about three (horrible) minutes, give or take

I was oddly impressed. "That's true. Or maybe you get impatient, and *then* stab her, to finish the job." I sighed again. "Either way, she's still dead."

He gave me a familiar look. "Anybody ever tell you you're morbid?"

I almost smiled. "Frequently."

Inspector Arkwright leaned against the opposite wall. The corridor was so tight, our boots were practically toe-to-toe. His moustache looked even more weasely than usual, the way he was watching me, eyes narrow.

"If there's one thing I hate," he said slowly, "it's—"

"Morbid little girls who interfere with your Investigation?"

He ignored this. "Being played. I don't like it."

"I'm not! I told you, I found her body. Look at Miss Judson's sketches again if you don't believe me." Figuring I could hardly get in any deeper, I forged ahead. "How much is Sir Quentin paying you to sweep this whole thing under the rug?"

"Now get this straight," he growled, pointing a finger straight at me. "*Nobody* accuses the Eastern Coastal Railway Police of corruption. We cannot be bought! And anyone who thinks we can has another think coming."

He turned on his heel and clipped out of the hallway, with me following behind. As we emerged into the main room, Constable Hoskiss was rising from his desk.

"Sir," he said, "that information you were waiting for's just come in." He handed Inspector Arkwright a slip of paper—a telegram, freshly delivered by his sister, no doubt.

The Inspector fairly snatched it from his hand. As he read, his unpleasant smile grew, dark eyes glittering. "Feast your eyes on this, missy." He handed me the slip, wherein were noted dates and locations: Eastbourne, Brighton, Southsea, along with the names of various hotels. I recognized them as the dates of the earlier seaside jewel thefts.

"What is it?" I said warily.

"Your aunt's travel schedule," he said. "Seems every time some jewelry goes missing hereabouts, a Miss *Helena* Hardcastle is right there."

For a moment I just stared at him, not comprehending. "But that's ridiculous," I said. "Why would Aunt Helena want to steal anything?" Murder, yes—that I could believe. Anyone could kill, if pressed. But Aunt Helena a *jewel thief*? That defied logic *and* imagination.

"The way I figure it," Inspector Arkwright said, "your dear old auntie wanted to liven up her dull existence by playing at a little petty crime. It seems to run in the family." This said with a Significant Look. "Mrs. Bloom was on to her, and when their paths crossed on the *Empress Express*, Miss Hardcastle knew she was out of time. It was either her or Bloom."

I wished I'd brought Miss Judson. That theory of the crime was so nonsensical I couldn't find the words to refute it. Except he had evidence. I stared at the telegram, as if it could explain everything.

"Face it, Little Miss Hardcastle," he said. "We've got the old woman dead to rights. She's going down for murder."

⁓

I found myself back outside in the chill evening air, considering the dizzying array of suspects that now confronted us. Each new clue we uncovered pointed to somebody different: Aunt Helena, Sir Quentin, Nurse Temby, Aunt Helena again. We'd managed to eliminate Mr. Coogan, at least. But how could we figure out the real culprit? There must be *proof.* I just had to find it.

More time had passed than I'd realized, and it was getting darker, lights blinking on in cottages up and down the hillsides. Even the ducks had gone home to roost. Wearily, I wandered down the hill, taking in the twilit village. In the half-light, the white cottages looked even more like a storybook, and it was easy to picture the smugglers from a century ago, disappearing among the jumbled houses with their barrels of French brandy and crates of lace and silk. Just like the murderer had. He was at large, even now. If he hadn't dropped off the train in the middle of the night, he might still be lurking about Eelscombe. Unless it was Aunt Helena, of course, locked up at Inspector Arkwright's pleasure. Or Sir Quentin, who didn't exactly seem the *lurking* sort.

I took a jagged turn in the road, suddenly suspicious of every looming shadow. A trellis of dead vines, a stack of empty fish barrels—any of those could hide Mrs. Bloom's killer. I hastened onward, clutching the tin pail to my chest and not heeding where I put my feet. A shadow rose abruptly from the gloom, and I shied away—slipping on the wet cobbles and turning my ankle.

Hands grabbed my shoulders. "Easy, there, missy."

I looked up—straight into the face of the man from Miss Ballingall's sketch.

18
LOCAL CURIOSITIES

The English countryside abounds with colorful local folk-lore and history. Many villages offer guidebooks or tours to the same, but some can only be found by chance.

—Hardcastle's Practical Travel Companion

I let out a shriek and struck out with the pail.

My attacker uttered a cry of surprise, like he'd caught a wild animal who'd turned on him. He sprang back, releasing me, and I struck again. The flimsy bucket hit oilcloth, and the man raised his arms to protect his face—although I could really only reach his chest. I finally realized he wasn't trying to kill me, and I stumbled backward, clutching the pail and panting. My ankle felt wobbly, and I sat down abruptly on a low stone wall, wanting to cry.

"Who are you?" I said, voice as wobbly as my ankle.

"McGuffin," he grunted. "Samuel." I recognized him now, at last. He was the old man we'd seen several times on the beach.

"What do you want?"

Mr. McGuffin looked around. "You ran into me," he pointed out. "Road's dangerous in th' dark."

So I'd noticed.

"Best get back to the 'otel now." He turned toward the village.

"Wait!" I cried. "I need to talk to you!" *What are you doing, Myrtle?*

He wheeled back slowly. "Eh?"

I hugged the pail tighter. "Um, somewhere public?"

Another grunt. Mr. McGuffin jerked his head toward the pie shop and set off at a pace I could scarcely keep up with. He had a long, ambling gait, and looked like he lived in his ancient weatherproof. Maybe he'd never got *his* luggage back either, I thought a little wildly.

I limped off after him, still not entirely trusting my ankle, but managed to catch up just as he headed for the shop next door to Mrs. Pettigrew's, The Revenue.

A public house.

"I can't go in there!" I squeaked.

"Pie shop's closed," he said, and swung open the tavern's door. I hesitated, but did not want to lose my suspect, now that I finally had him.

The door creaked shut behind me, leaving me in gloom. Oil lamps hung from the rafters, glowing through a smoky haze. Half of Eelscombe seemed to have assembled for their suppers—the male half. Fishermen of every age perched on stools and leaned on the bar, all faces turned my way with undisguised—and unfriendly—curiosity. Everyone recognized me as the Little Tourist Girl whose aunt had murdered Their Izzy.

Well, I'd asked for this. I scurried onward and nearly ran into Mr. McGuffin again when he stopped suddenly at the back of the tavern, near a glass display case and a paneled wall covered in framed pictures.

"Sit," he said, dragging out a bench for me. I sank onto it, and Mr. McGuffin followed suit, eyeing me strangely. I realized I was still holding on to the pail for dear life. I unclenched my fingers and set it beside me on the bench, feeling oddly vulnerable without it. "*Urchankliff?*" he asked, and I blinked at him, whereupon he enunciated, more slowly, "Did-you-'urt-your-foot?"

I shook my head. That didn't seem the sort of thing a murderer would say.

"You need sommat to eat? They do a middlin' fish pie 'ere."

"No, Mr. McGuffin—were you aboard the *Empress Express*? The train that came through here the other day?"

He scratched his shaggy head. "Can't say as I was," he said. "'Ardly been outside Eelscombe. Mam took me up to Lewes for a fair somewhen. That were . . ." He squinted. "Eighteen and forty-six."

"Eighteen forty-six," I echoed faintly. "So you weren't anywhere near the train on Saturday night? About two hundred and fifty miles up the coast?"

Mr. McGuffin looked like I'd asked if he'd been on the moon. "'Ow would I get there?" he said, genuinely curious.

"A boat, maybe?"

"Don't go out on the water anymore, along on account of the rheumatism."

"Oh."

"Why d'you ask?" He sat hunched in his coat, just a skinny old man letting a strange little girl pester him with odd questions.

"Someone saw—someone said she saw you there."

"On th' train?"

I kicked my heels against the legs of the bench and studied Mr. McGuffin's lined face and ragged beard. Maybe I'd been mistaken about the resemblance to Miss Judson's sketch. It was night and I'd been startled. They looked alike, but this couldn't possibly be The Man Temperance Saw. No wonder Constable Hoskiss had been surprised when we brought in his picture. I sighed.

"I'm sorry to bother you," I said, and started to slip from the bench.

"Don't you want to check my alibi, like they do in the stories?"

I blinked at the man. "Do—do you want me to?"

He breathed a rumbly sigh. "Nay, that's all right. Just seemed like it might be fun."

Unexpectedly, I grinned—and he grinned right back.

"You know," he said, tapping his gnarled finger thoughtfully on the table. "I were in Lewes somewhen else. In seventy-nine, 'twere. For the trial."

I sat down again. "The trial?"

He drew back slowly, indicating the framed pictures and the glass case. In the gloomy lamplight, I caught the shadowy images: newspaper clippings; a stately drawing of a steamship, copied—I realized—from the portrait in the Ballingall Arms lobby; a faded photograph of the Pier, cloth-wrapped bundles laid across the boardwalk.

"For the *Valkyrie*," he said. "I were one o' the witnesses."

My pulse sped up, and words tumbled out. "Mrs. Bloom was there, too—do you remember her?"

"Oh, surelye." A slow, sleepy smile. "Never forget 'er. Like a Valkyrie 'erself, I reckon, the way she fought for our folk. Real shame what happened to 'er, real shame."

Mr. McGuffin reached out and unlatched the case, lifting out a cold, ragged lump of iron, similar to the one we'd found while beachcombing with Miss Ballingall.

"From 'er bulk'ead." His voice was hushed. "She went down in Eels'ead Bay in October of seventy-eight. Explosion tore the boiler apart when she were docked at the Pier." He shook his head as if still haunted by the memory. "That's all that's left of 'er."

He handed it to me, and I turned it over in my hands. It was weighty and cold, its jagged edge fierce and sharp. I could imagine a piece like this striking poor Davey Hoskiss, flames on the water swallowing up little Molly.

I unhooked one of the photos from the wall. "Is this you?" It showed him dressed in his Sunday best, shaking the hand of a broadly smiling gentleman with side-whiskers. Mr. McGuffin had a shiny medal pinned to his chest.

Mr. McGuffin issued an embarrassed grunt, but fished around in the glass case and unearthed a heavy circle of brass, hung from a striped purple ribbon.

The medal showed the *Valkyrie* again, half submerged by waves. He held it up to the light, and I could make out the words: WRECK OF THE S.S. VALKYRIE. LOWELL STEAMER LINES, 1878. And on the other side: FOR GALLANT SERVICE & BRAVERY AFTER THE DISASTER.

"They give me that, along of I 'appened to pull the ship owner's daughter out o' the wreckage. Lucky little mite. Luckier than most, anyway."

"You saved Miss Lowell?" Who hadn't wanted to hear from Mrs. Bloom. I tilted the frame, trying to get a clearer view of the man awarding him the medal. "He looks familiar," I said. Although my record of identifying people from pictures was at an impressive low lately.

Mr. McGuffin gave his gruff chuckle. "Reckon so," he said. "You been in 'is company all week—stayin' at his big new 'otel."

I blinked, not quite understanding. But the flickering lamplight fell across the smiling man's face, golden and glowing, and now I recognized him. "That's Sir Quentin?"

"Well, dunno about that," he said. "Called 'isself Lowell, in those days. Surprised he come back 'ere again. Makin' up for everything, mebbe?"

Sir Quentin had owned the *Valkyrie*? "But why hasn't anyone said something?" I asked. "Why doesn't everyone in Eelscombe hate *him*?" My aunt only (maybe) killed *one* person Eelscombe loved, and they wanted to burn her at the stake. Sir Quentin had killed seventeen times that many!

A shrug. "Reckon they don't recognize 'im."

"What?" I took a closer look at the photograph. He did look very different now—a good four stone heavier, for one thing, not to mention much balder and jowlier. The man in the photograph was young and lean, with a full head of thick hair, and wearing sober business clothes, not an outrageous ringmaster's costume or safari suit. But you'd think being behind a deadly disaster might make a person fairly memorable, all the same. "Why not?"

"'E never come 'ere after," Mr. McGuffin explained. "I only met 'im at 'ospital in Brighton, visitin' the gell. Then he skipped town afore the trial—turned tail an' run, see, tryin' to escape the law." He tucked the medal and the metal safely back in their case. "Guess the only folk who *would* know 'im were me an' Mrs. Bloom."

∽

By the time I finally made it back to the Ballingall Arms, it was well and truly after dark, and a fierce autumn wind charged in from the sea. I was shivering and numb, but not with cold.

Mr. McGuffin had gallantly walked me back, regaling me with tales of smugglers and pirates in his gruff whisper. He was an excellent storyteller, probably not a murderer, and almost managed to distract me from my wild storm of thoughts. *Only me and Mrs. Bloom* would *know him.* It took me a disconcertingly long time to reconcile the last piece of Mr. McGuffin's account. The "lucky mite" he'd rescued, the unhappy Dorothea Lowell who had sent back Mrs. Bloom's letters unread and unopened—from their descriptions I'd somehow pictured a little girl. But she wasn't, not anymore—and not then, either. She was Temperance Ballingall.

Who'd pointed the finger at Mr. McGuffin, the only person left who could recognize her father.

Abruptly, all our theories and suppositions fell away, leaving only one that made sense and fit everything we'd learned. The killer had to be Sir Quentin. I'd been right from the very beginning—but I'd had the wrong motive. Or only part of the motive. Sir Quentin knew Mrs. Bloom planned to cancel his insurance policy, but he must *also* have feared she would expose him to the townspeople of Eelscombe, revealing that the benevolent developer of Fairhaven was really the man who'd destroyed so many families, and thereby shattering his plans for his great resort. And maybe she'd even meant to do so.

But somehow, I couldn't believe that of her. Her letters to Dorothea had been affectionate, not accusatory. Mrs. Bloom had considered Temperance one of *hers*—one of the people hurt by the *Valkyrie* that she took pains to keep in touch with, to take care of. She'd genuinely wished them well, even despite her disagreement with Sir Quentin about the tiara. Mr. McGuffin's and Mrs. Pettigrew's words echoed in my brain: *Ain't right. A real shame.* And my own, *unfair.*

I felt wild with anxiety when we reached the broad green lawn of the Ballingall Arms. Part of me wanted to drag poor Mr. McGuffin inside and insist he denounce the Ballingalls as frauds, but the more sensible part knew his story was still only circumstantial evidence, and that the more likely thing to happen would be Miss Ballingall shrieking hysterically, and Sir Quentin sending for Inspector Arkwright to lock Mr. McGuffin up and hang him alongside Aunt Helena.

Instead I thanked him and took the last stretch alone. A splotch of bright white out on the water caught my eye, too lumpy for a boat, too large to be human. A distant *Woomf! Woomf!* carried up along the wind.

"Copernicus?" What was he doing out so late? Was he swimming? Alone?

I limped to the terrace balustrade, trying to see by the light of the great hotel windows. I made out another shape, but it took a ghastly moment to understand what it was.

A wicker bath chair bobbed in the shallows, empty. My heart stopped—and that is not hyperbole, Dear Reader. The whole *world* stopped.

Poor Maudie was gone.

19
INEVITABLE DISCOVERY

Whitehall, London: Scotland Yard's Black Museum, maintained for the city's police forces, holds items acquired
by the Metropolitan Police during their Investigations,
including a letter from Jack the Ripper and the pistol
wielded by one of Queen Victoria's would-be assassins.
The public is occasionally admitted to view the artifacts;
enquire Chief Inspector Neame, Metropolitan Police.

—Hardcastle's Practical Travel Companion

Inside the hotel, there was chaos.

I had hobbled back in a stunned fog, expecting to
raise the alarm, but I was already too late. Everyone
knew that Maud was missing. She'd been in danger after
all. We hadn't been imagining things. But Miss Judson
had promised to look after her! What had gone wrong?

Mr. Penrose filled the great lobby with panic and
shouting. Sir Quentin boomed back, hurling incom-
prehensible orders at everyone and no one. The Bird

Ladies flitted about, eyes glittering with eager speculation. Temperance had fainted again, and Cicely and Nurse Temby were hunting for smelling salts. Aunt Helena ought to have been here. It wasn't quite the same without her bellowing in the mix, like an orchestra missing the low brass.

In the center of the storm, a small spot of calm, seated serenely on a graceful settee, was Miss Judson, watching everything with a look of cool detachment. She spotted me squeezing in. *Come here*, said her eyes, so I cautiously made my way to her side.

"What happened?" I gasped. "I saw—" I couldn't say it.

She lifted a finger to her lips. Reluctantly, impossibly, I held my tongue, though I had to sit on my hands to make myself hold still.

Gradually, the chaos resolved itself around a number of points of clarity.

". . . abducted!" shouted Mr. Penrose. "Must go after her . . . kill the man . . ."

I shot Miss Judson another look of alarm, but her serenity did not waver.

"Calm yourself, Edward. Think of your heart." That was Nurse Temby, a hand on Mr. Penrose's sleeve.

"Confound my heart!" he snapped. "He's taken her! Ballingall! Where're your pet coppers? I'll tear the coast up if I have to . . ." Mr. Penrose's stately calm had dissolved—and no wonder. But I gradually realized that behind his red face and raging, it wasn't *fear* I saw.

It was anger.

I turned again to Miss Judson, who lifted a fore-stalling finger. Clearly she had a plan, and I was not involved. I resolved to watch it play out.

As Sir Quentin tried to intervene, Miss Judson smoothly rose and glided into the fracas. "If I may," she said. Her calm voice cut through the shouting. She held up a folded letter, which she presented to Mr. Penrose.

"What the devil's this?" He snatched it from her and tore through it in a single glance. "Outrageous! I won't believe it!"

"Oh, I think you'll find everything's in order."

Doubt flashed across Nurse Temby's steely face, and she grappled the page from Mr. Penrose's hand. As she read, she turned ashen and clutched Mr. Penrose's arm. He shook her off, leaning over Miss Judson.

"What is the meaning of this? If you were involved in—in *spiriting away* my daughter, I will have the law on you. I'll—"

"No one has spirited anyone away, sir. If anything, Miss Penrose has spirited *herself* away, as she has every right to do. By this time tomorrow, she and Mr. Strand will be married, and there is nothing at all you can do about it."

The Bird Ladies gasped—*Married?*—and I think I gasped, too.

Miss Judson restrained herself, of course, but I recognized the quiet triumph in her otherwise placid expression.

For an apoplectic moment Mr. Penrose was speechless. "We'll see about that," he snarled, flinging the letter at her feet. "Temby!" He stalked off toward the lift, Nurse Temby following behind, looking adrift.

As the crowd dissolved, I ducked in and retrieved the note.

> *Father:*
> *By now you'll be aware of my plans to marry Mr. Victor Strand. Do not attempt to stop us. The Coast Guard have been alerted that we may be followed, and are directed to fire upon any vessel seen in pursuit. Mother's money is beyond your grasp. When I return, I shall draw up a settlement for you and Miss Temby, with the expectation that no word is ever spoken between us again. If you do not agree to these terms, I shall see you and Nurse Temby charged with Mother's murder.*
> *M. Penrose, soon-to-be Strand*

Mr. Strand? The motorcar salesman? I could scarcely believe it. And—how? How had all of this come about? My gaze lifted to Miss Judson, Observing Mr. Penrose's exit, hands hooked at her waist and looking entirely too pleased with herself. What had she *done*?

Mr. Penrose and Nurse Temby departed that very night, after a series of frantic telephone calls and bustling arrangements, handled with equanimity by Mr. Roberts. As we watched the spectacle unfold, they bundled themselves into a carriage that materialized from nowhere and set off, presumably in pursuit of Maud and Mr. Strand (and Copernicus), who—it turned out—were aboard a motorboat,* en route to catch a steamer that would carry them to the Channel Islands. They hadn't much of a head start, but Miss Judson seemed convinced they would make good their flight.

"I told Mr. Penrose they were setting sail from Hastings," she said—and something in her voice made me think Maud's father had set off in exactly the wrong direction.

At long last, when we were finally alone, Miss Judson confessed all. It was almost midnight, and Peony was furious, planting herself at Miss Judson's feet for a resentful wash and refusing to look at either of us. I was almost grateful for the distraction of Miss Judson's adventure. It gave me more time to assimilate everything I'd learned that day.

"You may have noticed," Miss Judson began, "that I have been some time of late in the company of young Mr. Strand."

I gave this the sour scowl it deserved.

* another of Mr. Strand's modern ventures, evidently

"Well, his attachment to Miss Penrose was swiftly made plain. Indeed, it could hardly have been missed." The look she gave me suggested my powers of Observation had been as poor as Inspector Arkwright's with the Tardieu spots. "Every breath from the poor fellow's lips had her name upon it, and I soon enough discovered the purpose for his and Maud's trip to Fairhaven."

"They always planned to elope?" It sounded romantic, yet there were in fact few actions more unforgivably scandalous that a Young Lady of Quality could take. Sensational novels—and reality—were full of the consequences, not always exaggerated: ruination, disownment, penury, death in the gutter. It would take someone exceptionally Irrepressible, not to mention resourceful, to pull it off without disaster.

"Always. Mr. Strand is no fortune hunter," she explained. "He's due to inherit a legacy as great as Maud's. They thought they'd hatched the perfect plan, but Nurse Temby and Mr. Penrose presented an obstacle."

"They foisted themselves on her at the last moment," I recalled. "She intended to come alone, but they wouldn't let her."

Miss Judson nodded. "Exactly. It was either escape their clutches in Fairhaven or be confined to a sanatorium. Or worse. She and Victor—Mr. Strand—despaired of making their getaway. Once their plight was explained—and her father's schemes exposed—I was happy to do what I could, which was little more than distracting the parties involved so the couple could slip off undetected." Miss Judson looked uncharacteristically delighted for having engineered such a heist, under everyone's gaze, with no one suspecting. She was a veritable criminal mastermind.

I sat down, my head spinning. "Mr. Penrose wants to *sue* you."

She merely laughed. "Oh, he'll reconsider. Maud wasn't wrong, you know." She was sober now. "It's very possible that they *did* kill her mother. There's no proof of it–and, no, I very much doubt they'll exhume the body to test it for arsenic, although you could certainly suggest it to their county coroner, if you feel strongly inclined. But Maud is willing to let the matter rest, so long as they leave her and Mr. Strand alone."

"Let the matter rest? But–" I couldn't form the rest of that sentence. Maud had been so frightened when she thought they were plotting to kill her. But they hadn't succeeded, and now she–and her fortune–were safe. Still, Mrs. Penrose deserved justice, too. "They can't just go free."

"I shouldn't worry about that." Miss Judson's voice was tinged with gleeful mischief, but she would explain no further.

❧

The next day, the previous night's excitement left the Ballingall Arms in a subdued daze, but I was still abuzz with worry—about the escaping newlyweds, about the escaping fortune-hunters-slash-murderers, and most of all about Sir Quentin. In a breathless rush last night, after Miss Judson's tale was well and truly put to bed, I'd finally explained everything I'd learned about the Ballingalls' past.

My sense of panic had scarcely lessened overnight, and I pressed my face to the terrace windows, trying to spot a figure in oilskin wandering about the shingle. "We need to find evidence that *proves* Sir Quentin's guilt," I said—for the fourteenth or fifteenth time. "Mr. McGuffin might be in danger. What if Inspector Arkwright decides to arrest him?"

Miss Judson was not as anxious as I on this front. "Then I'm sure he'll tell them the same tale he told you—with the picture from the pub to back up his story."

"Brilliant," I said. "Now we need to rescue another photograph."

"I'm not entirely convinced Temperance made that identification out of malice," Miss Judson said. "It's possible she doesn't even remember him, and only described him when we pressed her to make the sketch."

"So it's *your* fault," I said, voice sour.

Miss Judson sighed, scowling at her painting. "Mea culpa," she agreed. "This is not turning out right. Peony, pull that face again."

"*No.*"

At that, Miss Judson flung the brush down with a final sigh.

Happily, moments later, we were distracted by the first bit of good news in days: Mr. Blakeney had succeeded in convincing the railway to release our luggage.

"Replevin to the rescue," Miss Judson said, as we headed toward the lift.

Tom, the operator, and Peony greeted each other like a reunion of old friends. She covered his neat trouser leg in black fur and chattered to him as he blinked and tickled her.

"You're very good with animals," Miss Judson Observed.

Tom blushed, but beamed. "We used to have a—" but here he clammed up. "I'm not supposed to tell," he said.

"Then you'd best not." Miss Judson smoothed over the moment, and then we were in the lobby once more, where Cicely paced before the fishpond, like Peony awaiting an unreasonably delayed breakfast.

"I'd have had everything sent up, you know," Mr. Roberts was saying. "It's really no trouble. But Miss Highsmith said she'd like to collect it personally."

"Yes, she's been rather anxious about it," Miss Judson remarked.

"If the police confiscated anything of Aunt Helena's, she'll blame Cicely," I added.

Finally, we heard the rattle of carriage wheels, and Cicely let out a little cry and darted for the doors, just in time to meet the porters carting in a trolley full of trunks. I spotted my vile salmon pink one on the bottom, Miss Judson's practical set beside it, and atop it all, an overflowing array of trunks and boxes that must have belonged to the others. Cicely hovered fretfully as the trolley was loaded into the lift—with no room for us. She tried to squeeze in alongside it, and for a moment it seemed as though Tom might let her. But a gentle hand on her elbow from Mr. Roberts held her back.

"You'll be up there in a jiff, Miss Highsmith," he said in firm but kindly tones that brooked no objection, and she wrung her hands until the lift's return. I was half surprised that, given her state, she hadn't elected to go sprinting up the stairs instead.

Miss Judson and I exchanged curious glances, but perhaps Sir Quentin had not thought to include Cicely in his beneficence, showering *her* with lovely fresh underthings ordered in from Brighton, and this was simply the natural response of a Young Lady of Quality who desperately wanted clean stockings.

She fairly shot onto the lift when it arrived, Miss Judson and I smoothly at her heels.

Tom turned back with a half smile. "I can't make it go any faster," he apologized.

"It's quite all right," Miss Judson said, but the look Cicely gave him was murderous.

Finally, we all arrived back on our floor, Cicely disappearing behind the trolley into Aunt Helena's rooms. A few minutes later, the footmen brought our trunks to the Nile Rooms and settled them neatly in our respective bedchambers. They had to wade a bit around the sea of things that the Ballingalls had brought in.

"We'll have to give this all back now," I said, but Miss Judson was eyeing the paint set with something a bit like longing.

"It wouldn't do any harm to keep it," she protested.

"Investigators do not take *bribes*," I said, and shoved it under the bed. With a sigh, Miss Judson went to unpack.

I hauled my trunk to the wardrobe, knelt beside it, and opened the latches. Peony rubbed against it, reasserting her possession: *"Mine. And also mine. And Miss Judson's bags are mine, too."*

I flipped the lid and began unloading my books—but paused, one of my encyclopædias halfway out of the trunk. "Something's wrong." I had put the books in *below* the clothes, because it made sense to put the weightier items on the bottom, and because Miss Judson would have seen them if I'd left them on top. The Unmentionable Bathing Costume had been the last item I'd put in, besides my Wellies and slingshot. I called out to Miss Judson. "Do the contents of a trunk generally shift much in transit?"

"That depends upon how tightly they're packed, how rough the travel, and—why?" Miss Judson wandered over, one of her crisp shirtwaists held reverently to her face like a long-lost friend.

"Someone's searched my trunk." I felt a prickle at my neck—excitement, I think, mixed with a faint sense of violation.

Miss Judson was skeptical. "That seems improbable."

"Check yours," I commanded.

"Well, I've unpacked already," she said. "I didn't notice anything amiss, but . . ." She shifted her feet, with an apologetic grimace. "I wasn't looking for anything."

"Well, *someone* was," I said. "They've destroyed my penicillium samples!" I gingerly fished the spilt trays from among the books and clothes.

"I don't recall those being on the packing lists I prepared." Miss Judson's voice had a serves-you-right tone to it that I ignored. I set the now-worthless experiment to the side and resumed a more careful examination of the trunk.

"Why would anyone search my trunk?" I said.

"Well, that answer seems obvious," she said, with a hint of smugness. When I glared at her blankly, she added, "Your name."

I let out a wordless groan. Of course. Stamped upon the lid, for anyone to see, were my initials: HHM, with a name in script below: *Helena Hardcastle*.

Inspector Arkwright must have assumed my trunk was Aunt Helena's, then destroyed my samples out of negligence—or spite.

Miss Judson was sympathetic. "It should have taken but a moment to see this is the luggage of a child, not a woman in her sixties, and that they had the wrong trunk." Shaking her head, she returned to her own things.

I dug into my belongings, wondering why the police couldn't have managed to damage some of the silly traveling clothes, even just a little (they hadn't even got mold on the bathing costume). I was thus distracted and disgruntled, yanking books and waists from the trunk at random, when I froze. For a moment I merely stared stupidly, transfixed by an item that I had most certainly not packed—and which could not possibly have been overlooked by even the world's most inept policeman.

"Miss Judson?" It came out a strangled gasp. "Miss! Look!"

She hurried back and looked down into the trunk, face impassive. "Is that—" Her eyes darted to me, the only part of her betraying any emotion whatsoever.

I lifted it out as gingerly as my mold specimens—a bundle in black velvet, the cloth falling open as I held the item to the light, where it sparkled in all its icy blue-green glory.

"The Northern Lights," I breathed.

20
DO NOT DISTURB

Due caution in protecting one's belongings cannot be overstressed. Finer hotels offer modern locks on their rooms and guests can avail themselves of the hotel safe for additional security measures.

—Hardcastle's Practical Travel Companion

Miss Judson and I stared at the stolen (and evidently recovered!) tiara for a long moment. The stones had been freed from the arched wire frame that held them in shape as a headpiece, and the Northern Lights were now a slinky, glittering web of jewels on a white-gold chain, which poured through my hands like silk. Miss Judson frowned at them, willing them to explain themselves. (I knew that look. It generally produced the expected results, at least eventually.)

"How did it get there?" I asked, hoping the Socratic

Method might save us. "By which I mean, *who* put it there, and why?"

Her frown had not abated. "I think the confusion about your names answers the why," she said. "Whoever stashed that in your trunk clearly did so intending to put it in Aunt Helena's instead." She put out a tentative finger, like the jewels might bite her.

"But why? To frame her for the robbery?" Aunt Helena certainly wouldn't have mistaken my trunk for her own, and, "It clearly wasn't Nurse Temby." Having lost Maud, there was no way she'd have fled Eelscombe without at least second prize.

"Whoever wished to frame your aunt for all the robberies would have to have known her travel schedule." I slowly met her eyes, and we completed that thought together. *"Sir Quentin."*

Aunt Helena had been traveling with him on and off all summer. She was the perfect dupe—for the robbery *and* the murder.

"But—" Something still wasn't right. The swirling colors, commingling in the same stones, twisted at my brain. In the daylight from the terrace doors, the alexandrites shone sea green, sparking with a dark heart of violet so deep it was nearly red. Had we been looking at everything the wrong way? I moved my hands, watching the colors flash, trying to recapture the thought. There was an answer here. What was it?

"The whole robbery was engineered to distract us," I said slowly. "*All* of us. The passengers when the lights went out, and the guards with the fire in the dining car."

Miss Judson knelt beside me. "What are you saying?"

"I don't know." I almost knew. "Maybe we're *still* distracted." I wanted to get up and pace, but I could not stop staring at the mystifying colors. Looking one way, I saw green: a robbery, the stolen tiara. But from another angle, blood red: a murder—the death of Mrs. Bloom.

Or maybe I had that completely wrong. I shifted my grip on the tiara and the stones trembled, the deep inky red just tantalizingly out of reach, because it was hidden in bright daylight by the green.

Like a burst of white-violet fire in my brain, it came to me. "We've spent all this time trying to find the thief and the murderer—but we've missed the crime at the heart of everything!"

I sat back, spilling the stones into my lap. That was it, all along. The very crime Mrs. Bloom had come aboard the *Empress Express* to Investigate in the first place.

Insurance fraud.

Now I really couldn't sit still. "There was never any robbery. Five thousand pounds. Aunt Helena told us— Sir Quentin is in debt. How much does it cost to build a hotel, let alone buy a whole train? And all the rest of his grand plans? He orchestrated this whole thing, arranged to have the jewels 'stolen' for the insurance money."

"And he wanted his dear friend Helena and her family on hand as witnesses." Miss Judson could not hide her distaste.

"But he wasn't expecting his old nemesis to show up again." And Mrs. Bloom hadn't counted on Sir Quentin being prepared to kill for the money. I sat down heavily, the Northern Lights tumbling across my skirts. Even Peony was subdued.

"What are we going to do with them?" I said. "We can't keep them here, and we can't take them to the police. Finding the stolen jewels in a trunk with Aunt Helena's name on it? Inspector Arkwright will take that as incontrovertible proof of her guilt."

"I could wear them," Miss Judson suggested wistfully.

"I've had enough family members arrested this week, thank you. It needs to be somewhere safe, but not tied to us."

"Hmm," she said. "I might have an idea."

❧

Fifteen minutes later, we stood beside an unassuming little Eelscombe storefront, and I found myself wildly searching for the words *Safes to Let* among the other services advertised. It was well past teatime, and the little shop was closed, but in answer to our (somewhat panicked) knock, the door cracked open and a tiny, towheaded child of indeterminate gender peeked up at us with enormous brown eyes.

"Are you Robert's fwiends?"

"Robert's–?" Miss Judson swung the door open to reveal a scene of ordinary domestic chaos. Mrs. Pettigrew and Mr. Blakeney were installed in the bakery kitchen, barely visible amid a flurry of flour, whilst a gaggle of children and at least one duck wrestled on the floor. But with a look at us, Mrs. Pettigrew clapped her hands.

"Gells, out!"

In an instant, the children evaporated like mist, and Mr. Blakeney emerged from the kitchen, wiping his floury hands on a worn apron.

"I say, Stephen! This is unexpected. Didn't things work out with the luggage?"

"Not exactly." I glanced around the room, but Mrs. Pettigrew had given us some respectful distance and was puttering about the kitchen. "We've uncovered some–problematic evidence."

Mr. Blakeney's head cocked quizzically. Miss Judson held a simple reticule up for him to look inside.

He swore emphatically. "Oh, I do beg your pardon. I did not say that." Mr. Blakeney shoved a hand through his fair hair. "Although hypothetically speaking, that *is* what someone's legal counsel might say, should he be faced with such a Situation. So, erm, hypothetically speaking, that would hypothetically be—"

"The stolen tiara," I confirmed unnecessarily. "Somebody hid it in my trunk."

"Thinking it was Aunt Helena's trunk," Miss Judson added.

"Why did you bring it to me? Which you haven't done, because I've never seen it." It was obvious that Mr. Blakeney had immediately grasped the legal complications of being in possession of this evidence.

"We didn't know what else to do, I'm afraid." Miss Judson hastily explained our deductions about the insurance fraud, and the problems with the only alternatives we'd thought of.

"So naturally you thought of your friendly neighborhood post office and defense attorney." He sank down upon a bench.

"You *are* here to advise us," I said.

"How much is that thing worth?" He'd gone rather pale.

"It's insured for five thousand pounds." Miss Judson's voice was low—which, given the circumstances, did not make it particularly reassuring.

"And someone's been murdered over it. So you brought it to me." He muttered to himself, *"Next time, Blakeney, send a memorandum."*

"Can you keep it?" I said. "I mean, for a while? I mean, legally?"

He grimaced, unable to look away from the stones deep in Miss Judson's bag. "No, not really. I should turn this over to Arkwright."

Miss Judson snatched the bag back.

"All right," he said hastily. "Forget I said that." He got up and paced the cluttered common room, ducking the low beams in the ceiling. Finally, he snapped his fingers and swung back toward us. "But you've actually come to the right place. I have it on good authority that Pettigrew and company are, in fact, absolute masters of Hunt the Slipper."

I just stared at him. What was he on about?

"Huckle Buckle Beanstalk? Hot Boiled Beans?"

I shook my head.

But Miss Judson actually took a tiny jump and clapped her hands. "Oh! *Chaud ou froid!*" And suddenly I caught up to them. We'd played that at home. It meant "hot or cold" and was considerably less tedious than most parlor games. Father came up with the most inventive hiding places (we still hadn't tracked down one of Cook's silver teaspoons). But surely Mr. Blakeney couldn't mean what it sounded like he was suggesting.

Miss Judson sobered. "Are you sure? That seems . . ." She tossed up her hands. "No worse than any other idea we've come up with."

I had to agree. Looking around Mrs. Pettigrew's crowded shop, it seemed the last place in England that someone would look for a priceless tiara. Or the *first* place. Maybe she could post a sign! A mad little giggle escaped me.

"What say we all?" said Mr. Blakeney. "Shall we invite Mrs. Pettigrew into our little conspiracy?"

I glanced over to where Mrs. Pettigrew was doing a terrible job of pretending not to eavesdrop. I supposed this concerned her as much as anybody else, so I waved her over.

She looked skeptical, sidling toward us, her scarred face in shadow. Her reaction to the Northern Lights was rather less than dramatic.

"Huh. An' Mrs. Bloom were protectin' that?"

I nodded solemnly. "She was killed for it."

"Right, then," she said. "I've just the place." She scuttled over to the same shelf from whence she'd recently unearthed a perfectly preserved top hat. Mounting a stepstool, she waved an impatient hand at Miss Judson, who somewhat reluctantly handed over the jewels, reticule and all. "Doubt those coppers'll think to look there," Mrs. Pettigrew said, after shoving the hatbox to the back of the shelf, behind a tin of pickled herring and a pair of roller skates.

Mr. Blakeney watched her gravely, then voiced the same thought we all shared: "But who was the thief?"

❧

Hours later, I awoke from a dead sleep in my sarcophagus, groggy and bewildered. What had awakened me? A chilly breeze shifted the gauzy curtains, and

I heard a rustle, too large to be Peony. Theoretically, anyway.

"Peony?" I mumbled through a mouthful of fur. I shoved her away from my face and sat up, blinking in the darkness. I heard the rush of surf, felt the salty blast of sea air. I was quite sure I hadn't left the terrace doors open.

And then I saw her, silhouetted against the faint haze of light from the doors: a thin figure, a heavy fall of skirts. "Miss Judson!" That person wasn't Miss Judson, and I knew as much. Miss Judson didn't skulk. "*Miss Judson!*" I called.

The figure went on about her business, as if I hadn't spoken, not even caring that I knew she was here. She crept through the room toward the dressing area where we'd stashed my trunk. I scrambled out of bed, taking the blankets with me, landing in a loud heap on the floor. I didn't have a lamp handy, or matches, or anything useful, but it didn't matter. I had seen the intruder, and I knew exactly why she was here.

"It's *you*," I said, voice sharp with surprise. "It was you all along."

"Too darn clever for your own good," said Cicely— in a voice I didn't recognize, a far cry from her usual breathless wisp.

My brain stuttered, coming slowly to life. "You won't find it. It's not here." *Cicely* had stolen the tiara, hidden it in my luggage (by mistake, evidently), and confronted Mrs. Bloom in the baggage car. Motive, means, opportunity. "You killed Mrs. Bloom."

She slammed the lid of my trunk with a sound like a gunshot, shaking her head. "Not so clever after all." She wasn't armed—but she wasn't Cicely, either. At least, not the girl she'd been the last few days. Where was Miss Judson? Cicely took three impossibly fast steps across the room and grabbed me by the shoulders. I let out a little squeak.

"Where is it? Be a good girl and tell me what you've done with the tiara."

"We gave it to the police, of course," I said stoutly, but Cicely's face twisted in an ugly smile.

"You being best mates with Arkwright and all."

It was worth a shot, Dear Reader.

"You must've hid it somewhere. Clever thing like you, it won't be here in the hotel." She shook me again, but the answers didn't fall out. "Fine. Why don't you show me?"

"Why should I?"

"'Cos if you don't, my brother'll wake your precious Miss Judson."

"Brother?" I looked up in time to see another shape darken the terrace doors. The smart black uniform was gone, but I recognized him anyway: Tom, the lift operator. And now the resemblance was all too obvious. They had the same fair skin, wide dark eyes, thick eyebrows. They might have been twins. And he was holding a knife, its blade glinting silver in the moonlight.

My heart sank. "Is there anyone else?" I muttered—but I didn't dare disobey them. They'd killed Mrs. Bloom, after all. "Can I at least get my coat?"

"Get all your clothes, for all I care."

I bundled myself into my boots and coat, trying to make my sluggish brain respond. What should I do? Miss Judson hadn't heard me calling—and she was no match for a man with a knife. I still didn't know how they'd got into the room—from the terrace of Aunt Helena's room, probably. No sooner than I had one arm in a sleeve, Tom hauled me upright and pushed me forward, into the main corridor.

"Let's go," Cicely said. "Leave the cat."

"She goes where she wants." Peony darted ahead, streaking down the hallway. Tom hesitated.

"*Leave it,*" Cicely hissed.

A single electric lamp burned at the far end of the passage, barely more than a pinprick of light. They drove me in the other direction, away from the lifts, toward the servants' stair. Down we went, turning flight after flight through total darkness until I banged into a solid wall and no more stairs. No—a door. Tom gave it a none-too-kindly shove, revealing another corridor. And another. And another still, until finally we emerged into the gusty night. A light drizzle pattered down, making the pebbly beach slick and treacherous. I'd lost track of Peony.

"Now where?" Cicely asked. I thought fast—my best hope was people and safety. Give them what they want, and let them be on their way again. But Mrs. Pettigrew had four small children, and I didn't trust Tom—or that knife—at all.

"I hid it," I improvised. "At—on the Pier." Perfect. We could search there for hours, until Miss Judson finally noticed we were gone.

"Well, get going, then." Clutching my arm, Cicely dragged me across the slippery shingle, away from the hotel, away from light and civilization and help, and I began to wonder why I hadn't screamed my fool head off when I had the chance.

Out in the water, a light burned on a boat circling near. Tom paused to glance its way.

"Is that your ride?"

"You talk too much," Cicely growled. It was unfathomable, the change that had come over her. Gone was the meek creature trailing tearfully in Aunt Helena's wake and starting at nothing. In her place was someone I had no trouble imagining plunging a pair of scissors into Mrs. Bloom's back.

Or mine, if it came to that.

A streak of darkness darker than the rest of the beach flashed ahead of me, and I caught a glimpse of white signal-flare tail. Although there was little Peony could do to save me, I felt a little less desolate and abandoned. Ahead of us, the skeletal girders of the Pier made a dense shadow against the bleak sky and inky water, which crept inexorably ashore. It was around midnight, high tide, and the Pier stood knee deep in ocean.

"What are you going to do with the tiara?" I asked. "You can't sell it, you know." I didn't have any hope of stalling them, but I'd got this far—I wanted answers!

"Never you mind," said Tom.

"Police forces across Europe will be looking for it by now," I continued. "Sir Quentin had to report it stolen, to get the insurance money. Especially after you killed Mrs. Bloom. You'll be wanted for murder now, too." Cicely was right; I *did* talk too much.

"Can't you shut her up?" Tom pleaded.

"We didn't kill anybody," Cicely said.

"Yeah, Himself don't pay near enough for that."

Himself? That was what the hotel workers all called Sir Quentin. Belatedly, I recalled Cicely and Sir Quentin's overheard quarrel, him saying her work wasn't done. No wonder she'd been so frantic—she couldn't leave without the tiara.

Tom pushed me along, and the Pier grew closer. We could make out the wooden boardwalk and the ghostly shapes of the Amusement kiosks. I tried to put the pieces together as we made our stumbling procession, past the stone pilings with their memorial plaque, up between the faded ticket booths. Cicely pulled up the chain holding the gates closed, and Tom pushed me through. The Pier looked even more eerie and forbidding than it had by daylight. Pale clouds scudded overhead, casting the railings and lampposts in and out of moonlight. Dark water bubbled beneath us, licking the iron skeleton. Drizzle spattered the remains of the stalls, and the boards were slick, giving back wet reflections of the night.

"All right, where is it?"

Wind gusted my loose hair into an icy, whiplike spider's web, stinging my face. "You won't get away with this," I said, flinching as Tom's grip clenched harder. "How much is he paying you? Do you think he's going to let you walk away?" Now that I'd begun, I couldn't seem to stop, and the questions rattled out past my chattering teeth. "Killing Mrs. Bloom wasn't part of the plan, was it?" They looked at each other uncertainly. "Which one of you did that? It was Cicely, right? I don't remember you on the train," I said to Tom.

"Cis?" Tom's voice was doubtful, and he let his hand fall. I twisted free.

"Oh, shut up! Don't listen to her, Tom. I never killed anybody. Her aunt done that—she's just trying to confuse you."

Tom was staring at his sister in dismay. No—not twins after all. Cicely was older. Or perhaps Tom just looked to Cicely for guidance. And, probably, protection. Was she the mastermind of this pair?

"Did you kill someone, Cis?"

"No, I did not!" she barked. Tom's face crumpled, and I took a step back. "Oh, Tommy, don't worry." Cicely reached for her brother's arm. "It's going to be fine. *We're* going to be fine. I promised you I'd take care of everything, didn't I?"

Tom took a great sniff and wiped his nose with his sleeve.

"We'll get the tiara and sell it to Marceau, just like we planned."

"What about Himself?"

"You let me worry about that." Her voice was almost soothing—but she turned to me with an expression of iron. "Now get us the tiara, Myrtle. Where is it?"

I dared one more question. "Who's Marceau? Is he waiting on that boat back there?" Both their gazes flicked past me, out to sea, and I thought I must be correct. And with that, the last piece clicked into place. "You were planning to double-cross Sir Quentin! *That's* why you hid the tiara in my trunk, so you could retrieve it later. But Mrs. Bloom interrupted you when you went to get it back, so you had to kill her."

Cicely charged me, face twisted with anger. "For the last time, I *didn't kill her*! Do you think I'd be so stupid? Whoever did that almost cost me my chance at getting the tiara back. And I'm not missing another one, so if you please, show me where you've hidden it."

That wasn't a request. But if I could keep her talking—what? She'd get bored and have her brother kill me after all? Good plan, Myrtle. "How much did Marceau offer you for the tiara?"

"Five hundred pounds." Tom's voice rang with pride, and I gave his sister a look of outrage.

"It's worth ten times that!" Still, five hundred pounds would set them up nicely. How much did she earn as a Lady's Companion? How much did he make as a lift operator? Not that those were their real professions, obviously.

"Enough to keep us out of the workhouse." Cicely shrugged, and the look on Tom's face suggested he, at least, was no stranger to the horrific conditions that option offered.

"What happens if you don't turn the tiara over to your buyer?" Which was probably the stupidest question I might have asked, just then.

Cicely glared at me. "He kills all of us, so you'd better hope the tiara is where you say it is. Now go get it." She gave me a little shove forward, and I did the only thing I could think of—I ran.

21
Mare Apertum

The options for taking the waters at most seaside Resorts
are endless, but inexperienced bathers may consider
availing themselves of swimming lessons beforehand.

—Hardcastle's Practical Travel Companion

I didn't head sensibly back toward the beach and
safety. Even if I could have made it past Tom, they'd
catch me in an instant. Instead, I pounded down the
boardwalk, skidding on the wet planks. My dark coat
offered me scant advantage, as my footsteps sounded
like the heavy cavalry thundering down the Pier.

"Don't just stand there, Tom! Go get her! Myrtle,
don't be ridiculous. Come back and let's finish this."

I didn't like the way that sounded. To my left, the
leering clown's face of the skating parlor loomed,
mouth agape, tongue lolling. I scrambled inside, then
crawled through the broken boards to the ice cream

shop next door. Guano and trash littered the floor, and the going was slow. I'd lost the light, too. Hopefully that would help me. I pushed under a fallen wall, barely more than paper on a frame, and found myself in a jumbled kiosk full of coin-operated music boxes. I bumped into one, sending its mechanism shuddering in a cascade of tinny, broken notes that clanked overloud in the gloomy silence. I froze, hoping the Highsmiths hadn't heard that.

Plan, Myrtle. What was my plan? I didn't have a Marceau waiting on a handy boat to rescue me. The only thing I could think of now was to keep moving, put as much distance between me and Cicely—and Tom and his knife—as I could.

I crept through the shadows, among the run-down kiosks and weather-beaten Amusements. Between cracks in the boardwalk, black water winked the moonlight back at me, rippled and disorienting.

I heard a sharp metallic clang from across the Pier. It sounded like Cicely kicking the railing in frustration. "Enough games, Myrtle. We don't have all night."

I held my breath—I *did* have all night, actually, but Cicely's buyer might not wait forever.

"I'll tell you everything," she offered. "I know how curious you are. I'll confess the whole thing to you. Just come out where I can see you."

I was tempted. But I wasn't stupid. Still, the confusion of sounds on the Pier might work to my benefit.

By mad luck, I'd blundered into the vicinity of one end of the speaking tube system. In a few more feet, Cicely would be in range of the other, just as Clive and I had been the other day. The weathered copper fixture was dull in the moonlight. I crept closer.

"Go ahead." My skeptical voice disappeared down the tube running beneath the pier and rattled up beside Cicely, who jumped and spun round, looking for me. "What happened? How did Sir Quentin convince you to steal the tiara?"

Cicely uttered an Unladylike Word, a frustrated hand to her forehead. "Fine," she snapped. "You want to hear our sad story? How this toff and his daughter showed up one day in Brighton, all dolled up like they were on the grand tour? She was a sniveling thing, but she raised a holy fuss when her little pearl earrings went missing. And who do they blame but the housemaid?" She looked like she wanted to spit on the boardwalk. "Ballingall insisted I work for him, or he'd have me and Tom both down for hard labor. Or sent to Australia."

"England doesn't transport criminals anymore," I said. "Not since 1868."

She let out a laugh, high and sharp, which rang down the speaking tube. "Now she tells me."

My brain was buzzing, taking this in. "*You're* the Brighton Bandit?" I couldn't keep *all* the eagerness from my voice. "All those robberies Mrs. Bloom was

Investigating? And—Miss Penrose's jewels, too?" She'd been traveling with Aunt Helena—the perfect cover.

"You goin' to show me where that tiara is?"

Well, I supposed that was enough of an answer.

"Enough, Myrtle. Come on out, or I'll come find *you*."

I didn't ask what would happen then. She was poking her head around the kiosks. Soon enough she'd see the speaking tube—which plainly announced the location of its other end. Time to move on.

I crept away, daring a glance back up the Pier toward the beach. Why hadn't I sneaked *that* way instead? Cicely and Tom were fanned out, covering any escape, and Tom was getting closer, herding me toward the end of the Pier like the unfortunate sheep in Hardy.* To, no doubt, the same end.

"I've *earned* that money, Myrtle. You know I have. What's Sir Quentin done to deserve it? Let your aunt rot in jail? Blackmail a couple of kids?"

It was extortion, actually, but it didn't seem the moment to quibble with her.

I tried a different tack. "You know Tom will be charged with murder, too." I had to shout to be heard now, and then immediately scampered across the boardwalk to the other side of the Pier. I stumbled, scraping

---

* *Far from the Madding Crowd*, 1874. A depressing book, of little scientific merit, with only one lackluster murder. My friend Caroline recommended it.

my knee on a fallen board. Brilliant, now *I'd* die of tetanus. Assuming I made it off the Pier in one piece.

"Go *find her*!"

I heard Tom hesitate. "I ain't goin' down for murder, Cis."

Cicely released a little scream of frustration. She
must have been holding it in all week. "There was no
murder!"

Tom wheeled about to face his sister. "Don't you tell
me lies! I seen her! I had to help carry the body from
the train!" Evidently he'd been aboard the *Empress
Express* after all.

Cicely was distracted now, trying to soothe her
brother. "Yes, Tom, I know. *Someone* killed Mrs. Bloom,
but it wasn't me."

"Who was it, then?" Tom snuffled loudly enough
to be heard over the waves and wind.

"Well, I don't know," she said. "They've arrested
her aunt."

"That grand lady you was working for?"

Cicely looked like it took all her Exceptional
Forbearance not to smack him silly, but she clutched her
hands together and spoke in painfully slow words. "She
weren't no lady, Tom, and if we don't get Myrtle back,
we'll lose our five hundred pounds. So go an' get her."

But Tom didn't budge. "She *were* a lady," he insisted
tearfully. "She tipped me a shilling, she did, and called
me a smart lad."

Oh, sweet Helena! Of all the times to act like a real human.

"Tom, you *idiot*! Don't argue with me!"

With a shove that sent Cicely reeling, Tom shrilled, "Don't you call me that! Mam told you *never* call me that!" Having stood up to her, he turned on his heel and fled—straight toward my end of the Pier.

I backed up, bumping into the ruin of the concert hall with its larger-than-life Brighton Nightingale singing at us. The weak boards creaked ominously, and I froze, trying to hide against the garish colors of the poster. A mad laugh threatened, as I imagined myself a sort of Pier-colored chameleon. Tom was coming closer—and he still had the knife.

I cast about for some escape. There was no way I could dart past him, and despite all common sense screaming at me to stop, I kept backing up, closer and closer to the wrecked end of the Pier. Tom could see me clearly now.

"Tom! I'm sorry. Come back!" Cicely's voice was all over the place, as she spun round, trying to find us. "Myrtle!"

Tom spied me. He met my eyes, and raised a finger to his lips. *Shh*.

I felt Tom showed remarkably sound judgment.

He stepped closer to me, but the boards—or the iron pilings—screamed beneath his weight. He froze, and for a few deadly moments, neither of us dared breathe.

Cicely didn't seem to have heard. Finally, she called out, "Fine. If you won't help me, I'll just have to get Miss Judson to show me where you hid the tiara."

"That won't be necessary," said a glorious voice from the darkness. "Myrtle, are you down there?"

Weak with relief, I could barely scream loudly enough. "Miss! He has a knife!"

Tom whirled around, and I took the chance to edge out farther onto the Pier. Icy wind whipped my coat and hair. I held fast to the remains of the railing.

"Hang on, Stephen!" *Mr. Blakeney?*

"Don't move, Miss." That last voice could only belong to Constable Hoskiss. How had they *all* got here?

Cicely didn't take his advice. With an infuriated snarl, she turned and ran—straight for our end of the Pier. Was she mad?

"What are you doing?" Miss Judson cried. "There's nowhere to go!"

But Cicely barreled toward us like a human cannonball, heedless of the folly. Miss Judson followed, swift on her heels, Constable Hoskiss behind them, yelling for them to stop. I was yelling, too. Tom took a lunging step toward his sister, but the Pier shrieked again under his weight.

Cicely faltered, briefly, when the weakened structure swayed sickeningly, the wrenched metal pitching with a squeal that rattled my bones and set my teeth on edge.

"Miss Judson, don't come any closer!"

My warning came too late. She'd already stepped onto the unsound section. Unused to this much weight since the explosion years ago, the Pier made one last shuddering wail and surrendered. The last thing I saw was Miss Judson diving for Cicely.

Boards and railing fell away from me, and for a ghastly moment I was suspended in midair. But only a moment–I didn't even think to cry out.

Until it was too late, my head already under water. I swallowed a lungful of icy salt water, thrashing blindly, tangled in coat and nightgown and hair.

Then strong arms seized me, and I cried out again–this time with my head above the surface. Choking helplessly, I struggled, but Tom held me fast. "Easy," he said. "I've gotcher."

Ocean sloshed over me, into me, but Tom swam, one-handed, toward the pilings, ignoring my flailing. My arms were pinned to my sides, and it was all I could do to hold my breath–which was probably the most sensible course of action.

"Yer all right." We came to a stop, and Tom untangled me from his chest, wrapping my arms about a girder. I clung to the rough edges with frozen fingers, still sputtering and snorting up seawater. "It's shallow here. See?" Tom stood up. "I'm a good swimmer," he said proudly.

I just nodded, sagging gratefully against the piling.

A thunderous splashing, like every lawyer in England plowing through the shallows, crashed toward us.

"Hang on, Stephen. Here—" Mr. Blakeney plunged through the water, knee-deep and kicking wildly, not making much headway. But I fairly dived into his arms anyway, and he peeled me from the piling. Finally, with Tom bringing up the rear, we blundered back on shore and collapsed to the beach, pebbles crunching beneath us.

When I could think again, I looked out to sea, frantic—but there was Miss Judson, calmly treading water amid a shipwreck of broken Pier. Out of the wreckage, a small black-and-white head appeared, green eyes narrow, as Peony steadily cut through the surf like a tiny, unhappy motorboat.

Behind her, caught in the light from Marceau's boat, Cicely paused only a moment. She popped up from the surface, huge dark eyes making her look like a seal. She glanced back at us—at Tom, gaining the beach— then turned toward the boat and began to swim.

"She's a good swimmer, too." Tom's voice was mournful. "She has a medal." He raised a hand in a halfhearted farewell, watching his sister leave him behind.

22

WISH YOU
WERE HERE

*The conclusion of a holiday is just as important as its
outset. Embark upon your homeward journey in good
spirits, so that you will be eager to return.*

—*Hardcastle's Practical Travel Companion*

We sat shivering by the huge police station fireplace,
heaped with tartan blankets and Constable Hoskiss's
restorative tea (I was even starting to appreciate its
fishy aroma).

"I believe that's your hair," Miss Judson murmured.

"Yours, too," I returned—and sneezed.

Hours had passed. Constable Hoskiss had rounded
us all up, and we'd made our sloshing way up the hill to
the police station, Tom in handcuffs. My improbable
tale had poured out as the tea poured in, beginning

with the discovery of the Northern Lights tiara in my trunk, and culminating with our inglorious plunge into Eelshead Bay. I'd outlined the fundamental elements of Sir Quentin's scheme to defraud Albion Casualty by staging the robbery aboard the *Empress Express.* Cicely's dramatic flight and the sorrowful confession of Tom made that part of the story convincing.

We'd stopped at the pie shop on the way, to retrieve the Northern Lights. Mrs. Pettigrew had handed them over solemnly to her brother, who had simply stared in starstruck wonder. He even let Tom have a peek, which I thought awfully sporting.

Inspector Arkwright hadn't wanted to believe it. Dragged from his bed in the middle of the night, he was in no better spirits than usual. But the four soaking-wet witnesses and the reticule full of dismantled tiara in the gaolhouse soon changed his mind, and before the night was quite over, he stalked off to arrest Sir Quentin himself. I was sorry to miss that.

As we waited for them to return, Mr. Blakeney explained his appearance on the Pier in time to witness my dramatic—er—escape from Tom and Cicely.

"*Felis catus* to the rescue," he said. "She turned up at the pie shop. Wouldn't have known, but she roused the ducks, and they sounded the alarm." Rubbing his face, he watched Peony—now bathing before the fire—with awe. "That's not an ordinary cat, is it?"

Peony raised her face to him and blinked. *"No."*

"But how did you find us?" I asked Miss Judson.

Patiently, she enumerated the clues: "The terrace doors were open, and your coat and boots were gone, so you'd clearly gone outside. Cicely wasn't in her room, either, so it was easy to deduce you'd gone somewhere together. I went down to the beach, but when I couldn't see you, the Pier was the logical conclusion. We'll discuss the transgression later."

I snuggled happily into my blanket. It wasn't exactly how I'd pictured bathing with Miss Judson on our holiday, but it would do.

When Constable Hoskiss processed Tom's arrest, Mr. Blakeney stepped up to supervise, looking the very picture of a big-city solicitor with his wet curly hair, dripping trouser-cuffs, and wooly shawl bundled about his shoulders. I wondered how much of the insurance fraud plot Tom really knew. With Cicely gone, we were again left with only circumstantial evidence, and the courts might decide that Tom wasn't competent to testify against Sir Quentin. I hated to think that everything had been for naught, and Mrs. Bloom's killer would never be brought to justice.

"I can't believe she got away." I sighed. After everything, even having learned the truth and recovered the tiara, it still felt like we'd failed. We'd solved the murder, but the guilty party had escaped.

Inspector Arkwright returned with Sir Quentin just as Aunt Helena was released from her little tearoom empire. I was too snug and weary to get up, but the expression on her face would have kept me burrowed down anyway.

The chilly look she gave Sir Quentin was enough to freeze the whole police station. "*You!*" she roared, brandishing Mrs. Bloom's journal. "How dare you!"

"Now, Helena." He looked about nervously—for help or escape. "Helena, dear, I can explain—"

Aunt Helena marched herself up to Sir Quentin. "Explain this!" She smacked him soundly with the book. "You, sir, are a liar, a cheat, and a no-account scoundrel!"

He cringed away from her. "I'll—I'll get your money back!" he promised.

Her face went deadly pale. "My money? I'm not talking about money, you coward! Or the last few days of your nonsense. You involved *my niece* and her governess in your scheme!" Her voice hit a shrill octave, ringing off the stones. "You are lucky that Miss Judson knows how to swim, *Mr. Ballingall!*"

"And Tom," Miss Judson spoke up from our little corner.

"And Tom!" She held the book up for everyone to see. "It's all in here," she announced. "Mrs. Bloom recorded everything."

Sir Quentin's lip twitched in a sneer. "That woman didn't *know* anything," he began, but Aunt Helena cut him off.

"Really. Let's let the police decide what 'that woman' did or did not know, shall we?" She flipped to a page in the middle. "Mrs. Bloom wasn't fooled by your charade. She knew all about your real identity." Red crept up her cheeks, but she kept going. "She made notes of her conversations with an M. Étienne LeClerq of the House of Jolie, about how you bribed him to let you transport the tiara aboard your train." She turned another page. "Shall I go on?"

"Please don't." Sir Quentin forced the words through gritted teeth.

"Please do," said Inspector Arkwright. He sounded almost happy.

"Mrs. Bloom was on to you," Aunt Helena said. "She was about to expose your little scheme, so you killed her."

"Now, wait just a minute—"

"I think this has everything you need, Inspector." She presented the journal to Inspector Arkwright, who received it with something like awe. "It's a good thing my niece was clever enough to recover this, or that man might have got away with everything."

My ears must have been plugged with seawater. I couldn't possibly have heard Aunt Helena pay me a compliment.

With a final sniff, Aunt Helena pushed past Sir Quentin. "You great fraud. You're not even a real baronet." She brushed her hands together as though washing them of Sir Quentin. If I had not been so utterly astounded by this performance, I'd have been on my feet, applauding along with Mr. Blakeney.

"Brava," said Miss Judson softly.

Aunt Helena settled herself across from us, her back to the lot of them. Her bulk made the cozy spot seem even more private, despite the bustle of police procedure going on behind her. She met my gaze, and apparently I got sea salt in my eyes, too, because I thought I saw her wink at me! Peony took the opportunity for a moment of Exceptional Felinity and leaped into Aunt Helena's lap, getting wet black fur all over her mushroom-colored skirts. Aunt Helena pretended not to notice.

A moment later, we heard a cough. "Er, beggin' your pardon, ladies, but I believe this belongs to you." We glanced up to see Constable Hoskiss beside us, holding a leather valise. *My* valise! I stared at him.

"But how—?"

"It were delivered 'ere this morning. It had gone astray on the train, wound up in their lost property, and only just found its way back down to Fair'aven Station. I'm guessing from the initials, it belongs to one of you two ladies." He held it toward my aunt and me.

"Yes," I said. "It's mine. I—must have left it on the train. By mistake."

"Course," said the constable easily. "Figured as much. Night, ladies." With a touch of his phantom helmet brim, he stepped away again.

"Well, wonders never cease," Miss Judson said, as I set the bag beside me on the bench and flipped open the latches.

"Helena Myrtle," Aunt Helena hissed. "Your—things!"

She meant my stockings and drawers and petticoats—all the spare underthings I'd shoved into my valise to make room in my trunk for more important items. But no one was paying any attention to us anyway, and something else caught my eye: a thick black book with a worn cover and a cracked spine: *Figures of Characteristic British Fossils.*

"Mrs. Bloom's book," I said, voice reverent. I'd forgotten all about it. I touched its bent and softened corners, then gripped it hard. "We did it," I said to her. "We solved your last case." The Northern Lights tiara would be returned to its rightful owners, and the finders would receive a handsome reward.*

"More than that," Miss Judson said. "You also

---

* enough, as it turned out, to keep the Ballingall Arms hotel—now the Eel's Head—running, under new ownership, and to put a little extra into patching up the Pier. It would reopen by summer, just in time to welcome a positive army of holidaymakers. Investigators do not solve crimes for monetary glory, so credit for the recovery went to the townsfolk.

uncovered the plot against Miss Penrose and likely prevented another murder. Mrs. Bloom would be proud."

Gingerly, I let the book fall open in my lap, to a page marked with a folded piece of paper.

"What's that?" asked Aunt Helena, a notable lack of acid in her voice. An attempt to be conversational? Wonders never *did* cease.

It was another copy of the Brighton Nightingale opera poster, this one complete, the singer's name in bold bright letters across the bottom: DOROTHEA LOWELL. Like Mrs. Bloom, I felt sorry for Miss Ballingall, having her life ruined by her father's crimes. Twice, now. All the travel in the world hadn't let her reinvent herself, after all.

I ran my fingers down the still-brilliant colors, cracks in the ink from being creased for so many years, coming to rest on a graceful swirl of handwriting, an autograph scrawled across the bottom.

"Love, Dolly," Aunt Helena read aloud.

At that moment, the heavy police station door wrenched open with its ancient groan, admitting one last member of our Excursion.

"Father! What's going on?" The former Miss Lowell stood in the doorway in her frumpy plaid cape, looking so much like, yet so very different to, the young woman in the poster.

My hand slipped off the book, and another scrap of paper fell out, this one a folded note on fine vellum stationery labeled MISS TEMPERANCE BALLINGALL. With numb fingers, I opened it. *I need to speak with you.* *~DL*

I looked up—to meet Aunt Helena's gaze, her wide eyes searching, questioning. There was no date, no incriminating addition of *where* to meet. It could mean nothing. But—?

"Aunt Helena," I whispered, as we watched Miss Ballingall simper her way over to her father. "What happened to your scissors?"

Aunt Helena was staring at Temperance-Dorothea, mouth open wide enough to catch flies, as she would say. "I gave them to Temperance. She said she needed to fetch something from her luggage, and she'd pack them for me. But how could *she* . . . ? Her arm . . . ?" Her face was contorted with a mix of anger, confusion, and dismay.

Miss Judson leaned in to explain. "We think she's been faking that. Or exaggerating its weakness, at least."

"But how do we prove it?" I said urgently. "This is all still just circumstantial. Even with Mrs. Bloom's ledger, the way things are going, they'll peg Cicely as the actual killer, and poor Tom will take the blame as an accomplice after the fact!" That could mean hard labor, not the noose—but even so. I thought he was entirely innocent of everything but his sister's cruel manipulation.

"We'll see about that," Aunt Helena declared, snatching the playbill from me. Temperance-Dorothea was in the middle of the room, looking distraught. There were lines of worry at her eyes, and her thin mouth was pressed tight.

"Temperance, dearest!" Aunt Helena waddled over, leaning heavily on her stick.

"Oh, Helena!" Miss Ballingall turned to her, anguished face crumpled. "Is it really true—they caught the jewel thief?" She put an anxious hand— her left—to her temple, as if feeling the grip of Cicely wrenching the tiara off her head once more. I wondered how much she had known of her father's plans. Was she simply a brilliant actress? Or had any of her histrionics been real?

Aunt Helena's face was hard. "That ungrateful girl got away," she fumed. "But they caught her accomplice, and the Coast Guard are looking for the boat she made her escape on. To think that I let her into my confidence, made her my bosom friend!" With a sob, she pressed the playbill into Miss Ballingall's hand. "And all this time, I've been forsaken, left to languish like a criminal! I—oh, dear me—"

Aunt Helena clutched her chest, gasping. I surged to my feet, but Miss Judson held me back. Mr. Blakeney blinked in surprise.

As we watched, Aunt Helena's eyes rolled back in her head, and she stumbled heavily against Miss Ballingall.

"Oh, help!" Miss Ballingall gasped. "She's fainted!" With her left hand full of playbill, she had no choice but to react without thinking, grabbing Aunt Helena by the arm before she was bowled over herself. Miss Ballingall had both hands full of fungus-colored jacket when something seized her right wrist with a grip like a lobster. Miss Ballingall could not even let go.

Aunt Helena's eyes fluttered open, and she had a malicious glint in her eye. "Got you," she said.

Miss Ballingall let out one of her signature earsplitting shrieks.

It brought the house down. Everyone in the room turned to stare at her, as she wailed, flailing—one-handedly—at Aunt Helena.

"That's enough, dear." A sour voice cut through the siren, and Inspector Arkwright pulled the two women apart. "We all saw you."

Aunt Helena's face was aglow with dark triumph as she backed off and let Inspector Arkwright have his way with Miss Ballingall. Miss Lowell, rather.

"It's not my fault." Miss Ballingall was sobbing.

In the background, hands shackled, Sir Quentin watched this unfold, his ruddy face turning pale. "Dolly—" His voice was husky. "What did you do?"

She raised her head and faced him, dry-eyed. "What did *I* do? What did *you* do? You were going to stand by and let that woman ruin us. Again!"

"Did you kill Mrs. Bloom?" Five simple words from Inspector Arkwright.

"I *had* to. She was going to destroy everything! Just like the last time!"

Inspector Arkwright had uncrumpled the opera poster. I hopped up to fill in the details of the tragic backstory: how a young Dorothea Lowell, up-and-coming opera singer–the Brighton Nightingale–was injured when a paddle steamer owned by her father, Harold Lowell, had exploded. She'd suffered wounds to her arm, and thanks to the financial disaster and ensuing scandal, all her hopes for her dazzling future had gone up in flames, too. Fleeing a wrongful-death lawsuit, the Lowells had disappeared, only to reemerge, some years later, as the Ballingalls. New name, new enterprise–same old Insurance Investigator dogging their heels.

"I couldn't let her do it again, don't you see?" Miss Ballingall was pleading with us now. "But she wouldn't see reason. I offered her money–my share of the takings from the tiara–but she *refused to see reason*. What was I supposed to do?"

Sir Quentin looked crushed, colorless, a shadow of himself. "But I'd called it all off. When Mrs. Bloom showed up, I told Cicely–" Here he stopped, before incriminating himself.

Miss Ballingall gave her father a savage glare. "You were a *coward*," she said. "Just like always. I took care of things properly this time. I made *doubly sure* she wouldn't get in our way." She regarded her audience loftily, making sure we'd caught her meaning: that she'd both stabbed *and* strangled Mrs. Bloom.

Inspector Arkwright looked stunned. He stood back a pace, staring at her, rubbing the bridge of his nose. Constable Hoskiss sprang forward.

"Miss—er—Ballingall," he said. "You are under arrest for suspicion of murder." There wasn't a third set of handcuffs in the Eelscombe Constabulary, apparently, but Miss Ballingall was at center stage at long last, drawing out the final act in her starring role as the Tragic Heroine. Her shoulders straight, she let the constable lead her away, more gently than she deserved.

"She ruined us," she said, her final declaration.

Sir Quentin's face was crumpled. "No, Dolly. *I* ruined us." Softer, to himself, he added, "I ruined you."

I watched them both go with a heavy heart. None of this had turned out like it was supposed to. The ringleader of the crimes was a pathetic figure, his ambitions as much a wreck as the Pier. The jewel thief was a poor girl being blackmailed, and the ruthless murderer was just a bitter woman with a long-simmering disappointment. And we'd got Aunt Helena back.

"Now, can we wrap this up so the lot of you can get out of here? I'm tired of you crowding up my station."

"Inspector Arkwright." Constable Hoskiss reappeared and looked at him evenly. "It's *my* station, and if you don't mind, I'm very busy solvin' an 'omicide, unravelin' a case of insurance fraud, and breakin' up a ring of jewel thieves."

❧

After that, there didn't seem to be much point in finishing the holiday. We technically still had a whole week booked at the hotel, not to mention fresh clothes to enjoy it in, but we'd all rather had our fill of sea air and Family Amusements. In a somber mood, we packed up our belongings—old and new*—and set off for the railway station the next morning. Even Peony seemed content to burrow back into the hatbox, and she snored faintly away as we bundled her up with the rest of the luggage. I let her keep her purple collar.

Clive was in the lobby with his photography kit. It was, at last, a dazzlingly fine morning—sunlight glittering the beach and a cloudless sky turning the water alexandrite blue. A perfect day for beach photography. As Miss Judson and Aunt Helena headed for the doors, I paused to meet him.

"Look here," he said. From a stack in his hand, he passed me an image of the hotel, printed on a sturdy card. On its back was the word POSTCARD and several lines—presumably for an address. "Like they have in France, see?" he said. "You'll have to mail it in an envelope, but I reckon it'll get to your father well

---

* If a set of Winsor & Newton watercolors somehow found its way into Miss Judson's trunk, I'm sure I don't know anything about it.

enough." I Observed a label across the bottom reading ROBERTS'S FINE PHOTOGRAPHY, BRIGHTON & FAIRHAVEN. "I've made a whole series of 'em. Got the hotel, and the carousel, and the Pier, before you destroyed what was left of it. . . ."

"Very enterprising." I was impressed. "I'm sorry the police seized your crime scene pictures. You might be able to get them back after the trial."

"Don't want 'em," he declared. "Being a news-paperman is too dangerous for my blood. Have you heard about those new Kinetoscopes they're making in America? I think Fairhaven's just the place for a motion-picture kiosk. Too bad I missed the collapse of the Pier." A moment later, he gave me his easy grin and unslung his camera. "Go an' stand by the tiger."

෴

Mr. Blakeney did not accompany us back home. Standing on the platform at Fairhaven Station, hold-ing his box of files, he said, "I'm headed to Lewes for the sessions. Somebody needs to look after Tom. I'd hate to see the lad go down for what his sister and Sir Quentin did."

Miss Judson squeezed his arm. "That's very noble." Even Aunt Helena looked approving.

"Well," he said with a grin, "he did save Stephen's life."

The Bird Ladies had flocked to the platform, hav-ing recovered from some of their disappointment at missing the excitement on the Pier. "We're going, too," Miss Causton announced breathlessly, clutching her valise with her lace gloves. "We've never seen a trial before."

"Or such a handsome lawyer," added Miss Cabot, making Mr. Blakeney turn red.

Constable Hoskiss and Mrs. Pettigrew (and several assorted children and ducks) came to see us off.

Mrs. Pettigrew handed me a slip of paper. "You've a telegram from Manchester," she said, then gave my shoulder a little pat. My fingers trembled and I almost couldn't unfold it.

ATTENTION MISS MYRTLE HARDCASTLE. MY DEEPEST GRATITUDE FOR ASSISTANCE GIVEN TO MY IZZY. KNEW FRIENDS IN EELSCOMBE WOULD NEVER LET HER DOWN. YOURS IN SORROW, BERTRAM BLOOM, MANCHESTER.

All at once, I wanted to cry, and hugged the hat-box tighter.

Once I'd recovered, tucking the precious message inside Mrs. Bloom's fossil book, Mrs. Pettigrew presented us with a hamper full of food. "Plum heavies and herring. You can't trust that rubbish they serve on the railway."

She pressed the hamper upon Aunt Helena—who received it with uncommon grace, after giving

Constable Hoskiss a kiss on each cheek and asking him when he was going to find a nice girl and settle down. It was a very different sort of assemblage from the last time we'd gathered on this platform as a group, although the misty air still had its fishy tang. Was it possible I would miss that?

Constable Hoskiss had brought news. "We've had a wire from France. Miss Highsmith were spotted at the ferry terminal at Cherbourg, but they weren't able to apprehend her. She were traveling with a man."

"Marceau," I said. Poor Tom. "They've put out bulletins to the *Sûreté* and local police, right? We have an extradition treaty—" A hand fell on my arm, and I looked up to see Miss Judson giving me a peaceable look. I fell silent. She was right. France had its own criminals to deal with. I'd be watching, though. There was a lot more to that story than we'd been able to learn. One of these days, "Marceau" would resurface, and the Brighton Bandit with him. She couldn't be planning to abandon Tom forever. I would keep a weather eye on the newspapers—for Mrs. Bloom's sake.

"Thank you, Constable," I said.

He was nodding, rocking back on his heels. "And I thought you'd like to know, I've gone and rung up the Metropolitan Police. They'll be sending two members of the Detective Bureau down to take the Ballingalls—er, the Lowells, rather—off our hands."

"But you solved the case," I said. Or it happened

on his watch, at any rate. "You ought to get the credit for it."

He waved that away. "I've plenty o' work here." Two of the ducks were currently herding one of the Pettigrew children, pinching at her (his?) hems as she (he?) squealed in dismay.

The constable looked solemnly at Aunt Helena and cleared his throat. "Miss Hardcastle," he said, voice deep and somber. "On behalf of the Eelscombe Constabulary, I'm to offer our formal apology for your being wrongfully arrested."

"Ah, pish," she said—and there was an alarming twinkle in her eye. "You were the very picture of hospitality, Daniel."

The constable blushed and lifted his helmet. "Ladies," he said, with a little bow. "Duty calls." And he strolled off, whistling and spinning his truncheon, shooing the ducks off the platform.

Miss Judson had her sketchbook out—the very one originally seized by Inspector Arkwright, which Mr. Blakeney had wheedled free—and was taking in our final view of Eelscombe: a wink of blue water between towering cliffs, and the white sparkle of the Ballingall Arms perched atop the promontory.

Aunt Helena Observed this, lips tight.

Peony made an encouraging burble, so I ventured into Uncharted Territory. I edged up to Aunt Helena and gave as polite a little cough as I could.

Her head whipped round, and for a moment her eyes narrowed. I braced myself for a command not to be impertinent, but it did not come. "I'm sorry about your holiday, Aunt Helena. About what happened with Sir Quentin. I know it's not how you wanted things to go."

She was silent a long moment, scrutinizing me. I summoned all my Exceptional Forbearance and did not fidget. Not even a twitch. Finally, she reached out and curled a strand of limp puce ribbon from my hat back into place, fingers lingering longer than necessary.

"I will *never* forgive that man for this," she said, voice scarcely more than a murmur. "Prison is too good for him, after what he did—putting you and Judson in harm's way."

"Not to mention framing you for murder," Miss Judson put in mildly.

"Nonsense." Aunt Helena straightened her own hat, adjusting the stuffed bird to a more intimidating angle. She looked like she was about to come down hard on the local Duck Gang. There was a mad gleam in her dark eye. "That was the most fun I've had in twenty years. Pity Arthur had to miss it."

She hooked us each by the arm and steered us toward the train. "After this," she added in a voice I did not recognize, "Christmas is going to be frightfully dull."

The Investigation Will Continue
in
Cold-Blooded Myrtle

A NOTE FROM THE AUTHOR

The first real woman (so far as we know . . .) murdered on an English train was thirty-three-year-old business-woman Elizabeth Camp, bludgeoned to death in 1897, a few years after this story is set. The motive was believed to be robbery, as Camp was known to carry significant amounts of cash. A combined investigation by Scotland Yard and the London & South-Western Railway Police produced a wealth of physical evidence, including the murder weapon (a large pharmacist's pestle, for grinding medicine) and multiple suspects. Despite their efforts, Camp's murder was never solved.

The French criminology conference Mr. Hardcastle attends is fictional, but France did lead the way in international symposia on the subject. Pioneering criminologist Dr. Alexandre Lacassagne founded a series of regular conferences much like the one described, the

International Congress on Criminal Anthropology, in which cutting-edge techniques and case studies were presented and debated. The series continued every few years from 1885 until World War I brought it to a halt in 1916. Inconveniently for the timing of Myrtle's holiday, it was not held in 1893.

My thanks and appreciation go to Elise Howard and the rest of the brilliant team at Algonquin Young Readers, for their ongoing support of Myrtle and her adventures. Especial thanks to Susan Wilkins—humbug! And proper thanks go out to Sussex native Keely Parrack, along on account of her help with local dialect. Pond pudding's on me.